MURDER AT CHRISTMAS

'Twixt the Cup and the Lip by Julian Symons—There's a jewel heist going down at Orbin's store and only a pair of department store Santas know whodunit.

Auggie Wren's Christmas Story by Paul Auster—A lost wallet, a blind woman, and a juvenile shoplifter provide all the trimmings for an unforgettable holiday feast—and solve a twenty-year-old mystery.

Christmas Gift by Robert Turner—Two hardened cops on a Christmas eve stakeout show an unexpected bit of holiday spirit.

Father Crumlish Celebrates Christmas by Alice Scanlan Reach—It's up to a sleuthing priest to follow the trail of a broken lamb, a man on a ledge, and a crying child to solve a baffling murder case.

AND 6 MORE SUSPENSEFUL TALES OF CHRISTMAS CRIMES AND MISDEMEANORS

MURDER
AT
CHRISTMAS
and Other Stories

from *Ellery Queen's
Mystery Magazine*
and *Alfred Hitchcock's
Mystery Magazine*

Edited by Cynthia Manson

A SIGNET BOOK

SIGNET
Published by the Penguin Group
Penguin Books USA Inc., 375 Hudson Street,
New York, New York 10014, U.S.A.
Penguin Books Ltd, 27 Wrights Lane,
London W8 5TZ, England
Penguin Books Australia Ltd, Ringwood,
Victoria, Australia
Penguin Books Canada Ltd, 10 Alcorn Avenue,
Toronto, Ontario, Canada M4V 3B2
Penguin Books (N.Z.) Ltd, 182–190 Wairau Road,
Auckland 10, New Zealand

Penguin Books Ltd, Registered Offices:
Harmondsworth, Middlesex, England

First published by Signet,
an imprint of New American Library,
a division of Penguin Books USA Inc.

First Printing, November, 1991
10 9 8 7 6 5 4 3 2 1

Grateful acknowledgment is made to the following for permission to reprint
their copyrighted material:

MISS CRINDLE AND FATHER CHRISTMAS by Malcom Gray, Copyright
© 1990 by Davis Publications, Inc. Reprinted by permission of Curtis Brown,
Ltd.; THE THEFT OF THE CHRISTMAS STOCKING by Edward D.
Hoch, Copyright © 1989 by Davis Publications, Inc. Reprinted by permission

The following page constitutes an extension of this copyright page.

CONTENTS

INTRODUCTION

Murder at Christmas And Other Stories

The popularity of last year's *Mystery for Christmas* prompted the decision to publish a second volume. This collection of stories culled once again from the pages of *Ellery Queen's Mystery Magazine* and *Alfred Hitchcock's Mystery Magazine* comprises a diversified cast of characters. They are a sister who steals from her scrooge-like brother to give to the poor, a father who leaves clues not gifts in his daughter's Christmas stocking, a thief who wears a Santa Claus disguise, and a department store of talking toys. The authors include such well-known mystery writers as Julian Symons, John Mortimer, Georges Simenon, Alice Scanlan Reach, and Edward D. Hoch.

The author not published in our mystery magazines is Paul Auster, whose "Auggie Wren's Christmas Story" first appeared in *The New York Times*. It is included here because, unlike most mystery and detective stories which end with the resolution of the crime, this one presents a victim who is true to the spirit of Christmas in his pursuit of the perpetrator.

May the stories in *Murder at Christmas* bring you the gift of reading pleasure!

THE THEFT OF THE CHRISTMAS STOCKING

Edward D. Hoch

It always seemed more like Christmas with snow in the air, even if there were only fat white flakes that melted as they hit the sidewalk. Walking briskly along Fifth Avenue at noon on Christmas Eve, Nick Velvet was aware of the last-minute crowds clutching red-and-green shopping bags that must have delighted the merchants. When he turned in at the building on the corner of Fifty-fourth Street, he wasn't surprised to see that the pre-Christmas festivities had spread even here, within the confines of one of Manhattan's most exclusive private clubs.

The slender, sour-faced man behind the desk inside the door eyed Nick for an instant and asked, "Are you looking for the Dellon-Simpson Christmas party?"

"Mr. Charles Simpson," Nick confirmed. "I have an appointment with him here."

The guardian of the door consulted his list. "You'd be Mr. Velvet?"

"That's right."

"You'll find Mr. Simpson in the library, straight ahead. He's expecting you."

Nick crossed the marble floor, past a curving staircase that led up to a surprisingly noisy party, and entered the library through tall oak doors that shut out virtually all sound. Inside was a club-room from a hundred years ago, complete with an elderly member dozing in front of the fireplace.

"Mr. Velvet?" a voice asked, and Nick turned and saw a figure rising from the shadow of an oversized wing chair.

11

"That's correct. You'd be Charles Simpson?"

"I would be." By the flickering firelight, Nick could make out a tall man with a noble face and furry white sideburns. He looked to be a vigorous sixty or so and his handshake was a grip of steel. "Thank you for coming."

"I'm keeping you from your firm's Christmas party."

"Nonsense. Business before pleasure, even on Christmas Eve. I want you to steal something for me, Mr. Velvet."

"That's my business. You understand the conditions? Nothing of value, and my fee—"

"I was told in advance. But it must be done tonight. Is that a problem?"

"No. What's the object?"

Simpson's face crinkled into a tight-lipped smile. "A Christmas stocking. I want you to steal the Christmas stocking hanging from the fireplace at my granddaughter's. Any time after midnight."

"Does it contain something valuable?"

"The gift inside will be valueless, but I want that, too."

"Where does she live?"

"With her mother in a duplex apartment on upper Fifth Avenue." He produced a piece of paper from his pocket. "Here's the address. I warn you, the building has tight security."

"I'll get in."

"Phone me at this number if you're successful." He walked Nick to the lobby, and as Nick started for the door he said, "Oh, and Mr. Velvet—"

Nick turned. "Yes?"

"Merry Christmas."

After explaining on the phone to Gloria why he wouldn't be home until well after midnight, Nick journeyed up Fifth Avenue to the address he'd been given. It proved to be a fine old building with a doorman, and a security guard seated behind a bank of television monitors. There would be a TV camera in each of the elevators, at the service entrance, and probably in the stairwell.

Nick walked around the block and thought about it. The most likely way to gain access to the building would be to pose as a delivery man. He could rent a uniform, buy a poinsettia, and walk right past the doorman as if he were delivering it to one of the apartments. It wouldn't work after midnight, of course. He'd have to gain access to the building much earlier and find a hiding place out of range of the TV cameras.

Surprisingly—or not—as Nick again approached the front of the building, a florist's van pulled up in front of the building. A young man got out, walked quickly around to the rear, and opened the doors. He brought out a huge poinsettia that almost hid his face and walked into the lobby with it. Nick stopped on the sidewalk to light a cigarette and pause as if in thought.

The doorman immediately took the plant from the young man, checked the address tag, and sent him on his way. He picked up the house phone and presently one of the building employees appeared to complete the plant's delivery. Through it all, the security man never left his post behind the TV monitors.

Nick sighed and strolled away. A delivery wouldn't gain him access to the apartment, not even on Christmas Eve. It would have to be something else. He glanced again at the note he carried in his pocket: Florence Beaufeld, it read. Apt. 501.

The name was not Simpson, he'd noticed at once. If the child was his granddaughter, that meant the mother she lived with was probably Charles Simpson's daughter, separated, widowed, or divorced. Nick wondered why Simpson couldn't go to the apartment himself on Christmas Day and perform his own stocking theft.

Nick wasn't paid to think too much about the motives of his clients—that had gotten him into trouble enough in the past—but he did feel he should know whether Florence was the mother's or the daughter's name. The phonebook showed only one

Beaufeld at that address: Beaufeld, F. It seemed likely that Florence was the child's mother, Florence Simpson Beaufeld.

None of which would help him gain entrance to the apartment after midnight. He crossed Fifth Avenue and tried to get a better view of the building from Central Park. Assuming Apartment 501 was on the fifth floor, it had to face either the side street or the park. The other two sides of the building abutted adjoining buildings on Fifth Avenue and the side street. But the top stories of all three buildings were set back, so there was no access between them across the rooftops. No one could have reached the top of any of the buildings except Santa Claus.

The more Nick thought about it, the more convinced he became that it would have to be Santa Claus.

At eleven-thirty that night, he approached the front door of the building. The padding of the Santa Claus suit was warm and uncomfortable, smelling faintly of scented powder, and the bag of fancily wrapped gifts he'd slung over his shoulder weighed more than he'd expected. The doorman saw him coming and held open the portals for him. That was the first good sign. Santa was expected.

"Ho ho ho!" Nick thundered in the heartiest voice he could manage.

The doorman smiled good-naturedly. "Got a gift for me, Santa?"

"Ho ho ho!" Nick took out one of the gifts he'd bought to fill the top of the sack. "Right here, sonny!"

The doorman smiled and accepted the slim flat box. "Looks like a necktie to me. Thanks a lot, Santa. Which party do you want, the Brewsters or the Trevensons?"

"Brewsters," Nick decided.

"Seventeenth floor."

Nick glanced toward the security guard and saw him looking through the early edition of the following morning's *Times*. He entered the nearest elevator and pressed the button for seventeen. As soon as the door closed and the elevator started to rise, he hit the fifth-floor button, too. The TV camera might spot him getting off at the wrong floor, but it was less of a risk than being seen running down the stairwell with his bag of tricks.

The corridor on the fifth floor was silent and deserted, lit only by an indirect glow from unseen fixtures near the ceiling. There were only three doors, so he knew 501 was going to be a large apartment. He glanced at his watch and saw that it wasn't yet midnight. Then he listened at the door of 501. Hearing nothing, he reached deep into his bag and extracted a leather case of lock picks. It took him just forty-five seconds to unlock the door. He was mildly surprised that the chain lock wasn't latched, but the reason quickly became obvious. The woman of the house, Florence Beaufeld, was preparing to go out.

By the glow of a twelve-foot Christmas tree standing near the spiral staircase in the duplex, he saw a handsome brown-haired woman of around forty adjusting a glistening earring. It was her hair, done in an unusual style that evoked the idea of a layered helmet, that caught his attention. She finished adjusting the earring, straightened the neckline of her red-velvet dress, and picked up a sequined purse.

Nick slipped into the dining area, taking shelter in the shadows behind a china cabinet, as the woman stepped to the foot of the staircase and called out, "I'm going up to the Brewsters' party, Michelle. Go to bed now, it's almost midnight. And don't peek at your gifts!" There was a mumbled reply from upstairs as Mrs. Beaufeld let herself out of the apartment.

Nick waited, sweating in his Santa suit, until he heard a grandfather clock chime midnight. Then he left his hiding place and moved silently across the carpeted floor toward the lighted Christmas tree. A fireplace was beyond the tree, along an inside wall, and above it was an oil portrait of Florence Beaufeld seated with a protective arm around a lovely young girl about eight years old. Below it, taped to the mantel, was a single red Christmas stocking, bulging with an unseen gift.

Carefully setting down the bag, Nick moved to the mantel. He reached out and took the stocking in his hand, carefully pulling the tape away from the wood. As he did, he heard the slightest of sounds behind him and turned to see a young woman in a short night-gown and bare legs standing at the foot of the stair-case, a tiny automatic held firmly in her right hand.

"Get your hand off my stocking, Santa," she said, "or I'll send you back to the North Pole in a wooden box . . ."

Nick did as he was told. "Come now," he said gruffly, "you don't want to point that thing at Santa."

She motioned slightly with the pistol. "Take off the hat and beard. I like to see who I'm talking to."

He tossed the red hat on the floor and pulled the sticky beard away from his skin.

"Satisfied now?" he asked in his normal voice.

"Say, you're not bad-looking. Who are you?"

"Do you mind if I take off this coat and padding before we talk? It's really quite uncomfortable."

"Sure, but don't try anything. I've seen all the mov-ies." She watched him while he dropped the coat on the floor with the rest and then pulled the padding from his pants. He'd worn jeans and a black turtle-neck under the Santa suit in case he had to shed it to make his escape. With the padding out, the red pants fell by themselves and he stepped out of them.

"Now, what was your question?"

"Who are you?"

She spoke with an educated, private-school voice, even when her words were tough and gritty. Nick guessed Michelle Beaufeld was now in her late teens.

"I'm a friend of your grandfather," he told her.

"Charles Simpson?" The truth seemed to dawn on her. "Oh, no!" She started to laugh. "He wanted you to steal the gift!"

"Well, the stocking the gift is in."

She shook her head. "Santa Claus, the thief! Won't

that make a story for the papers? Grandpa Tries To Steal Child's Christmas Gift."

"You're no child," Nick pointed out. "Why don't you put away that gun? I'm not going to hurt you."

She motioned toward the Santa Claus outfit on the floor. "Put your pants back on."

"They're too big for me without the padding."

"That's the idea. If you try to rush me, they'll trip you up."

When he'd done as she ordered, she sat in an easy chair and carefully set the pistol down on an end table by her side. "Now we can talk," she said. "I know Grandpa wouldn't send anyone to harm me, but I can understand his wanting to get his hands on that gift. Let's have a look at it—toss the stocking over here. No funny business now!"

Nick did as he was told, convinced now that she wouldn't think of shooting him any more than he'd think of harming her. The stocking landed on the chair by her side and she picked it up, withdrawing the gift in its holiday wrapping. As she worked at unwrapping it, she reminded Nick of her mother adjusting the earring earlier. She had her mother's high cheekbones and pouting lips, and was well on her way to becoming a great beauty. Putting aside the wrapping, she held up a little plastic pig for Nick to see. It was a gift more suitable for a child of five or six. "There we go! I'll put it with the others."

"What others?"

"Didn't Grandpa tell you? They're gifts from my father. He sends one every Christmas."

"Does he know how old you are?"

"Of course he does. They have a special meaning."

"Oh?"

"*That's* what Grandpa's dying to find out—what their special meaning is."

"Do *you* know?" he asked.

"Well—not yet," she admitted. "It's about something I'm supposed to get when I'm eighteen."

"How old are you now?"

"Seventeen. My birthday's next month."

"Does your father ever come to see you?"

She shook her head. "Not since I was twelve. The only time I hear from him is at Christmas, and then it's just the gift in the stocking. There hasn't been a note since the first time."

"How does he deliver them? I know you don't believe in Santa Claus."

That brought a genuine smile. "I don't know. I suppose Mother must put them there, although she's always denied it."

"What does your grandfather have to do with any of this?"

Her face showed exasperation, then uncertainty. "Why am I telling you my family history when I should be calling the police?"

"Because you wouldn't want to call the police and implicate your grandfather. You told me yourself how funny the headline would look. Besides, I might be able to help you."

"How?"

"It seems to me you've got a real mystery on your hands. If I can solve it for you, there'd be no need for you to keep this little pig, would there?"

"What do you mean?"

"You'd have the answer to your mystery and I'd have the gift to deliver to your grandfather in the stocking."

"He's paying you for this, isn't he?"

"Yes," Nick admitted.

"How much?"

"A great deal. It's how I make my living."

She picked up the automatic and for a split second he thought she was going to shoot him, after all. "Take off those foolish red pants," she said, "and let's have a beer."

The kitchen had a sleek contemporary look that clashed with the rest of the apartment. Michelle opened the refrigerator and brought out two bottles of a popular German beer. "Aren't you a bit young to be drinking beer?" Nick asked as she poured two glasses.

"Aren't you a bit old to be a thief?"

"All right," he agreed with a smile, "let's get down to business. Tell me about your father."

"His name is Dan Beaufeld. When I was a child, he ran a charterboat business in Florida. He was away from New York most of the time, especially in the winter when he had a lot of tourist business. Sometimes my mother would take me down to visit him and we'd get to ride on one of his deep-sea-fishing boats. I was twelve the last time I saw him, five years ago. That was when my mother divorced him. At the time I had no idea what it was all about. Somehow I blamed myself, which I guess a lot of kids do. My mother had bought this apartment with her own money, so she stayed here. My father moved to Florida year-round."

"Did you understand what caused the divorce?"

"Not at first. I knew my grandfather had been part of it. I thought he'd poisoned my mother's mind against my father. Once when he found me sobbing in my room, he told me I shouldn't cry over my father because he was a bad man—an evil man."

Charter boats in Florida in the mid-1980s suggested only one thing to Nick. "Could your father have been involved in drug traffic?"

"That's what Grandpa finally told me, just last year. He said he'd made a lot of money using his boats for drug smuggling and that the police were still looking for him. That was why Grandpa forced my mother to divorce him. He was afraid the family would be tainted or something."

"What about these mysterious gifts?"

"They started when I was thirteen. There was a note attached to the first one. It was from my father and he said I was always in his thoughts. He said to keep the gifts, and when I was eighteen they'd make me wealthy. The gifts have appeared in my stocking every Christmas, but there were never any more notes."

"What were the gifts?"

"The first was a little toy bus with a greyhound on the side. Then there was a copy of Poe's poem "The Raven," which I loved when I was fourteen. The third year was an apple, and I ate that. Last year there was a snapshot of Mother my father had taken when they were still married. Now there's this plastic pig."

"An odd combination of gifts," Nick admitted. "I can't see—"

"Who the hell are *you*?" a voice asked from the doorway.

Nick turned to see Florence Beaufeld standing wide-eyed at the kitchen door, taking in the scene before her.

He stood up, more as a reflex action than from any real fear of attack. "I'm pleased to meet you, Mrs. Beaufeld. My name is Nick Velvet."

"What are you doing here with my daughter?"

"Mother—"

"Were you sent by her father? Are you this year's Christmas gift?"

"He was sent to steal the gift, Mother! I caught him by the fireplace dressed up like Santa Claus."

"And you're sitting here chatting with him? Where are the police?"

"I didn't call them."

"My God, Michelle!"

"I'm perfectly all right, Mother. Please."

"Go upstairs and put on some clothes. I'll attend to Mr. Velvet."

Michelle hesitated and then decided to obey her mother's command. She left the kitchen without a word and went up the staircase, taking the automatic with her. Florence Beaufeld turned back to Nick. "Now tell me the truth. What are you doing here?"

"I was hired by your father, Mrs. Beaufeld."

"I should have guessed as much. Whenever I mentioned those Christmas gifts from Dan it threw him into a frenzy. I vowed not to tell him if there was one this year, but he had to know. He said Dan was planning to give Michelle a large sum of illegal drug money."

"Why would he do that?"

Mrs. Beaufeld shook her head. "Only because he loves her, I suppose, and she's his daughter. He's been hiding out from the police for over five years now, and he's never seen her in all that time."

"What do *you* make of these gifts?"

"I suppose they're a message of some sort, like a child's puzzle, but I haven't been able to read it. Was there another gift tonight?"

"A plastic pig. But perhaps I don't have to tell you that—your daughter suspects you're the one who leaves them for her."

"I swear I'm not! I have no contact with Dan. That stocking was empty earlier this evening. I looked."

"At what time?"

"Shortly before ten, I think."

"Who was in the apartment after that?"

"Only Michelle and me."

"No one else?"

"I have a woman who cooks and cleans for us. She left at about that time. I can't remember whether I looked at the stocking before or after she let herself out."

"Would you give me her name and address?"

"Are you a detective of some sort?"

"Only a professional trying to earn some money. I was hired to bring your father the stocking with the latest gift. Maybe if I solve the riddle for your daughter, she'll let me have it. Then everyone will be happy."

"Well, I'm certain Agnes isn't involved, but you can have her address if you want." She wrote it on a piece of notepaper.

"One other thing. Before I leave, could I see the gifts your daughter received? She told me she ate the apple, but the others?"

She studied him through narrowed eyes. "You have a way with you, Mr. Velvet. For all I know you're nothing but a common thief, yet you charmed my daughter and now you seem to be doing the same with me. Come upstairs. I'll ask Michelle to show you the gifts."

He followed her up the staircase and waited discreetly in the hallway while she checked to see that her daughter was wearing a robe. Then he entered the girl's bedroom. All seventeen years of her life seemed to be crammed haphazardly into it. Michelle led him to a bookcase where a rock star's poster dominated shelves of alphabet books and stuffed toys. There the four objects were lined up, just as she had described them—the toy bus, the Poe poem, the snapshot of Mrs. Beaufeld, and now the pig.

"Michelle will be eighteen next month," Nick said. "It's my understanding the message must be complete, whatever it is, if it's to direct her to a fortune by then."

"But how is he able to get in here to leave these things?"

"I'm hoping Agnes can tell me that," Nick said.

The clock was chiming one as he left the apartment.

Downstairs, a different doorman and security guard were on duty. Nick slipped the doorman a ten-dollar bill. "Merry Christmas."

"Thank you, sir. Are you a resident here?"

"Only a visitor. I was wondering if you've worked here long enough to remember Dan Beaufeld. He was in Apartment 501 before his divorce about five years ago."

"Sorry, I just started last year." He called over to the security guard watching the television monitors. "Larry, were you here five years ago?"

The man shook his head. "Just over four years. The old-timers get the day and evening shifts."

"Thanks anyway," Nick said. He went out into the cold night air and took a cab home. Gloria was waiting up for him, to exchange gifts over a bottle of champagne.

The Beaufeld maid and cook, Agnes Wilson, lived on Fifth Avenue, too, but far uptown in Harlem. It was noon on Christmas Day when Nick visited the housing project where her apartment was located. Her husband eyed him suspiciously and asked, "What do you want with Agnes?"

"I just have a couple of questions. It won't take a minute."

"You a cop?"

"Do I look like one? I'm a friend of the Beaufeld family."

Agnes Wilson was small and pretty, with deep-brown eyes and a friendly smile. "I never knew Mr. Beaufeld," she said. "They were still married when I started there, but he was always in Florida. I never saw him."

"Mrs. Wilson, someone left a Christmas toy in Michelle's stocking by the fireplace last night. Do you know anything about it?"

"No."

"You didn't leave it? You weren't paid to leave it?"

"No one paid me to do anything."

"Not Dan Beaufeld?"

"Not him or anyone else."

Nick leaned forward in his chair. "Michelle has received gifts in her stocking for five years now—a toy bus, a poem, an apple, a photograph, and a plastic pig. Do these mean anything to you?"

"No, they don't." She seemed genuinely surprised. "I didn't know about the gifts. A couple of years back I mentioned to Mrs. Beaufeld that I thought Michelle was pretty old to be hanging a stocking on the fireplace Christmas Eve, but she just shrugged it off. It wasn't any of my business, so I shut up. Maybe it wasn't so odd, after all. I worked for a German family once that hung stockings on the fireplace for St. Nicholas every Christmas—all of them, even the parents.

"Did any strangers come to the door this week when Michelle or her mother were out?"

"No strangers get by the doorman in that building. They've got TV cameras in the elevators and everything."

Nick got up to leave, handing her a folded ten-dollar bill. "Thank you for your time, Mrs. Wilson. I hope you and your husband have a Merry Christmas."

Agnes's husband saw him to the door. "You always go calling on Christmas Day?"

"Just like Santa Claus," Nick told him with a smile.

He telephoned Charles Simpson from a pay phone at the corner. "Are you having a good holiday?" he asked.

"Is that you, Velvet? What luck have you had?"

"Fair. I had the stocking in my hands, but I don't have it now."

"What was in it?"

"If I tell you, do I get paid?"

"A partial payment. I won't know if I need the stocking and the gift until I see them."

"All right. I'll try to have them tonight, or tomorrow morning for sure."

He hung up and grabbed a bus heading downtown. Ten minutes later he was back at the Beaufelds' building. The doorman was the same one who'd been on duty the previous day when he'd first scouted the building. Nick asked him if he'd known Dan Beaufeld.

The doorman told him he'd only been there three years.

Nick asked the security guard the same question.

"Me? I've been here a year. I know the mother and daughter, not the ex-husband. He never comes around, does he?"

"Not lately," Nick agreed. "Do you have keys to all the apartments?"

"We have one set of master keys, but they never leave this locked desk unless they have to be used in an emergency."

"And there's always someone on duty here?"

"Always," the guard said, beginning to look suspiciously at Nick. "The doorman and I are never away at the same time."

"That certainly speaks well for the security here. No one gets in who isn't expected."

"Including you," the doorman said. "Who are you here to see, anyway?"

"Florence Beaufeld."

The doorman called up on the phone and then sent Nick up on the elevator.

Florence Beaufeld met him at the door with word that they'd be leaving soon to have Christmas dinner with her father. "He'll be picking us up in his car."

"This won't take long. Are you likely to discuss the gift in Michelle's Christmas stocking?"

"No chance of that."

Michelle came down the stairs. "Are *you* back again?" She was wearing a sparkling green party dress with a flared skirt. "Have you solved the riddle yet?"

"I may have. But first I'd like to see a picture of your father. A snapshot, anything."

"I threw them all away after the divorce," Florence said.

"I have one," Michelle told him and went off to get it. She returned with a snapshot of a handsome man with a moustache and a broad grin, squinting into the camera.

Nick studied it for a moment and nodded. "Now I can tell you about the gifts. It's just a theory, but I think it's correct. Here's my proposition. If I'm right, you give me the stocking and the latest gift to deliver to your grandfather."

"All right," Michelle agreed, and her mother nodded, gripping her hands together.

"I had no idea what the five gifts meant until I glimpsed those old alphabet books in your room, Michelle. I imagine your dad used to read to you from those when you were learning the alphabet." Michelle nodded silently. "Those books always use simple objects or animals to stand for the letters. Many of them start out 'A is for Apple.' "

Her mother took it up. "Of course! 'B is for Bus,' 'R is for Raven,' 'A is for Apple'—but then there was the photo of me."

"Mother?" Nick said. " 'M is for Mother,' 'P is for Pig.' "

"Bramp?" Michelle laughed. "What does that mean?"

"That stumped me, too, until I remembered it wasn't just any bus. It had a greyhound on the side. 'G is for Greyhound.' That would give us gramp."

"Gramp," Florence Beaufeld said.

"Gramp!" her daughter repeated. "You mean Grandpa? The money was to come from him?"

"Obviously out of the question," Nick agreed. "He'd never act as a channel for your father's money, not when he opposed the whole thing so vigorously. He even hired me in the hope of learning the location of the money before you found it."

"But gramp certainly means grandfather," Florence pointed out. "It has no other meaning that I know of."

"True enough. But remember that your former husband was limiting himself to a five-letter word by using this system of symbolic Christmas gifts. The word had to be completed by today, a month before Michelle's eighteenth birthday. If gramp stands for grandfather, could the word grandfather itself signify something other than Michelle's flesh-and-blood grandfather?"

He saw the light dawn on Michelle's face first. "The grandfather clock!"

Nick smiled. "Let's take a look."

In the base of the clock, below the window where the pendulum swung, they found the package. Inside were neatly banded packages of hundred-dollar bills.

Florence Beaufeld stood up, breathing hard. "There's close to a half million dollars here."

"He couldn't risk entering this apartment too many times, so he hid the money in advance. If you hadn't found it, he'd probably have found a way to give you a more obvious hint."

"You mean Dan has been in this apartment?"

Nick nodded. "For the last five Christmas Eves."

"But—"

She was interrupted by the buzzer, and the doorman's voice announced the arrival of Mr. Simpson's car.

"Go on," Nick urged them. "I'll catch you up on the rest later."

It was shortly before midnight when Nick stepped from the shadows near the building and intercepted the man walking quickly toward the entrance. "Larry?"

The night-security man turned to stare at Nick. "You're the fellow who was asking all those questions."

"That's right. I finally got some answers. You're Dan Beaufeld, aren't you?"

"I—"

"There's no point in denying it. I've seen your picture. You shaved off your moustache, but otherwise you look pretty much the same."

"Where did I slip up? Or was it just the photo?" There was a tone of resignation in his voice.

"There were other things. If Dan Beaufeld was leaving those Christmas gifts himself, he had to have a way into the apartment. A building employee seemed likely in view of the tight security, and one of the security men seemed most likely. There are master keys in the security desk and it would have been easy for you to have one duplicated. The gifts were always left shortly before midnight on Christmas Eve, and that implied someone who might start work on the midnight shift. You couldn't leave your post after midnight. Last night as I was leaving, you told me you'd been here just over four years—enough to cover the last five Christmases. You also said old-timers got the day and evening shifts, yet the day security man told me he's only been here a year. That made me wonder if you preferred the midnight shift so you'd be less likely to be seen and recognized by people who might know you. Of course you spent most of your time in Florida, even before the divorce, and without the moustache it was doubtful any of the other employees or residents would recognize you. On those occasions when Michelle or her mother came in after midnight, you could simply hide your face behind a newspaper or bend down behind the TV monitors."

"I had to be close to her," Dan Beaufeld admitted. "I had to watch my daughter growing up, even if it meant risking arrest. I'd see her going off to school or to parties, watching from across the street, and that was enough. Working here made me feel close to them both. Michelle had a custom of hanging up her Christmas stocking, so I started leaving the gifts every year to let her know I was near and to prepare her for the money she'd get when she turned eighteen.

"I knew the maid let herself out around ten o'clock, and Florence never bothered to relatch the chain lock until bedtime. I entered with my master key, making certain they weren't in the downstairs rooms, and left the gift in the stocking before midnight. Last year I had to come back twice because they were sitting by the fireplace, but usually Florence was out at someone's Christmas party and it was all clear."

"Last night you left the money, too—in the grandfather clock."

Beaufeld grinned. "So they read the clues properly."

"It's drug money, isn't it?"

"Some of it, but I'm out of that now. I used some fake ID to start a new life, a clean life."

"Charles Simpson still wants you in prison."

Dan Beaufeld took a deep breath. "Sometimes I think about turning myself in. Some of the crimes are beyond the statute of limitations now, and a lawyer told me that if I surrendered I'd probably get off with a lenient sentence."

"Why don't you talk it over with Florence and Michelle? They don't want your money, they want you. They're waiting up there for you now."

Dan Beaufeld turned his eyes skyward, toward the lighted windows he must have looked at hundreds of times before. "What are *you* getting out of this?" he asked.

Nick Velvet, who had serious doubts about collecting his fee from Charles Simpson, merely answered, "I don't need to get anything out of this one. It's Christmas."

'TWIXT THE CUP AND THE LIP

Julian Symons

"A beautiful morning, Miss Oliphant. I shall take a short constitutional."

"Very well, Mr. Payne."

Mr. Rossiter Payne put on his good thick Melton overcoat, took his bowler hat off its peg, carefully brushed it, and put it on. He looked at himself in a small glass and nodded approvingly at what he saw.

He was a man in his early fifties, but he might have passed for ten years less, so square were his shoulders, so ruler-straight his back. Two fine wings of gray hair showed under the bowler. He looked like a retired Guards officer, although he had, in fact, no closer relationship with the Army than an uncle who had been cashiered.

At the door he paused, his eyes twinkling. "Don't let anybody steal the stock while I'm out, Miss Oliphant."

Miss Oliphant, a thin spinster of indeterminate middle-age, blushed. She adored Mr. Payne.

He had removed his hat to speak to her. Now he clapped it on his head again, cast an appreciative look at the bow window of his shop, which displayed several sets of standard authors with the discreet legend above—*Rossiter Payne, Bookseller. Specialist in First Editions and Manuscripts*—and made his way up New Bond Street toward Oxford Street.

At the top of New Bond Street he stopped, as he did five days a week, at the stall on the corner. The old woman put the carnation into his buttonhole.

"Fourteen shopping days to Christmas now, Mrs. Shankly. We've all got to think about it, haven't we?"

A ten shilling note changed hands instead of the usual half crown. He left her blessing him confusedly.

This was perfect December weather—crisply cold, the sun shining. Oxford Street was wearing its holiday decorations—enormous gold and silver coins from which depended ropes of pearls, diamonds, rubies, emeralds. When lighted up in the afternoon they looked pretty, although a little garish for Mr. Payne's refined taste. But still, they had a certain symbolic feeling about them, and he smiled at them.

Nothing, indeed, could disturb Mr. Payne's good temper this morning—not the jostling crowds on the pavements or the customary traffic jams which seemed, indeed, to please him. He walked along until he came to a large store that said above it, in enormous letters, ORBIN'S. These letters were picked out in colored lights, and the lights themselves were festooned with Christmas trees and holly wreaths and the figures of the Seven Dwarfs, all of which lighted up.

Orbin's department store went right round the corner into the comparatively quiet Jessiter Street. Once again Mr. Payne went through a customary ceremony. He crossed the road and went down several steps into an establishment unique of its kind—Danny's Shoe Parlor. Here, sitting on a kind of throne in this semi-basement, one saw through a small window the lower halves of passers-by. Here Danny, with two assistants almost as old as himself, had been shining shoes for almost 30 years.

Leather-faced, immensely lined, but still remarkably sharp-eyed, Danny knelt down now in front of Mr. Payne, turned up the cuffs of his trousers, and began to put an altogether superior shine on already well-polished shoes.

"Lovely morning, Mr. Payne."

"You can't see much of it from here."

"More than you think. You see the pavements, and if they're not spotted, right off you know it isn't raining. Then there's something in the way people walk,

you know what I mean, like it's Christmas in the air."
Mr. Payne laughed indulgently. Now Danny was
mildly reproachful. "You still haven't brought me in
that pair of black shoes, sir."

Mr. Payne frowned slightly. A week ago he had
been almost knocked down by a bicyclist, and the
mudguard of the bicycle had scraped badly one of the
shoes he was wearing, cutting the leather at one point.
Danny was confident that he could repair the cut so
that it wouldn't show. Mr. Payne was not so sure.

"I'll bring them along," he said vaguely.

"Sooner the better, Mr. Payne, sooner the better."

Mr. Payne did not like being reminded of the bicycle incident. He gave Danny half a crown instead of
the ten shillings he had intended, crossed the road
again, and walked into the side entrance of Orbin's,
which called itself unequivocally "London's Greatest
Department Store."

This end of the store was quiet. He walked up the
stairs, past the grocery department on the ground
floor, and wine and cigars on the second, to jewelry
on the third. There were rarely many people in this
department, but today a small crowd had gathered
around a man who was making a speech. A placard
at the department entrance said: "The Russian Royal
Family Jewels. On display for two weeks by kind permission of the Grand Duke and Grand Duchess of
Moldo-Lithuania."

These were not the Russian Crown Jewels, seized
by the Bolsheviks during the Revolution, but an inferior collection brought out of Russia by the Grand
Duke and Grand Duchess, who had long since become
plain Mr. and Mrs. Skandorski, who lived in New Jer-
sey, and were now on a visit to England.

Mr. Payne was not interested in Mr. and Mrs.
Skandorski, nor in Sir Henry Orbin who was stum-
bling through a short speech. He was interested only
in the jewels. When the speech was over he mingled
with the crowd round the showcase that stood almost
in the middle of the room.

The royal jewels lay on beds of velvet—a tiara that

looked too heavy to be worn, diamond necklaces and bracelets, a cluster of diamonds and emeralds, and a dozen other pieces, each with an elegant calligraphic description of its origin and history. Mr. Payne did not see the jewels as a romantic relic of the past, nor did he permit himself to think of them as things of beauty. He saw them as his personal Christmas present.

He walked out of the department, looking neither to left nor right, and certainly paying no attention to the spotty young clerk who rushed forward to open the door for him. He walked back to his bookshop, sniffing that sharp December air, made another little joke to Miss Oliphant, and told her she could go out to lunch. During her lunch hour he sold an American a set of a Victorian magazine called *The Jewel Box*.

It seemed a good augury.

In the past ten years Mr. Payne had engineered successfully—with the help of other, and inferior, intellects—six jewel robberies. He had remained undetected, he believed, partly because of his skill in planning, partly because he ran a perfectly legitimate book business, and partly because he broke the law only when he needed money. He had little interest in women, and his habits were generally ascetic, but he did have one vice.

Mr. Payne developed a system at roulette, an improvement on the almost infallible Frank-Konig system, and every year he went to Monte Carlo and played his system. Almost every year it failed—or rather, it revealed certain imperfections which he then tried to remedy.

It was to support his foolproof system that Mr. Payne had turned from bookselling to crime. He believed himself to be, in a quiet way, a mastermind in the modern criminal world.

Those associated with him were far from that, as he immediately would have acknowledged. He met them two evenings after he had looked at the royal jewels, in his pleasant little flat above the shop, which could

be approached from a side entrance opening into an
alley.

There was Stacey, who looked what he was, a thick-
nosed thug; there was a thin young man in a tight suit
whose name was Jack Line, and who was always called
Straight or Straight Line; and there was Lester Jones,
the spotty clerk in the Jewelry Department.

Stacey and Straight Line sat drinking whiskey, Mr.
Payne sipped some excellent sherry, and Lester Jones
drank nothing at all, while Mr. Payne in his pedantic,
almost schoolmasterly manner, told them how the robbery was to be accomplished.

"You all know what the job is, but let me tell you
how much it is worth. In its present form the collection is worth whatever sum you'd care to mention—a
quarter of a million pounds perhaps. There is no real
market value. But alas, it will have to be broken up.
My friend thinks the value will be in the neighborhood
of fifty thousand pounds. Not less, and not much
more."

"Your friend?" the jewelry clerk said timidly.

"The fence. Lambie, isn't it?" It was Stacey who
spoke. Mr. Payne nodded. "Okay, how do we split?"

"I will come to that later. Now, here are the diffi-
culties. First of all, there are two store detectives on
each floor. We must see to it that those on the third
floor are not in the Jewelry Department. Next, there
is a man named Davidson, an American, whose job
it is to keep an eye on the jewels. He has been
brought over here by a protection agency, and it is
likely that he will carry a gun. Third, the jewels are
in a showcase, and any attempt to open this showcase
other than with the proper key will set off an alarm.
The key is kept in the Manager's Office, inside the
Jewelry Department."

Stacey got up, shambled over to the whiskey de-
canter, and poured himself another drink. "Where do
you get all this from?"

Mr. Payne permitted himself a small smile. "Lester
works in the department. Lester is a friend of mine."

Stacey looked at Lester with contempt. He did not like amateurs.

"Let me continue, and tell you how the obstacles can be overcome. First, the two store detectives. Supposing that a small fire bomb were planted in the Fur Department, at the other end of the third floor from Jewelry—that would certainly occupy one detective for a few minutes. Supposing that in the department that deals with ladies' hats, which is next to Furs, a woman shopper complained that she had been robbed—this would certainly involve the other store detective. Could you arrange this, Stace? These—assistants, shall I call them?—would be paid a straight fee. They would have to carry out their diversions at a precise time, which I have fixed as ten thirty in the morning."

"Okay," said Stacey. "Consider it arranged."

"Next, Davidson. He is an American, as I said, and Lester tells me that a happy event is expected in his family any day now. He has left Mrs. Davidson behind in America, of course. Now, supposing that a call came through, apparently from an American hospital, for Mr. Davidson. Supposing that the telephone in the Jewelry Department was out of order because the cord had been cut. Davidson would be called out of the department for the few minutes, no more, that we should need."

"Who cuts the cord?" Stacey asked.

"That will be part of Lester's job."

"And who makes the phone call?"

"Again, Stace, I hoped that you might be able to provide—"

"I can do that." Stacey drained his whiskey. "But what do you do?"

Mr. Payne's lips, never full, were compressed to a disapproving line. He answered the implied criticism only by inviting them to look at two maps—one the layout of the entire third floor, the other of the Jewelry Department itself. Stacey and Straight were impressed, as the uneducated always are, by such evidence of careful planning.

"The Jewelry Department is at one end of the third

floor. It has only one exit—into the Carpet Department. There is a service lift which comes straight up into the Jewelry Department. You and I, Stace, will be in that. We shall stop it between floors with the Emergency Stop button. At exactly ten thirty-two we shall go up to the third floor. Lester will give us a sign. If everything has gone well, we proceed. If not, we call the job off. Now, what I propose . . ."

He told them, they listened, and they found it good. Even the ignorant, Mr. Payne was glad to see, could recognize genius. He told Straight Line his role.

"We must have a car, Straight, and a driver. What he has to do is simple, but he must stay cool. So I thought of you." Straight grinned.

"In Jessiter Street, just outside the side entrance to Orbin's, there is a parking space reserved for Orbins' customers. It is hardly ever full. But if it is full you can double park there for five minutes—cars often do that. I take it you can—acquire a car, shall I say?— for the purpose. You will face away from Oxford Street, and you will have no more than a few minutes' run to Lambie's house on Greenly Street. You will drop Stace and me, drive on a mile or two, and leave the car. We shall give the stuff to Lambie. He will pay on the nail. Then we all split."

From that point they went on to argue about the split. The argument was warm, but not really heated. They settled that Stacey would get 25 per cent of the total, Straight and Lester 12½ per cent each, and that half would go to the mastermind. Mr. Payne agreed to provide out of his share the £150 that Stacey said would cover the three diversions.

The job was fixed six days ahead—for Tuesday of the following week.

Stacey had two faults which had prevented him from rising high in his profession. One was that he drank too much, the other that he was stupid. He made an effort to keep his drinking under control, knowing that when he drank he talked. So he did not even tell his wife about the job, although she was safe enough.

But he could not resist cheating about the money, which Payne had given to him in full.

The fire bomb was easy. Stacey got hold of a little man named Shrimp Bateson, and fixed it with him. There was no risk, and Shrimp thought himself well paid with twenty-five quid. The bomb itself cost only a fiver, from a friend who dealt in hardware. It was guaranteed to cause just a little fire, nothing serious.

For the telephone call Stacey used a Canadian who was grubbing a living at a striptease club. It didn't seem to either of them that the job was worth more than a tenner, but the Canadian asked for twenty and got fifteen.

The woman was a different matter, for she had to be a bit of an actress, and she might be in for trouble since she actually had to cause a disturbance. Stacey hired an eighteen-stone Irish woman named Lucy O'Malley, who had once been a female wrestler, and had very little in the way of a record—nothing more than a couple of drunk and disorderlies. She refused to take anything less than £50, realizing, as the others hadn't, that Stacey must have something big on.

The whole lot came to less than £100, so that there was cash to spare. Stacey paid them all half their money in advance, put the rest of the £100 aside, and went on a roaring drunk for a couple of days, during which he somehow managed to keep his mouth buttoned and his nose clean.

When he reported on Monday night to Mr. Payne he seemed to have everything fixed, including himself.

Straight Line was a reliable character, a young man who kept himself to himself. He pinched the car on Monday afternoon, took it along to the semilegitimate garage run by his father-in-law, and put new license plates on it. There was no time for a respray job, but he roughed the car up a little so that the owner would be unlikely to recognize it if by an unlucky chance he should be passing outside Orbin's on Tuesday morning. During this whole operation, of course, Straight wore gloves.

He also reported to Mr. Payne on Monday night.

Lester's name was not really Lester—it was Leonard. His mother and his friends in Balham, where he had been born and brought up, called him Lenny. He detested this, as he detested his surname and the pimples that, in spite of his assiduous efforts with ointment, appeared on his face every couple of months. There was nothing he could do about the name of Jones, because it was on his National Insurance card, but Lester for Leonard was a gesture toward emancipation.

Another gesture was made when he left home and mother for a one-room flat in Notting Hill Gate. A third gesture—and the most important one—was his friendship with Lucille, whom he had met in a jazz club called The Whizz Fizz.

Lucille called herself an actress, but the only evidence of it was that she occasionally sang in the club. Her voice was tuneless but loud. After she sang, Lester always bought her a drink, and the drink was always whiskey.

"So what's new?" she said. "Lester-boy, what's new?"

"I sold a diamond necklace today. Two hundred and fifty pounds. Mr. Marston was very pleased." Mr. Marston was the manager of the Jewelry Department.

"So Mr. Marston was pleased. Big deal." Lucille looked round restlessly, tapping her foot.

"He might give me a raise."

"Another ten bob a week and a pension for your fallen arches."

"Lucille, won't you—"

"No." The peak of emancipation for Lester, a dream beyond which his thoughts really could not reach, was that one day Lucille would come to live with him. Far from that, she had not even slept with him yet. "Look, Lester-boy, I know what I want, and let's face it, you haven't got it."

He was incautious enough to ask, "What?"

"Money, moolah, the green folding stuff. Without it you're nothing, with it they can't hurt you."

Lester was drinking whiskey too, although he didn't really like it. Perhaps, but for the whiskey, he would never have said, "Supposing I had money?"

"What money? Where would you get it—draw it out of the Savings Bank?"

"I mean a lot of money."

"Lester-boy, I don't think in penny numbers. I'm talking about real money."

The room was thick with smoke; the Whizz Fizz Kids were playing. Lester leaned back and said deliberately, "Next week I'll have money—thousands of pounds."

Lucille was about to laugh. Then she said, "It's my turn to buy a drink, I'm feeling generous. Hey, Joe. Two more of the same."

Later that night they lay on the bed in his one-room flat. She had let him make love to her, and he had told her everything.

"So the stuff's going to a man called Lambie in Greenly Street?"

Lester had never before drunk so much in one evening. Was it six whiskies or seven? He felt ill, and alarmed. "Lucille, you won't say anything? I mean, I wasn't supposed to tell—"

"Relax. What do you take me for?" She touched his cheek with red-tipped nails. "Besides, we shouldn't have secrets, should we?"

He watched her as she got off the bed and began to dress. "Won't you stay? I mean, it would be all right with the landlady."

"No can do, Lester-boy. See you at the club, though. Tomorrow night. Promise."

"Promise." When she had gone he turned over on to his side and groaned. He feared that he was going to be sick, and he was. Afterwards, he felt better.

Lucille went home to her flat in Earl's Court which she shared with a man named Jim Baxter. He had been sent to Borstal for a robbery from a confectioner's which had involved considerable violence. Since then he had done two short stretches. He listened to what she had to say, then asked, "What's this Lester like?"

"A creep."

"Has he got the nerve to kid you, or do you think it's on the level, what he's told you?"

"He wouldn't kid me. He wants me to live with him when he's got the money. I said I might."

Jim showed her what he thought of that idea. Then he said, "Tuesday morning, eh. Until then, you play along with this creep. Any change in plans I want to know about it. You can do it, can't you, baby?"

She looked up at him. He had a scar on the left side of his face which she thought made him look immensely attractive. "I can do it. And Jim?"

"Yes?"

"What about afterwards?"

"Afterwards, baby? Well, for spending money there's no place like London. Unless it's Paris."

Lester Jones also reported on Monday night. Lucille was being very kind to him, so he no longer felt uneasy.

Mr. Payne gave them all a final briefing and stressed that timing, in this as in every similar affair, was the vital element.

Mr. Rossiter Payne rose on Tuesday morning at his usual time, just after eight o'clock. He bathed and shaved with care and precision, and ate his usual breakfast of one soft-boiled egg, two pieces of toast, and one cup of unsugared coffee. When Miss Oliphant arrived he was already in the shop.

"My dear Miss Oliphant. Are you, as they say, ready to cope this morning?"

"Of course, Mr. Payne. Do you have to go out?"

"I do. Something quite unexpected. An American collector named—but I mustn't tell his name even to you, he doesn't want it known—is in London, and he has asked me to see him. He wants to try to buy the manuscripts of—but there again I'm sworn to secrecy, although if I weren't I should surprise you. I am calling on him, so I shall leave things in your care until—" Mr. Payne looked at his expensive watch—"not later than midday. I shall certainly be back by then. In the meantime, Miss Oliphant, I entrust my ware to you."

She giggled. "I won't let anyone steal the stock, Mr. Payne."

Mr. Payne went upstairs again to his flat where, laid out on his bed, was a very different set of clothes from that which he normally wore. He emerged later from the little side entrance looking quite unlike the dapper, retired Guards officer known to Miss Oliphant.

His clothes were of the shabby nondescript ready-to-wear kind that might be worn by a City clerk very much down on his luck—the sleeve and trouser cuffs distinctly frayed, the tie a piece of dirty string. Curling strands of rather disgustingly gingery hair strayed from beneath his stained gray trilby hat and his face was gray too—gray and much lined, the face of a man of sixty who has been defeated by life.

Mr. Payne had bright blue eyes, but the man who came out of the side entrance had, thanks to contact lenses, brown ones. This man shuffled off down the alley with shoulders bent, carrying a rather dingy suitcase. He was quite unrecognizable as the upright Rossiter Payne.

Indeed, if there was a criticism to be made of him, it was that he looked almost too much the "little man." Long, long ago, Mr. Payne had been an actor, and although his dramatic abilities were extremely limited, he had always loved and been extremely good at make-up.

He took with him a realistic-looking gun that, in fact, fired nothing more lethal than caps. He was a man who disliked violence, and thought it unnecessary.

After he left Mr. Payne on Monday night, Stacey had been unable to resist having a few drinks. The alarm clock wakened him to a smell of frizzling bacon. His wife sensed that he had a job on, and she came into the bedroom as he was taking the Smith and Wesson out of the cupboard.

"Bill." He turned round. "Do you need that?"

"What do you think?"

"Don't take it."

"Ah, don't be stupid."

"Bill, please. I get frightened."

Stacey put the gun into his hip pocket. "Won't use it. Just makes me feel a bit more comfortable, see?"

He ate his breakfast with a good appetite and then telephoned Shrimp Bateson, Lucy O'Malley, and the Canadian, to make sure they were ready. They were. His wife watched him fearfully. Then he came to say goodbye.

"Bill, look after yourself."

"Always do." And he was gone.

Lucille had spent Monday night with Lester. This was much against her wish, but Jim had insisted on it, saying that he must know of any possible last-minute change.

Lester had no appetite at all. She watched with barely concealed contempt as he drank no more than half a cup of coffee and pushed aside his toast. When he got dressed his fingers were trembling so that he could hardly button his shirt.

"Today's the day, then."

"Yes. I wish it was over."

"Don't worry."

He said eagerly, "I'll see you in the club tonight."

"Yes."

"I shall have the money then, and we could go away together. Oh, no, of course not—I've got to stay on the job."

"That's right," she said, humoring him.

As soon as he had gone, she rang Jim and reported that there were no last-minute changes.

Straight Line lived with his family. They knew he had a job on, but nobody talked about it. Only his mother stopped him at the door and said, "Good luck, son," and his father said, "Keep your nose clean."

Straight went to the garage and got out the Jag. 10:30.

Shrimp Bateson walked into the Fur Department with a brown-paper package under his arm. He strolled about pretending to look at furs, while trying to find a place to put down the little parcel. There were several shoppers and he went unnoticed.

He stopped at the point where Furs led to the stairs, moved into a window embrasure, took the little metal cylinder out of its brown-paper wrapping, pressed the switch which started the mechanism, and walked rapidly away.

He had almost reached the door when he was tapped on the shoulder. He turned. A clerk was standing with the brown paper in his hand.

"Excuse me, sir, I think you've dropped something. I found this paper—"

"No, no," Shrimp said. "It's not mine."

There was no time to waste in arguing. Shrimp turned and half walked, half ran, through the doors and to the staircase. The clerk followed him. People were coming up the stairs, and Shrimp, in a desperate attempt to avoid them, slipped and fell, bruising his shoulder.

The clerk was standing hesitantly at the top of the stairs when he heard the *whoosh* of sound and, turning, saw flames. He ran down the stairs then, took Shrimp firmly by the arm and said, "I think you'd better come back with me, sir."

The bomb had gone off on schedule, setting fire to the window curtains and to one end of a store counter. A few women were screaming, and other clerks were busy saving the furs. Flack, one of the store detectives, arrived on the spot quickly, and organized the use of the fire extinguishers. They got the fire completely under control in three minutes.

The clerk, full of zeal, brought Shrimp along to Flack. "Here's the man who did it."

Flack looked at him. "Firebug, eh?"

"Let me go. I had nothing to do with it."

"Let's talk to the manager, shall we?" Flack said, and led Shrimp away.

The time was now 10:39.

* * *

Lucy O'Malley looked at herself in the glass, and at the skimpy hat perched on her enormous head. Her fake-crocodile handbag, of a size to match her person, had been put down on a chair nearby.

"What do you feel, madam?" the young saleswoman asked, ready to take her cue from the customer's reaction.

"Terrible."

"Perhaps it isn't really you."

"It looks bloody awful," Lucy said. She enjoyed swearing, and saw no reason why she should restrain herself.

The salesgirl laughed perfunctorily and dutifully, and moved over again toward the hats. She indicated a black hat with a wide brim. "Perhaps something more like this?"

Lucy looked at her watch. 10:31. It was time. She went across to her handbag, opened it, and screamed.

"Is something the matter, madam?"

"I've been robbed!"

"Oh, really, I don't think that can have happened."

Lucy had a sergeant-major's voice, and she used it. "Don't tell me what can and can't have happened, young woman. My money was in here, and now it's gone. Somebody's taken it."

The salesgirl, easily intimidated, blushed. The department supervisor, elegant, eagle-nosed, blue-rinsed, moved across like an arrow and asked politely if she could help.

"My money's been stolen," Lucy shouted. "I put my bag down for a minute, twenty pounds in it, and now it's gone. That's the class of people they get in Orbin's." She addressed this last sentence to another shopper, who moved away hurriedly.

"Let's look, shall we, just to make sure." Blue Rinse took hold of the handbag, Lucy took hold of it too, and somehow the bag's contents spilled onto the carpet.

"You stupid fool," Lucy roared.

"I'm sorry, madam," Blue Rinse said icily. She

picked up handkerchief, lipstick, powder compact, tissues. Certainly there was no money in the bag. "You're sure the money was in the bag?"

"Of course I'm sure. It was in my purse. I had it five minutes ago. Someone here has stolen it."

"Not so loud, please, madam."

"I shall speak as loudly as I like. Where's your store detective, or haven't you got one?"

Sidley, the other detective on the third floor, was pushing through the little crowd that had collected. "What seems to be the matter?"

"This lady says twenty pounds has been stolen from her handbag." Blue Rinse just managed to refrain from emphasizing the word "lady."

"I'm very sorry. Shall we talk about it in the office?"

"I don't budge until I get my money back." Lucy was carrying an umbrella, and she waved it threateningly. However, she allowed herself to be led along to the office. There the handbag was examined again and the salesgirl, now tearful, was interrogated. There also Lucy, having surreptitiously glanced at the time, put a hand into the capacious pocket of her coat, and discovered the purse. There was twenty pounds in it, just as she had said.

She apologized, although the apology went much against the grain for her, declined the suggestion that she should return to the hat counter, and left the store with the consciousness of a job well done.

"Well," Sidley said. "I shouldn't like to tangle with her on a dark night."

The time was now 10:40.

The clock in the Jewelry Department stood at exactly 10:33 when a girl came running in, out of breath, and said to the manager, "Oh, Mr. Marston, there's a telephone call for Mr. Davidson. It's from America."

Marston was large, and inclined to get pompous. "Put it through here, then."

"I can't. There's something wrong with the line in this department—it seems to be dead."

Davidson had heard his name mentioned, and came over to them quickly. He was a crew-cut American, tough and lean. "It'll be about my wife, she's expecting a baby. Where's the call?"

"We've got it in Administration, one floor up."

"Come on, then." Davidson started off at what was almost a run, and the girl trotted after him. Marston stared at both of them disapprovingly. He became aware that one of his clerks, Lester Jones, was looking rather odd.

"Is anything the matter, Jones? Do you feel unwell?"

Lester said that he was all right. The act of cutting the telephone cord had filled him with terror, but with the departure of Davidson he really did feel better. He thought of the money—and of Lucille.

Lucille was just saying goodbye to Jim Baxter and his friend Eddie Grain. They were equipped with an arsenal of weapons, including flick knives, bicycle chains, and brass knuckles. They did not, however, carry revolvers.

"You'll be careful," Lucille said to Jim.

"Don't worry. This is going to be like taking candy from a baby, isn't it, Eddie?"

"S'right," Eddie said. He had a limited vocabulary, and an almost perpetual smile. He was a terror with a knife.

The Canadian made the call from the striptease club. He had a girl with him. He had told her that it would be a big giggle. When he heard Davidson's voice—the time was just after ten thirty-four—he said, "Is that Mr. Davidson?"

"Yes."

"This is the James Long Foster Hospital in Chicago, Mr. Davidson, Maternity floor."

"Yes?"

"Will you speak up, please. I can't hear you very well."

"Have you got some news of my wife?" Davidson

said loudly. He was in a small booth next to the store switchboard. There was no reply. "Hello? Are you there?"

The Canadian put one hand over the receiver, and ran the other up the girl's bare thigh. "Let him stew a little." The girl laughed. They could hear Davidson asking if they were still on the line. Then the Canadian spoke again.

"Hello, hello, Mr. Davidson. We seem to have a bad connection."

"I can hear you clearly. What news is there?"

"No need to worry, Mr. Davidson. Your wife is fine."

"Has she had the baby?"

The Canadian chuckled. "Now, don't be impatient. That's not the kind of thing you can hurry, you know."

"What have you got to tell me then? Why are you calling?"

The Canadian put his hand over the receiver again, said to the girl, "You say something."

"What shall I say?"

"Doesn't matter—that we've got the wires crossed or something."

The girl leaned over, picked up the telephone. "This is the operator. Who are you calling?"

In the telephone booth sweat was running off Davidson. He hammered with his fist on the wall of the booth. "Damn you, get off the line! Put me back to the Maternity Floor."

"This is the operator. Who do you want, please?"

Davidson checked himself suddenly. The girl had a Cockney voice. "Who are you? What's your game?"

The girl handed the telephone back to the Canadian, looking frightened. "He's on to me."

"Hell." The Canadian picked up the receiver again, but the girl had left it, uncovered, and Davidson had heard the girl's words. He dropped the telephone, pushed open the door of the booth, and raced for the stairs. As he ran he loosened the revolver in his hip pocket.

The time was now 10:41.

Straight Line brought the Jaguar smoothly to a stop in the space reserved for Orbin's customers, and looked at his watch. It was 10:32.

Nobody questioned him, nobody so much as gave him a glance. Beautiful, he thought, a nice smooth job, really couldn't be simpler. Then his hands tightened on the steering wheel.

He saw in the rear-view mirror, standing just a few yards behind him, a policeman. Three men were evidently asking the policeman for directions, and the copper was consulting a London place map.

Well, Straight thought, he can't see anything of me except my back, and in a couple of minutes he'll be gone. There was still plenty of time. Payne and Stacey weren't due out of the building until 10:39 or 10:40. Yes, plenty of time.

But there was a hollow feeling in Straight's stomach as he watched the policeman in his mirror.

Some minutes earlier, at 10:24, Payne and Stacey had met at the service elevator beside the Grocery Department on the ground floor. They had met this early because of the possibility that the elevator might be in use when they needed it, although from Lester's observation it was used mostly in the early morning and late afternoon.

They did not need the elevator until 10:30, and they would be very unlucky if it was permanently in use at that time. If they were that unlucky—well, Mr. Payne had said with the pseudo-philosophy of the born gambler, they would have to call the job off. But even as he said this he knew that it was not true, and that having gone so far he would not turn back.

The two men did not speak to each other, but advanced steadily toward the elevator by way of inspecting chow mein, hymettus honey, and real turtle soup. The Grocery Department was full of shoppers, and the two men were quite unnoticed. Mr. Payne reached the elevator first and pressed the button. They were in luck. The door opened.

Within seconds they were both inside. Still neither man spoke. Mr. Payne pressed the button which said 3, and then, when they had passed the second floor, the button that said Emergency Stop. Jarringly the elevator came to a stop. It was now immobilized, so far as a call from outside was concerned. It could be put back into motion only by calling in engineers who would free the Emergency Stop mechanism—or, of course, by operating the elevator from inside.

Stacey shivered a little. The elevator was designed for freight, and therefore roomy enough to hold twenty passengers; but Stacey had a slight tendency to claustrophobia which was increased by the thought that they were poised between floors. He said, "I suppose that bloody thing will work when you press the button?"

"Don't worry, my friend. Have faith in me." Mr. Payne opened the dingy suitcase, revealing as he did so that he was now wearing rubber gloves. In the suitcase were two long red cloaks, two fuzzy white wigs, two thick white beards, two pairs of outsize horn-rimmed spectacles, two red noses, and two hats with large tassels. "This may not be a perfect fit for you, but I don't think you can deny that it's a perfect disguise."

They put on the clothes, Mr. Payne with the pleasure he always felt in dressing up, Stacey with a certain reluctance. The idea was clever, all right, he had to admit that, and when he looked in the elevator's small mirror and saw a Santa Claus looking back at him, he was pleased to find himself totally unrecognizable. Deliberately he took the Smith and Wesson out of his jacket and put it into the pocket of the red cloak.

"You understand, Stace, there is no question of using that weapon."

"Unless I have to."

"There is no question," Mr. Payne repeated firmly. "Violence is never necessary. It is a confession that one lacks intelligence."

"We got to point it at them, haven't we? Show we mean business."

Mr. Payne acknowledged that painful necessity by a downward twitch of his mouth, undiscernible beneath the false beard.

"Isn't it time, yet?"

Mr. Payne looked at his watch. "It is now ten twenty-nine. We go—over the top, you might call it—at ten thirty-two precisely. Compose yourself to wait, Stace."

Stacey grunted. He could not help admiring his companion, who stood peering into the small glass, adjusting his beard and mustache, and settling his cloak more comfortably. When at last Mr. Payne nodded, and said, "Here we go," and pressed the button marked 3, resentment was added to admiration. He's all right now, but wait till we get to the action, Stacey thought. His gloved hand on the Smith and Wesson reassured him of strength and efficiency.

The elevator shuddered, moved upward, stopped. The door opened. Mr. Payne placed his suitcase in the open elevator door so that it would stay open and keep the elevator at the third floor. Then they stepped out.

To Lester the time that passed after Davidson's departure and before the elevator door opened was complete and absolute torture.

The whole thing had seemed so easy when Mr. Payne had outlined it to them. "It is simply a matter of perfect timing," he had said. "If everybody plays his part properly, Stace and I will be back in the lift within five minutes. Planning is the essence of this, as of every scientific operation. Nobody will be hurt, and nobody will suffer financially except—" and here he had looked at Lester with a twinkle in his frosty eyes—"except the insurance company. And I don't think the most tender-hearted of us will worry too much about the insurance company."

That was all very well, and Lester had done what he was supposed to do, but he hadn't really been able

to believe that the rest of it would happen. He had
been terrified, but with the terror was mixed a sense
of unreality.

He still couldn't believe, even when Davidson went
to the telephone upstairs, that the plan would go
through without a hitch. He was showing some costume jewelry to a thin old woman who kept roping
necklaces around her scrawny neck, and while he did
so he kept looking at the elevator, above which was
the department clock. The hands moved slowly, after
Davidson left, from 10:31 to 10:32.

They're not coming, Lester thought. It's all off. A
flood of relief, touched with regret but with relief pre-
dominating, went through him. Then the elevator
door opened, and the two Santa Clauses stepped out.
Lester started convulsively.

"Young man," the thin woman said severely, "it
doesn't seem to me that I have your undivided attention. Haven't you anything in blue and amber?"

It had been arranged that Lester would nod to signify that Davidson had left the department, or shake
his head if anything had gone wrong. He nodded now
as though he had St. Vitus's Dance.

The thin woman looked at him, astonished. "Young
man, is anything the matter?"

"Blue and amber," Lester said wildly, "amber and
blue." He pulled out a box from under the counter
and began to look through it. His hands were shaking.

Mr. Payne had been right in his assumption that no
surprise would be occasioned by the appearance of
two Santa Clauses in any department at this time of
year. This, he liked to think, was his own characteris-
tic touch—the touch of, not to be unduly modest
about it, creative genius. There were a dozen people
in the Jewelry Department, half of them looking at
the Russian Royal Family Jewels, which had proved
less of an attraction than Sir Henry Orbin had hoped.
Three of the others were wandering about in the idle
way of people who are not really intending to buy
anything, and the other three were at the counters,
where they were being attended to by Lester, a sales-

girl whose name was Miss Glenny, and by Marston himself.

The appearance of the Santa Clauses aroused only the feeling of pleasure experienced by most people at sight of these slightly artificial figures of jollity. Even Marston barely glanced at them. There were half a dozen Santa Clauses in the store during the weeks before Christmas, and he assumed that these two were on their way to the Toy Department, which was also on the third floor, or to the Robin Hood in Sherwood Forest tableau, which was this year's display for children.

The Santa Clauses walked across the floor together as though they were in fact going into Carpets and then on to the Toy Department, but after passing Lester they diverged. Mr. Payne went to the archway that led from Jewelry to Carpets, and Stacey abruptly turned behind Lester toward the Manager's Office.

Marston, trying to sell an emerald brooch to an American who was not at all sure his wife would like it, looked up in surprise. He had a natural reluctance to make a fuss in public, and also to leave his customer; but when he saw Stacey with a hand actually on the door of his own small but sacred office he said to the American, "Excuse me a moment, sir," and said to Miss Glenny, "Look after this gentleman, please"—by which he meant that the American should not be allowed to walk out with the emerald brooch—and called out, although not so loudly that the call could be thought of as anything so vulgar as a shout, "Just a moment, please. What are you doing there? What do you want?"

Stacey ignored him. In doing so he was carrying out Mr. Payne's specific instructions. At some point it was inevitable that the people in the department would realize that a theft was taking place, but the longer they could be kept from realizing it, Mr. Payne had said, the better. Stacey's own inclination would have been to pull out his revolver at once and terrorize anybody likely to make trouble; but he did as he was told.

The Manager's Office was not much more than a cubbyhole, with papers neatly arranged on a desk; behind the desk, half a dozen keys were hanging on the wall. The showcase key, Lester had said, was the second from the left, but for the sake of appearances Stacey took all the keys. He had just turned to go when Marston opened the door and saw the keys in Stacey's hand.

The manager was not lacking in courage. He understood at once what was happening and, without speaking, tried to grapple with the intruder. Stacey drew the Smith and Wesson from his pocket and struck Marston hard with it on the forehead. The manager dropped to the ground. A trickle of blood came from his head.

The office door was open, and there was no point in making any further attempt at deception. Stacey swung the revolver around and rasped, "Just keep quiet, and nobody else will get hurt."

Mr. Payne produced his cap pistol and said, in a voice as unlike his usual cultured tones as possible, "Stay where you are. Don't move. We shall be gone in five minutes."

Somebody said, "Well, I'm damned." But no one moved. Marston lay on the floor, groaning. Stacey went to the showcase, pretended to fumble with another key, then inserted the right one. The case opened at once. The jewels lay naked and unprotected. He dropped the other keys on the floor, stretched in his gloved hands, picked up the royal jewels, and stuffed them into his pocket.

It's going to work, Lester thought unbelievingly, it's going to work. He watched, fascinated, as the cascade of shining stuff vanished into Stacey's pocket. Then he became aware that the thin woman was pressing something into his hand. Looking down, he saw with horror that it was a large, brand-new clasp knife, with the dangerous-looking blade open.

"Bought it for my nephew," the thin woman whispered. "As he passes you, go for him."

It had been arranged that if Lester's behavior

should arouse the least suspicion he should make a pretended attack on Stacey, who would give him a punch just severe enough to knock him down. Everything had gone so well, however, that this had not been necessary, but now it seemed to Lester that he had no choice.

As the two Santa Clauses backed across the room toward the service elevator, covering the people at the counters with their revolvers, one real and the other a toy, Lester launched himself feebly at Stacey, with the clasp knife demonstratively raised. At the same time Marston, on the other side of Stacey and a little behind him, rose to his feet and staggered in the direction of the elevator.

Stacey's contempt for Lester increased with the sight of the knife, which he regarded as an unnecessary bit of bravado. He shifted the revolver to his left hand, and with his right punched Lester hard in the stomach. The blow doubled Lester up. He dropped the knife and collapsed to the floor, writhing in quite genuine pain.

The delivery of the blow delayed Stacey so that Marston was almost up to him. Mr. Payne, retreating rapidly to the elevator, shouted a warning, but the manager was on Stacey, clawing at his robes. He did not succeed in pulling off the red cloak, but his other hand came away with the wig, revealing Stacey's own cropped brown hair. Stacey snatched back the wig, broke away, and fired the revolver with his left hand.

Perhaps he could hardly have said himself whether he intended to hit Marston, or simply to stop him. The bullet missed the manager and hit Lester, who was rising on one knee. Lester dropped again. Miss Glenny screamed, another woman cried out, and Marston halted.

Mr. Payne and Stacey were almost at the elevator when Davidson came charging in through the Carpet Department entrance. The American drew the revolver from his pocket and shot, all in one swift movement. Stacey fired back wildly. Then the two Santa Clauses were in the service elevator, and the door closed on them.

Davidson took one look at the empty showcase, and shouted to Marston, "Is there an emergency alarm that rings downstairs?"

The manager shook his head. "And my telephone's not working."

"They've cut the line." Davidson raced back through the Carpet Department to the passenger elevators.

Marston went over to where Lester was lying, with half a dozen people round him, including the thin woman. "We must get a doctor."

The American he had been serving said, "I am a doctor." He was bending over Lester, whose eyes were wide open.

"How is he?"

The American lowered his voice. "He got it in the abdomen."

Lester seemed to be trying to raise himself up. The thin woman helped him. He sat up, looked around, and said, "Lucille." Then blood suddenly rushed out of his mouth, and he sank back.

The doctor bent over again, then looked up. "I'm very sorry. He's dead."

The thin woman gave Lester a more generous obituary than he deserved. "He wasn't a very good clerk, but he was a brave young man."

Straight Line, outside in the stolen Jag, waited for the policeman to move. But not a bit of it. The three men with the policeman were pointing to a particular spot on the map, and the copper was laughing; they were having some sort of stupid joke together. What the hell, Straight thought, hasn't the bleeder got any work to do, doesn't he know he's not supposed to be hanging about?

Straight looked at his watch. 10:34, coming up to 10:35—and now, as the three men finally moved away, what should happen but that a teen-age girl should come up, and the copper was bending over toward her with a look of holiday good-will.

It's no good, Straight thought, I shall land them right in his lap if I stay here. He pulled away from the parking space, looked again at his watch. He was obsessed by the need to get out of the policeman's sight.

Once round the block, he thought, just once round can't take more than a minute, and I've got more than two minutes to spare. Then if the copper's still here I'll stay a few yards away from him with my engine running.

He moved down Jessiter Street and a moment after Straight had gone, the policeman, who had never even glanced at him, moved away too.

By Mr. Payne's plan they should have taken off their Santa Claus costumes in the service elevator and walked out at the bottom as the same respectable, anonymous citizens who had gone in; but as soon as they were inside the elevator Stacey said, "He hit me." A stain showed on the scarlet right arm of his robe.

Mr. Payne pressed the button to take them down. He was proud that, in this emergency, his thoughts came with clarity and logic. He spoke them aloud.

"No time to take these off. Anyway, they're just as good a disguise in the street. Straight will be waiting. We step out and into the car, take them off there. Davidson shouldn't have been back in that department for another two minutes."

"I gotta get to a doctor."

"We'll go to Lambie's first. He'll fix it." The elevator whirred downward. Almost timidly, Mr. Payne broached the subject that worried him most. "What happened to Lester?"

"He caught one." Stacey was pale.

The elevator stopped. Mr. Payne adjusted the wig on Stacey's head. "They can't possibly be waiting for us, there hasn't been time. We just walk out. Not too fast, remember. Casually, normally."

The elevator door opened and they walked the fifty feet to the Jessiter Street exit. They were delayed only by a small boy who rushed up to Mr. Payne, clung to his legs and shouted that he wanted his Christmas present. Mr. Payne gently disengaged him, whispered to his mother, "Our tea break. Back later," and moved on.

Now they were outside in the street. But there was no sign of Straight or the Jaguar.

Stacey began to curse. They crossed the road from Orbin's, stood outside Danny's Shoe Parlor for a period that seemed to both of them endless, but was, in fact, only thirty seconds. People looked at them curiously—two Santa Clauses wearing false noses—but they did not arouse great attention. They were oddities, yes, but oddities were in keeping with the time of year and Oxford Street's festive decorations.

"We've got to get away," Stacey said. "We're sitting ducks."

"Don't be a fool. We wouldn't get a hundred yards."

"Planning," Stacey said bitterly. "Fine bloody planning. If you ask me—"

"Here he is."

The Jag drew up beside them, and in a moment they were in and down Jessiter Street, away from Orbin's. Davidson was on the spot less than a minute later, but by the time he had found passers-by who had seen the two Santa Clauses get into the car, they were half a mile away.

Straight Line began to explain what had happened, Stacey swore at him, and Mr. Payne cut them both short.

"No time for that. Get these clothes off, talk later."

"You got the rocks?"

"Yes, but Stace has been hit. By the American detective. I don't think it's bad, though."

"Whatsisname, Lester, he okay?"

"There was trouble. Stace caught him with a bullet."

Straight said nothing more. He was not one to complain about something that couldn't be helped. His feelings showed only in the controlled savagery with which he maneuvered the Jag.

While Straight drove, Mr. Payne was taking off his own Santa Claus outfit and helping Stacey off with his. He stuffed them, with the wigs and beards and noses, back into the suitcase. Stacey winced as the robe came over his right arm, and Mr. Payne gave him a handkerchief to hold over it. At the same time he suggested that Stacey hand over the jewels, since Mr. Payne would be doing the negotiating with the fence. It was a mark of the trust that both men still reposed in Mr. Payne that Stacey handed them over without a word, and that Straight did not object or even comment.

They turned into the quiet Georgian terrace where Lambie lived. "Number Fifteen, right-hand side," Mr. Payne said.

Jim Baxter and Eddie Grain had been hanging about in the street for several minutes. Lucille had learned from Lester what car Straight was driving. They recognized the Jag immediately, and strolled toward it. They had just reached the car when it came to a stop in front of Lambie's house. Stacey and Mr. Payne got out.

Jim and Eddie were not, after all, too experienced. They made an elementary mistake in not waiting until Straight had driven away. Jim had his flick knife out and was pointing it at Mr. Payne's stomach.

"Come on now, Dad, give us the stuff and you won't get hurt," he said.

On the other side of the car Eddie Grain, less subtle, swung at Stacey with a shortened length of bicycle chain. Stacey, hit round the head, went down, and Eddie was on top of him, kicking, punching, searching.

Mr. Payne hated violence, but he was capable of defending himself. He stepped aside, kicked upward, and knocked the knife flying from Jim's hand. Then he rang the doorbell of Lambie's house. At the same

time Straight got out of the car and felled Eddie Grain
with a vicious rabbit punch.

During the next few minutes several things happened simultaneously. At the end of the road a police
whistle was blown, loudly and insistently, by an old
lady who had seen what was going on. Lambie, who
also saw what was going on and wanted no part of it,
told his manservant on no account to answer the doorbell or open the door.

Stacey, kicked and beaten by Eddie Grain, drew his
revolver and fired four shots. One of them struck
Eddie in the chest, and another hit Jim Baxter in the
leg. Eddie scuttled down the street holding his chest,
turned the corner, and ran slap into the arms of two
policemen hurrying to the scene.

Straight, who did not care for shooting, got back
into the Jag and drove away. He abandoned the Jag
as soon as he could, and went home.

When the police arrived, with a bleating Eddie in
tow, they found Stacey and Jim Baxter on the ground,
and several neighbors only too ready to tell confusing
stories about the great gang fight that had just taken
place. They interrogated Lambie, of course, but he
had not seen or heard anything at all.

And Mr. Payne? With a general melee taking place,
and Lambie clearly not intending to answer his doorbell, he had walked away down the road. When he
turned the corner he found a cab, which he took to
within a couple of hundred yards of his shop. Then, an
anonymous man carrying a shabby suitcase, he went in
through the little side entrance.

Things had gone badly, he reflected as he again
became Mr. Rossiter Payne the antiquarian bookseller, mistakes had been made. But happily they were
not his mistakes. The jewels would be hot, no doubt;
they would have to be kept for a while, but all was
not lost.

Stace and Straight were professionals—they would
never talk. And although Mr. Payne did not, of
course, know that Lester was dead, he realized that

the young man would be able to pose as a wounded hero and was not likely to be subjected to severe questioning.

So Mr. Payne was whistling *There's a Silver Lining* as he went down to greet Miss Oliphant.

"Oh, Mr. Payne," she trilled. "You're back before you said. It's not half-past eleven."

Could that be true? Yes, it was.

"Did the American collector—I mean, will you be able to sell him the manuscripts?"

"I hope so. Negotiations are proceeding, Miss Oliphant. They may take some time, but I hope they will reach a successful conclusion."

The time passed uneventfully until 2:30 in the afternoon when Miss Oliphant entered his little private office. "Mr. Payne, there are two gentlemen to see you. They won't say what it's about, but they look— well, rather funny."

As soon as Mr. Payne saw them and even before they produced their warrant cards, he knew that there was nothing funny about them. He took them up to the flat and tried to talk his way out of it, but he knew it was no use. They hadn't yet got search warrants, the Inspector said, but they would be taking Mr. Payne along anyway. It would save them some trouble if he would care to show them—

Mr. Payne showed them. He gave them the jewels and the Santa Claus disguises. Then he sighed at the weakness of subordinates. "Somebody squealed, I suppose."

"Oh, no. I'm afraid the truth is you were a bit careless."

"*I* was careless." Mr. Payne was genuinely scandalized.

"Yes. You were recognized."

"Impossible!"

"Not at all. When you left Orbin's and got out into the street, there was a bit of a mixup so that you had to wait. Isn't that right?"

"Yes, but I was completely disguised."

"Danny the shoeshine man knows you by name, doesn't he?"

"Yes, but he couldn't possibly have seen me."

"He didn't need to. Danny can't see any faces from his basement, as you know, but he did see something, and he came to tell us about it. He saw two pairs of legs, and the bottoms of some sort of red robes. And he saw the shoes. He recognized one pair of shoes, Mr. Payne. Not those you're wearing now, but that pair on the floor over there."

Mr. Payne looked across the room at the black shoes—shoes so perfectly appropriate to the role of shabby little clerk that he had been playing, and at the decisive, fatally recognizable sharp cut made by the bicycle mudguard in the black leather.

DEATH IN THE CHRISTMAS HOUR

James Powell

In the first hour of Christmas morning animals can talk and toys come to life provided no humans are lurking about.

Several minutes after the last stroke of midnight had tolled over the snowy Christmas city, a Welsh corgi named Owen Glendower could be seen leading a young man on a leash past the houseware windows of McTammany's Department Store.

Austin W. Metcalfe, as this young person called himself, possessed a round face cluttered with glasses and a short-stemmed, fat-bowled pipe whose operation he had not yet mastered. A burgundy muffler was tucked up neatly under his chin. His hands and feet were warm in fleece-lined leather. Every button of his dark-blue overcoat was buttoned. He moved with a sedate and serious air, having by dint of application and high purpose risen to be second assistant curator of the Metropolitan Museum of Toys.

In other words—as Owen Glendower would be the first to admit—Metcalfe was a very, very pompous young ass. The dog looked back over its shoulder as if about to unload a considerable burden of complaint. Poor square Metcalfe really needed his corners knocked off. The dog hoped some girl would come along crazy enough to take a liking to him and do the job before it was too late. Recently Metcalfe had met one who seemed to fit the bill. Owen Glendower had used his considerable powers of thought transference to inspire a phone call. (Half the good ideas humans get come from their pets. Owen Glendower didn't know where the other half came from.) But the young stick-in-the-mud wouldn't budge. The dog turned to mutter at a hydrant.

Though the wind was picking up, Metcalfe waited patiently in the falling snow, conscious of being a kindly and, he was sure, a beloved master. He'd have enjoyed dwelling on that but his pipe went out again and he had to struggle to relight it.

Meanwhile, around the corner and just ten feet from where he stood, the occupants of the largest of McTammany's toy windows were enjoying a fashion show. The Dick and Jane dolls were displaying their extensive wardrobes to an appreciative audience of frogs in frill collars, sows in dresses, and a variety of robots, those metal facsimiles of humanity who beeped, hummed, and flashed their approval in the most amazing manner considering that batteries were not included.

When Owen Glendower was ready, he coughed to warn the toys to freeze in their tracks and then led the young man around the corner so the whole window could see what an honest corgi had to put up with all year long. As for Metcalfe, he'd seen the window many times before. The museum had loaned its popular toy display and the young man's personal creation, "A Victorian Christmas," to McTammany's for the holidays. Metcalfe came daily to admire his handiwork on exhibit in the next window. But he always stopped here first. The antique toys never suffered from the comparison.

Unwilling to interrupt the toys' Christmas Hour any longer, Owen Glendower coughed again and led the way to Metcalfe's window. The young man's design represented a Victorian living room centering on a small alabaster fireplace. To its left stood a Christmas tree hung with brightly painted wooden ornaments and topped by a caroling angel.

Before the tree was a music-box ballerina on tiptoe and a blue-and-yellow jack-in-the-box. On the hearth rug stood a Punch and Judy show with two fine hand puppets. The right of the fireplace was occupied by a grass-green wing chair and a matching hassock topped with a most elegant Victorian dollhouse whose porcelain mistress stood at the door in a plum-colored hoop skirt. At the base of the hassock a nutcracker captain of hussars with fierce grin and drawn saber led a formation of toy soldiers in scarlet coats and bearskin hats.

Rather, that was how Metcalfe had laid out the exhibit. But tonight someone else's hand had been at work. The soldiers were nowhere to be seen. The hussar and the rest of the toys stood in a circle in front of the jack-in-the-box looking down at Judy, lying on the red Turkey carpet, a limp and strangely lifeless figure looking somehow less than a hand puppet without a hand in it.

And there was more uncanniness. The jack-in-the-box was out and nodding on its spring. But traffic vibrations sometimes triggered the box latch. And the hussar seemed atremble as though it had just snapped to attention. Still, that might have been Metcalfe's imagination. But where did that Sherlock Holmes doll come from? And why did Metcalfe have the distinct impression the little detective was on the verge of pointing an accusing finger?

Then he saw the teddy bear at Holmes' side and the light dawned. Miss Tinker, a department-store window dresser who'd helped him set up the museum display, said she always put her Teddy in one of the toy windows and please couldn't she sit him there on the wing chair? Well, Metcalfe'd had to laugh at that and explain how every toy, ornament, and piece of furniture in the display was an authentic Victorian artifact. Teddy bears were Edwardian. With bad grace she had accepted his compromise that she wrap up the bear and put it under the tree where more presents were needed. Why, he wondered, were the pretty ones all so feather-headed?

On the other hand, he hadn't been completely honest with her. The museum didn't have a Victorian Christmas-tree angel. Mr. Jacoby, their toy repair and reproduction wizard, had fashioned this one from parts of an Amelia Earhart doll damaged when the wire that held its monoplane to the ceiling above the Toys Conquer the Clouds display had broken. Metcalfe'd been tempted to call her up and confess. Now he was rather glad he hadn't. A Sherlock Holmes doll, indeed! Metcalfe relit his pipe and rocked back and forth on his heels, puffing with his hands clasped behind his back. Yes, he would definitely have to speak to the young lady about this. And about how the teddy bear got there, too.

Metcalfe might have stayed for some time, fuming, imagining his righteousness at this confrontation, but Owen Glendower gave a sigh of tedium and led him away, knowing that Mr. Metropolitan, the generous Armenian who was the museum's director and principal endower, had asked his second assistant curator to make an early-morning visit to the toy reliquary at the museum. Last Christmas morning the night watchman had reported discovering three dead alligators in a pool of blood in the Victorian Wing.

Asked to produce the carcasses, the man insisted he'd burned them in the furnace after cleaning up the mess. Asked to explain the disappearance of one of the finest of the Victorian dolls, the night watchman had professed ignorance. Metcalfe had been commissioned to drop in and smell the night watchman's breath to determine, as Mr. Metropolitan put it, "if the man's on the Christmas sauce."

As for where Teddy came from, the answer was the Midwest. Miss Ivy Tinker had brought him with her as a mascot when she moved East to take the job with McTammany's. For Teddy, mascoting was a kind of lonely, fallow time, waiting for Miss Ivy Tinker to get married and have children so he could get back to toying again. Teddy had spent his first Christmas Hour here in the East alone, pacing up and down with his paws in his pockets and nothing to do but kick at a corner of the rug.

To insure that wouldn't happen again, he had furrowed his brow and directed his powers of thought transference at Miss Ivy Tinker's sleeping head behind the bedroom door. The next morning over toast she announced that she'd dreamed she'd included him in one of her Christmas toy windows. And why not? The perfect cachet for a Tinker-dressed window. The stuffed bear wasn't surprised a bit. Half the good ideas humans get come from their toys. Teddy didn't know where the other half came from.

Teddy hadn't spent a boring Christmas Hour since. Last year he'd been right in the middle of McTammany's stuffed-animal window. On the stroke of midnight, in clopped the team of stuffed Clydesdales, the kangaroo pulled the spigot out of his pouch and told the old one about Australian beer being made out of kangaroo hops, and a great time'd been had by all. Teddy'd worn a hangover and a lopsided grin for the rest of the year.

And now it was the Christmas Hour again. Stretching at the first rush of vital power, Teddy felt the noisy paper and some constricting bond. His paw found the seam in the wrapping, located the end of the velvet bow, and pulled. With the toll of midnight sounding dimly in the distance, he emerged and found himself standing among a pile of presents under a Christmas tree. Farther out in the room he could see other toys coming to life. He was just about to join them when the sound of a muffled violin made him stop.

He lay his ear to the gay boxes one by one until he found the source. He stripped back the paper. The lid illustration on the box depicted night and fog and a doorway from another era. The number on the door was 221B. The name on the lamppost was Baker Street. Large bright letters declared: THE ORIGINAL SHERLOCK HOLMES DOLL. ANOTHER WONDERFUL CREATION FROM DOYLE TOYS.

Teddy opened the box. The doll inside wore a deer-stalker cap and a coat with a cape. In addition to its violin and bow, which the doll lay aside with a smile, the other accessories included a magnifying glass, a calabash pipe, and a Persian slipper stuffed with shag.

"Thank you, my dear sir," said Sherlock Holmes,

taking Teddy's proffered paw to help himself out of the box. "I've spent I don't know how many Christmases wedged down behind a radiator in the toy-department stockroom. I'm the sole survivor of an unpopular and long-forgotten line of dolls. I don't know whom to thank for being here."

"Miss Ivy Tinker needed more boxes for under the tree," said Teddy, introducing himself.

"Ursus arctus Rooseveltii? I hardly think so," said the detective. "And I did publish an anonymous monograph on stuffed animals." Reaching for his glass, he examined Teddy's eyes and the seam on his shoulder. "Your eyes are French glass manufactured by Homard et Fils. Your seams are a double stitch called English nightingale because, like that bird, it is only found in England east of the Severn and south of the Trent.

"Homard et Fils supplied only one company in that area, Tiddicomb and Weams. That firm produced stuffed bears only once. On the birth of Queen Victoria's son, Prince Leopold, in 1854, Tiddicomb and Weams presented the child with a papier-mâché replica of the House of Lords, complete with twelve stuffed bears dressed in stars and garters and full pontificals to represent the lords spiritual and temporal. This wonderful toy the teenaged prince later donated to an auction in aid of the victims of the great Chicago fire and it disappeared from sight in America. You, Teddy, are a Bear of the Realm."

Teddy's chest swelled with pride and his voice grew husky. "I believed it when Miss Ivy Tinker said I was a teddy bear. We stuffed animals are notoriously absent-minded."

"Well, come along, old fellow," said Holmes, taking his arm. "It's the Christmas Hour. The game's afoot. Time to wrap ourselves around a good stiff drink."

Teddy needed no urging. They strolled from under the tree together, walking to the beat of the carol being sung by the silver-voiced angel atop the tree—

who, in the nature of Christmas-tree angels, preferred to spend the hour singing hymns of joy and praise.

Suddenly a captain of hussars blocked their way, a dozen redcoats at his back. The officer raised a suspicious eyebrow at Teddy and lay the point of his saber against his hairy breast. "Well, you ain't no alligator but you could be a rat in disguise," said the hussar, gnashing his teeth in a most threatening manner.

Teddy knocked the saber aside and growled as a Bear of the Realm might. "What I am is a bear."

Impressed by this lack of meekness, the officer said, "You mean one of those stuffed-animal chappies? Then welcome aboard. Captain Rataplan here. We can use anyone with spunk enough to stand beside us in this damned business."

"And just what business is that, Captain?" asked Holmes.

"Let's save that for over a drink once we've got the perimeter secure," said the hussar. "I see old Punch has opened for business."

Holmes followed the officer's finger over to the hearth rug where the two hand puppets were converting their stage into a bar, Punch polishing the counter with a rag while Judy set up the bottles and glasses.

But Teddy's gaze couldn't get past the music-box ballerina only a few feet away. She had the dancer's classic features, small head, large eyes, and long legs. Teddy tried to catch her attention by wiggling his ears. "A fine figure of a woman," agreed Captain Rataplan. "That's Allegretta. Gretta, we call her. Likes to play hard to get, don't you know. Well, I don't mind that in a woman. Faint heart ne'er won fair lady, eh?" He snorted fiercely and marched his men away.

Holmes and Teddy headed off across the carpet in the direction of the bar. As they passed the closed jack-in-the-box, Holmes remarked, "Jack seems to be a slug-a-bed."

Then they stopped and introduced themselves to the ballerina, who sat nursing a foot in her lap. "Come and join us for a drink," urged Teddy, wiggling his ears outrageously. "Tempus fugit."

"I'll be right along, okay?" she said through chewing gum. "Boy, are my dogs barking."

"After a year on tiptoe, dogs that didn't bark would be quite a clue indeed," observed Holmes with a smile which she answered with a blank stare.

At the bar Punch greeted them with a "What'll it be, gents?" in a squeaking batlike voice.

"Something with a splash of the old gasogene, Landlord, if you please," said Holmes. "A scotch whisky, I think."

"Make mine a gibson," said Teddy. The cocktail vice had spread quickly among creatures who only came to life one hour a year.

"So be it, gents," said Punch. But as the hunchback reached for the scotch he shouted over his shoulder, "Judy, where are you off to?"

"The olives," squeaked his female partner.

"Onions for gibsons, old hoss," scolded Punch. He mixed their drinks and when Judy came back from the icebox carrying a pickled onion on the point of an ice pick he served them. "Your health, gents," he declared, raising his own mug of beer. As they clinked their drinks, Punch turned once again to Judy and demanded, "Where now, old hoss?"

"An olive," she said, waving the ice pick. "Here comes Captain Rataplan for his martooni."

But the hussar heard her and shook his head. "My men come first. Twelve mugs of the nut-brown ale." Judy put the ice pick in the pocket of her smock and obediently set to filling the mugs.

Turning to Holmes and his bear companion, Captain Rataplan said, "Getting back to the alligator situation, the damned things feed on sewer rats all year round. So come Christmas Hour we're a delicious change of pace and they swarm up and make a try for us. No problem. We can give as good as we get. And alligators are a stupid, muscle-bound crew.

"But then there are the rats. Cowards, but smart as whips. Gentlemen, one of these years the rats are going to talk the alligators into an alliance. What I see coming against us is an army of alligators each with a rat riding on its neck whispering orders in its ear. Mark my words, when that day dawns toydom will vanish from human memory and dogs and cats won't be far behind."

"A grim prospect, Captain," said Holmes gravely. "Let's hope the rats never get the idea."

But as Rataplan left with his mugs of ale on a tray, some of the gloom went with him. After a few pulls at his drink, Holmes leaned back with his elbows on the bar and said, "Rat masterminds astride alligators or not, Teddy, it's great to be alive again. I miss only one thing: a mystery to be solved. No, I'm a liar, Teddy. Two things."

"And what's the other, Holmes?" asked Teddy, chewing the onion from his gibson.

Sherlock Holmes did not answer. He straightened up. "Speak of the devil!" he exclaimed. "Excuse me, old man, won't you?" And taking off his cap, the detective strode across to the hassock where a woman stood smiling at him. Not a woman but *the* woman. "Can it be you, Miss Adler? I mean, Mrs. Godfrey Norton." For that indeed was the married name of the heroine of *A Scandal in Bohemia*.

"Good morning, Mr. Holmes," smiled the woman. "And it is Irene Adler. I assumed my professional name when my husband's death obliged me to return to the operatic stage."

"Allow me to offer you my arm, Miss Adler," urged the detective. "Let us walk a bit apart. I must know how you come to be here. I was just telling my friend Teddy that there are only two things I miss: Miss Irene Adler and a good mystery."

"In that order, Mr. Holmes?"

"Indeed," insisted the detective.

Irene Adler laughed gaily at the lie. Then they picked out a design in the carpet to use as a path and walked together toward the big window. "I'm from the Diva series of dolls," she explained, "each a replica of a prima donna of a European opera house. The museum has us displayed on the stage of a Victorian doll opera house.

"Well, last year there was that terrible business when the alligators swarmed in on us right at the start of the Christmas Hour, shouting their vile sewer language. If it hadn't been for Captain Rataplan and his thin red line of soldiers which bestrode the aisle and Punch who backed them up with his club no one would have had time to find high ground. The rest of the Victorian Christmas people sought refuge up on the hassock. But in the excitement Lady Gwendolyn, the mistress of the dollhouse, fell over the edge into the midst of the alligators and was swallowed up in a single gulp."

Holmes and the woman had reached the window. They stood in silence, contemplating the darkness beyond the glass and watching the wind swirl the snow beneath the streetlights. Then Irene Adler said, "So here I am. I was chosen to take Lady Gwendolyn's place. Personally, I found the Diva Christmas Hours oppressive, with all the ladies trying to upstage each other. I have always preferred the company of men." Then she said, "But come, tell me how you come to be here?"

But before the detective could answer, Teddy came up behind them. "My dear Holmes," he said in a voice which had become progressively more British since he'd learned of his ancestry, "there's been a terrible thing. Judy's been murdered."

Judy was quite dead. There was evidence of a severe contusion under her hooked chin. But death had come another way. Concealed within the folds of the voluminous smock hand puppets wear was the handle of the ice pick which had found her heart.

Holmes rose from his examination of the corpse and surveyed the horrified toys who stood around it, including a newcomer, a young man in a cap with bells and a particolored suit. This would be Jack. His box stood wide open and empty.

Irene Adler was pale. "Are we toys capable of murder?" she asked.

"And of seeing that justice is done, as I assure you it will," nodded Holmes grimly. "Now, what happened here?"

Gretta said, "Judy came running up to Jack's box, giggling like a goose and squeaking something about olives. Next thing you know it's whacko!"

"I guess she was leaning over the box when I popped out and the lid caught her under the chin," said Jack. "A nasty rap, Mr. Holmes. And it knocked her out. But she wasn't dead. I sent Gretta for a wet cloth." Here the young man broke down and buried his face in his hands. "Oh Judy, Judy, Judy," he sobbed.

"When Punch and I ran back with the wet cloth Captain Rataplan here was bending over her," said the ballerina. "Then he jumped up quick and started an argument with Jack."

"I thought the scoundrel'd hit her, Mr. Holmes," said the hussar. "I accused him of striking a woman. Not that it surprised me. The man's an utter coward. He proved that last year, lurking in his box when there were alligators to be driven off. I lost my temper and tried to throttle him, I admit it. But Punch leaped up from taking care of Judy and pulled me off."

"The cloth fell from Judy's head," said Gretta. "I leaned over to put it back on and that's when I saw the ice pick. That's when your stuffed friend came running up."

"I was on the hassock getting some tables and chairs from the house for the ladies," said Teddy. "You know me. Anything to help the festivities along. I saw the fight from up there and came on the double."

"Any chance it was an accident?" asked Punch. "We'd all warned the dumb old hoss not to carry the ice pick around in her pocket."

"This was no accident," said Holmes. Then he paused for a thoughtful moment. "Gretta," he asked, "did you examine Judy before you ran off for the cloth?" When the ballerina shook her head he added, "So she might have been dead already?"

The young woman shrugged.

"And you, Captain Rataplan," asked Holmes, "could you swear July was alive when you bent over her?"

"I didn't look further than the mark on her chin and flew off the handle," admitted the fierce hussar. "This Jack fellow's an upstart."

"You can say that again," mused Holmes.

Rataplan did and added, "This fellow whose trouser legs aren't even the same color had the brass to have his eye on Lady Gwendolyn, who lived in the big house on the hassock. Last year I slew three alligators and left them as dead as luggage. And only the brave deserve the fair. But I would never, never have aspired to the hand of so fine a lady."

Rataplan paused to clear his throat. "Of course my heart is elsewhere," he said. Here, like many brave men he was overcome by an attack of shyness and averted his eyes. Holmes was quick to observe that it was the ballerina's unsympathetic gaze he was avoiding. The emotional lives of toys with only an hour of life each year lay close to the surface, like those of young people in wartime.

Holmes looked at Punch. "Landlord, was Judy alive or dead when you put the cloth on her forehead?"

"Search me, guv," said the hunchback. "I mean, the fracas broke out right away."

"And yet you were certainly attached to Judy."

"A strictly professional relationship," insisted Punch. "I mean, did you ever see the snoot on her?"

"You're rather well endowed in that department yourself," observed Holmes.

"But I don't have to look at me, you see," said Punch quickly. "And while we're on the subject, you've got something of a beak yourself."

Holmes turned to confront Jack. "And just what was your relationship with the deceased?" he demanded.

"We all need someone, Mr. Holmes," said Jack.

"But why do you in particular need someone?"

Jack turned white. He lay a hand on the detective's arm and murmured, "Could I have a word in private, Mr. Holmes?"

"If you'll be more straightforward than you have been up to now," replied Holmes.

The bells on Jack's cap jingled as he swore he would be. When they had moved off a bit from the others Jack said, "I'm sure you realize that I can't trigger my lid latch from the inside."

"I am quite familiar with the Wunderbar jack-in-the-box mechanism," said the detective.

"But the others aren't, you see," said Jack. "My lid latch is defective. Traffic can trigger it and out I pop. 'Surprise!' They think I do it myself, but I can't. When the Christmas Hour comes I can't even get out of my box myself. That's a humiliating situation for a grown toy. That's my dark secret. My first Hour here in the Victorian Christmas exhibit I was lucky. A passing subway train triggered my latch. But I couldn't depend on that. I had to tell my secret to someone. I chose Lady Gwendolyn because she was so kind and good. Every Christmas Hour after that she'd slip over here first thing and let me out.

"But last year the alligators attacked and she fell to her death. In fact, I'd still be in the damned box if Rataplan hadn't come storming over after the alligators turned tail. He called me a coward and beat on the lid with his bloody saber until he accidentally triggered the latch. But what about next year? Well, Judy'd always been a bit soft on me so I took the chance of explaining things to her. She was the one who thought up the olive business. Rataplan's martooni was always the first drink of the night. She'd tell Punch she was keeping the olives in my icebox."

"Your secret has cost the lives of two people," said the detective. "I cannot believe that to be a coincidence. Come, let us settle this matter."

They returned to the waiting circle of toys where Holmes said, "Ladies and gentlemen, Judy's murderer is a very resourceful and decisive person who has committed a perfect crime."

"Come now, Holmes," protested Teddy, "don't tell us you are baffled."

"Consider my dilemma," said Holmes. "There are four suspects: Jack, Captain Rataplan, Punch, and Gretta. All had the opportunity to kill her. There is no clue to tell us which one did. Ergo, a perfect crime."

"And so justice will not be done, Mr. Holmes," said Irene Adler.

"Ah, but it will be, Miss Adler," said Holmes. "It will be indeed. Our murderer's mistake was in committing two perfect crimes. You see, you all believed Lady Gwendolyn's tragic death an accident. But in fact she was murdered. Someone pushed her to her death. That was a perfect crime and the murderer would have escaped discovery except for killing again.

"Judy's murder, perfect though the crime was, points the unerring finger of guilt at Lady Gwendolyn's killer. Rataplan and Punch were fighting the alligators. Jack was in his box. Of the three toys on the hassock two are dead. Clearly the murderer is—" Holmes was about to point an accusing finger when a corgi coughed.

The Christmas-tree angel fell silent and the toys froze in their places. The figure of an owlish, self-satisfied-looking young man loomed on the other side of the window glass.

Under his breath Teddy whispered, "It's the second assistant curator from the toy museum, Holmes. Met him once. Something of a royal stuffed shirt, don't you know? Miss Ivy Tinker has spoken of him most severely to me."

"He looks invincibly square, old fellow," whispered Holmes, venturing a glance. "I'd say she's got her work cut out for her." After what seemed an interminable period of time, the human outside the window was led away and Holmes' accusing finger pointed.

But as quick as a cat, Gretta snatched the astonished Rataplan's saber away from him and knocked him to the floor with the flat of it. Punch made a grab for her but she wounded him in the arm. Jack turned pale and popped down in his box, pulling the lid shut after him.

"There are soldiers at all the exits. You can't escape, you know," said Holmes calmly.

"We'll see about that," said the ballerina, holding them at bay with the saber and moving slowly backward in the direction of the Christmas tree. Leaving Irene Adler to tend to the wounded, Holmes and Teddy kept pace as close as Gretta would allow.

"I killed them both, okay?" she boasted. "When fate brought Jack and me together I swore to myself I'd kill anyone who came between us."

"It wasn't fate," insisted Teddy. "It was the second assistant curator."

Gretta didn't hear him. "I knew Jack had something going with Lady Gwendolyn," she said. "I saw them whispering and he'd always pop out of his box the minute she came to visit. I waited for my chance. When the alligators broke in, I took it." She was directly under the tree now. She looked around her and then continued. "But right away he took up with Judy. Judy—can you imagine that? Tonight when she came waltzing over to the box, I saw red and applied my foot to the small of her back. It knocked her over the lid just as Jack popped out. I'd only meant to warn her off. But later when I saw I could get away with it, I said what the hell and slipped in the ice pick."

"And now the game's up, Gretta," said Holmes.

With a contemptuous laugh the woman put the saber between her teeth, leaped up into the tree and disappeared from sight.

"But surely she doesn't think she can get away, Holmes?" said the amazed bear.

"There's only one way to find out, old fellow," answered the detective clambering up the tree trunk.

"Onwards and upwards, then," said Teddy who was stuffed with excelsior.

But pursuit wasn't easy. As Gretta fled up the tree, she cut the strings on the wooden ornaments and sent them crashing down on her pursuers, obliging them to seek frequent shelter. And the dancer's excellent physical condition enabled her to leap from branch to branch like a monkey. She soon left them far behind. "Adios, okay, Mr. Holmes?" she shouted triumphantly.

"I've been a blind fool, Teddy," said the detective, ducking to avoid a falling ornament. "She's going to hijack the angel and make it fly her to the Cuban Mission to the United Nations."

"Political asylum?" puffed Teddy.

"More than that, you dumb animal!" shouted Gretta, who was now at the top of the tree with the blade of the saber across the angel's throat. "Before the clock strikes one tonight, the rats in the basement of the Cuban Mission will know of Rataplan's great fear because I will tell them. When you all come to life next Christmas Hour, an army of alligators with rat riders will be there to greet you. Hell hath no fury like a scorned toy."

With this cry, she vaulted onto the angel's back and slapped the creature's thigh with the flat of the saber. The angel flapped its wings and launched them both into space. It circled the top of the tree in a wide arc and then executed a barrel roll Amelia Earhart would have been proud of. Gretta fell head first the long distance to the floor.

The Victorian Christmas exhibit has been returned to the museum, where it continues to attract crowds. A Bo Peep with a velvet bow on her crook was Metcalfe's replacement for the broken music-box ballerina he passed on to Mr. Jacoby for repairs. "Listen, Metcalfe," said the overworked Mr. Jacoby, laying the doll in a small cardboard box and fastening the lid with a stout elastic band, "this goes on the shelf in the closet. If I get to it in twenty years it'll be lucky."

A new, less timid Judy has been found. They say it gives Punch as good as it gets. And sitting in the wing chair wearing the whole regalia of a Knight of the Garter is Teddy. A card nearby informs the world that it is in the presence of a rare Bear of the Realm on loan to the museum from Miss Ivy Tinker.

And here's how this dramatic change came about. When Metcalfe arrived at the museum that Christmas morning, the night watchman claimed more alligator sightings. The second assistant curator used an arch laugh he had developed to heap scorn on things. But since the man's breath passed muster he took a turn around the museum to see for himself.

In each wing of the museum Metcalfe experienced the uncanny feeling that he was interrupting a celebration. Worse than that, out in the corridors every shadow along the wall took on an amphibian shape and every night sound the building made became a vile mutter. Metcalfe was happy to let Owen Glendower lead him home. In spite of the late hour, he was so unsettled he had to read himself to sleep, choosing an old monograph on stuffed toys he'd picked up in a second-hand bookshop.

Later that day when he arrived at McTammany's for his confrontation with Miss Tinker, his indignation vanished when he noticed Teddy's English nightingale stitching and glass Homard et Fils eyes. Excited, he begged her to loan the priceless antique to the museum. She did not agree at once. They were obliged to return to the subject over several dinners and during numerous events about town. Metcalfe was also required to listen to her views on the dangers of extremism on matters of authenticity. To illustrate what she meant, one night she told him that in spite of when they were made, there was something about the Diva doll and the Sherlock Holmes doll that made them go together wonderfully. Metcalfe made the mistake of heaping scorn on this idea with that laugh of his. As a result, she swore she would not loan Teddy to the museum or set eyes on Metcalfe again until the Holmes doll had been rescued from the McTammany stockroom and was standing beside the Irene Adler doll in the Victorian Christmas exhibit.

Of course, Miss Tinker retained visiting rights to Teddy. Sometimes when she and Metcalfe would come to the museum in the evenings when it was closed, they would bring Owen Glendower along. The corgi rather liked her. The young woman hadn't knocked off all Metcalfe's corners yet but she was well on the way. And sometimes all three of them would stop in on the late-working Mr. Jacoby. In the middle of one of their discussions, Mr. Jacoby set his teacup down on the workbench, stroked his cat, and said, "Speaking of authentic, Metcalfe, how about this: suppose I make the broken Judy doll into a Victorian Christmas-tree angel?"

"Great," said Metcalfe, making an admiring gesture with his pipe. "Honestly, Mr. Jacoby, I don't know where you come up with your ideas."

Here Mr. Jacoby lowered his eyes modestly. But the cat and Owen Glendower were obliged to exchange glances.

AUGGIE WREN'S CHRISTMAS STORY

Paul Auster

I heard this story from Auggie Wren. Since Auggie doesn't come off too well in it, at least not as well as he'd like to, he's asked me not to use his real name. Other than that, the whole business about the lost wallet and the blind woman and the Christmas dinner is just as he told it to me.

Auggie and I have known each other for close to eleven years now. He works behind the counter of a cigar store on Court Street in downtown Brooklyn, and since it's the only store that carries the little Dutch cigars I like to smoke, I go in there fairly often. For a long time I didn't give much thought to Auggie Wren. He was the strange little man who wore a hooded blue sweatshirt and sold me cigars and magazines, the impish, wisecracking character who always had something funny to say about the weather or the Mets or the politicians in Washington, and that was the extent of it.

But then one day several years ago he happened to be looking through a magazine in the store, and he stumbled across a review of one of my books. He knew it was me because a photograph accompanied the review, and after that things changed between us. I was no longer just another customer to Auggie, I had become a distinguished person. Most people couldn't care less about books and writers, but it turned out that Auggie considered himself an artist. Now that he had cracked the secret of who I was, he embraced me as an ally, a confidant, a brother-in-arms. To tell the truth, I found it rather embarrassing.

Then, almost inevitably, a moment came when he asked if I would be willing to look at his photographs. Given his enthusiasm and good will, there didn't seem to be any way I could turn him down.

God knows what I was expecting. At the very least, it wasn't what Auggie showed me the next day. In a small, windowless room at the back of the store, he opened a cardboard box and pulled out twelve identical black photo albums. This was his life's work, he said, and it didn't take him more than five minutes a day to do it. Every morning for the past twelve years, he had stood at the corner of Atlantic Avenue and Clinton Street at precisely 7 o'clock and had taken a single color photograph of precisely the same view. The project now ran to more than four thousand photographs. Each album represented a different year, and all the pictures were laid out in sequence from January 1 to December 31, with the dates carefully recorded under each one.

As I flipped through the albums and began to study Auggie's work, I didn't know what to think. My first impression was that it was the oddest, most bewildering thing I had ever seen. All the pictures were the same. The whole project was a numbing onslaught of repetition, the same street and the same buildings over and over again, an unrelenting delirium of redundant images. I couldn't think of anything to say to Auggie, so I continued turning pages, nodding my head in feigned appreciation. Auggie himself seemed unperturbed, watching me with a broad smile on his face, but after I'd been at it for several minutes, he suddenly interrupted me and said, "You're going too fast. You'll never get it if you don't slow down."

He was right, of course. If you don't take the time to look, you'll never manage to see anything. I picked up another album and forced myself to go more deliberately. I paid closer attention to details, took note of shifts in the weather, watched for the changing angles of light as the seasons advanced. Eventually, I was able to detect subtle differences in the traffic flow, to anticipate the rhythm of the different days (the commotion of workday mornings, the relative stillness of weekends, the contrast between Saturdays and Sundays). And then, little by little, I began to recognize the faces of the people in the background, the passersby on their way to work, the same people in the same spot every morning, living an instant of their lives in the field of Auggie's camera.

Once I got to know them, I began to study their postures, the way they carried themselves from one morning to the next, trying to discover their moods from these surface indications, as if I could imagine stories for them, as if I could penetrate the invisible dramas locked inside their bodies. I picked up another album. I was no longer bored, no longer puzzled as I had been at first. Auggie was photographing time, I realized, both natural time and human time, and he was doing it by planting himself in one tiny corner of the world and willing it to be his own by standing guard in the space he had chosen for himself. As he watched me pore over his work, Auggie continued to smile with pleasure. Then, almost as if he had been reading my thoughts, he began to recite a line from Shakespeare. "Tomorrow and tomorrow and tomorrow," he muttered under his breath, "time creeps on its petty pace." I understood then that he knew exactly what he was doing.

That was more than two thousand pictures ago. Since that day, Auggie and I have discussed his work many times, but it was only last week that I learned how he acquired his camera and started taking pictures in the first place. That was the subject of the story he told me, and I'm still struggling to make sense of it.

Earlier that same week, a man from *The New York Times* called me and asked if I would be willing to write a short story that would appear in the paper on Christmas morning. My first impulse was to say no, but the man was very charming and persistent, and by the end of the conversation I told him I would give it

a try. The moment I hung up the phone, however, I
fell into a deep panic. What did I know about Christmas? I asked myself. What did I know about writing
short stories on commission?

I spent the next several days in despair, warring
with the ghosts of Dickens, O. Henry, and other masters of the Yuletide spirit. The very phrase "Christmas
story" had unpleasant associations for me, evoking
dreadful outpourings of hypocritical mush and treacle.
Even at their best, Christmas stories were no more
than wish-fulfillment dreams, fairy tales for adults,
and I'd be damned if I'd ever allowed myself to write
something like that. And yet, how could anyone propose to write an unsentimental Christmas story? It was
a contradiction in terms, an impossibility, an out-and-
out conundrum. One might just as well try to imagine
a racehorse without legs, or a sparrow without wings.

I got nowhere. On Thursday I went out for a long
walk, hoping the air would clear my head. Just past
noon, I stopped in at the cigar store to replenish my
supply, and there was Auggie, standing behind the
counter as always. He asked me how I was. Without
really meaning to, I found myself unburdening my
troubles to him. "A Christmas story?" he said after I
had finished. "Is that all? If you buy me lunch, my
friend, I'll tell you the best Christmas story you ever
heard. And I guarantee that every word of it is true."

We walked down the block to Jack's, a cramped and
boisterous delicatessen with good pastrami sandwiches
and photographs of old Dodgers teams hanging on the
walls. We found a table at the back, ordered our food,
and then Auggie launched into his story.

"It was the summer of '72," he said. "A kid came
in one morning and started stealing things from the
store. He must have been about nineteen or twenty,
and I don't think I've ever seen a more pathetic shoplifter in my life. He's standing by the rack of paperbacks along the far wall and stuffing books into the
pockets of his raincoat. It was crowded around the
counter just then, so I didn't notice him at first. But
once I noticed what he was up to, I started to shout.

He took off like a jackrabbit, and by the time I managed to get out from behind the counter, he was already tearing down Atlantic Avenue. I chased after him for about half a block, and then I gave up. He'd dropped something along the way, and since I didn't feel like running anymore, I bent down to see what it was.

"It turned out to be his wallet. There wasn't any money inside, but his driver's license was there along with three or four snapshots. I suppose I could have called the cops and had him arrested. I had his name and address from the license, but I felt kind of sorry for him. He was just a measly little punk, and once I looked at those pictures in his wallet, I couldn't bring myself to feel very angry at him. Robert Goodwin. That was his name. In one of the pictures, I remember, he was standing with his arm around his mother or grandmother. In another one, he was sitting there at age nine or ten dressed in a baseball uniform with a big smile on his face. I just didn't have the heart. He was probably on dope now, I figured. A poor kid from Brooklyn without much going for him, and who cared about a couple of trashy paperbacks anyway?

"So I held on to the wallet. Every once in a while I'd get a little urge to send it back to him, but I kept delaying and never did anything about it. Then Christmas rolls around and I'm stuck with nothing to do. The boss usually invites me over to his house to spend the day, but that year he and his family were down in Florida visiting relatives. So I'm sitting in my apartment that morning, feeling a little sorry for myself, and then I see Robert Goodwin's wallet lying on a shelf in the kitchen. I figure what the hell, why not do something nice for once, and I put on my coat and go out to return the wallet in person.

"The address was over in Boerum Hill, somewhere in the projects. It was freezing out that day, and I remember getting lost a few times trying to find the building. Everything looks the same in that place, and you keep going over the same ground thinking you're somewhere else. Anyway, I finally get to the apartment I'm looking for and ring the bell. Nothing happens. I assume no one's there, but I try again just to make sure. I wait a little longer and just when I'm about to give up, I hear someone shuffling to the door. An old woman's voice asks who's there, and I say I'm looking for Robert Goodwin. 'Is that you, Robert?' the old woman says, and then she undoes about fifteen locks and opens the door.

"She has to be at least eighty, maybe ninety, years old, and the first thing I notice about her is that she's blind. 'I knew you'd come, Robert,' she says. 'I knew you wouldn't forget your Granny Ethel on Christmas.' And then she opens her arms as if she's about to hug me.

"I didn't have much time to think, you understand. I had to say something real fast, and before I knew what was happening, I could hear the words coming out of my mouth. 'That's right, Granny Ethel,' I said. 'I came back to see you on Christmas.' Don't ask me why I did it. I don't have any idea. Maybe I didn't want to disappoint her or something, I don't know. It just came out that way, and then this old woman was suddenly hugging me there in front of the door, and I was hugging her back.

"I didn't exactly say that I was her grandson. Not in so many words, at least, but that was the implication. I wasn't trying to trick her, though. It was like a game we'd both decided to play—without having to discuss the rules. I mean, that woman *knew* I wasn't her grandson Robert. She was old and dotty, but she wasn't so far gone that she couldn't tell the difference between a stranger and her own flesh and blood. But it made her happy to pretend, and since I had nothing better to do anyway, I was happy to go along with her.

"So we went into the apartment and spent the day together. The place was a real dump, I might add, but what else can you expect from a blind woman who does her own housekeeping? Every time she asked me a question about how I was, I would lie to her. I told her I'd found a good job working in a candy store, I told her I was about to get married, I told her a hundred pretty stories, and she made like she believed every one of them. 'That's fine, Robert,' she would say, nodding her head and smiling. 'I always knew things would work out for you.'

"After a while, I started getting pretty hungry. There didn't seem to be much food in the house, so I went out to a store in the neighborhood and brought back a mess of stuff. A precooked chicken, vegetable soup, a bucket of potato salad, a chocolate cake, all kinds of things. Ethel had a couple of bottles of wine stashed in her bedroom, and so between us we managed to put together a fairly decent Christmas dinner. We both got a little tipsy from the wine, I remember, and after the meal was over we went out to sit in the living room, where the chairs were more comfortable. I had to take a pee, so I excused myself and went to the bathroom down the hall. That's where things took yet another turn. It was ditsy enough doing my little jig as Ethel's grandson, but what I did next was positively crazy, and I've never forgiven myself for it.

"I go into the bathroom, and stacked up against the wall next to the shower, I see a pile of six or seven cameras. Brand-new 35 millimeter cameras, still in their boxes, top-quality merchandise. I figure this is the work of the real Robert, a storage-place for one of his recent hauls. I've never taken a picture in my life, and I've certainly never stolen anything, but the moment I see those cameras sitting in the bathroom, I decide I want one for myself. Just like that. And without even stopping to think about it, I tuck one of the boxes under my arm and go back to the living room.

"I couldn't have been gone for more than three minutes, but in that time Granny Ethel had fallen asleep in her chair. Too much Chianti, I suppose. I went into the kitchen to wash the dishes, and she slept on through the whole racket, snoring like a baby. There didn't seem to be any point in disturbing her, so I decided to leave. I couldn't even write a note to say goodbye, seeing that she was blind and all, and so

I just left. I put her grandson's wallet on the table, picked up the camera again, and walked out of the apartment. And that's the end of the story."

"Did you ever go back to see her?" I asked.

"Once," he said. "About three or four months later. I felt so bad about stealing the camera, I hadn't even used it yet. I finally made up my mind to return it, but Ethel wasn't there anymore. I don't know what happened to her, but someone else had moved into the apartment, and he couldn't tell me where she was."

"She probably died."

"Yeah, probably."

"Which means that she spent her last Christmas with you."

"I guess so. I never thought of it that way."

"It was a good deed, Auggie. It was a nice thing you did for her."

"I lied to her, and then I stole from her. I don't see how you can call that a good deed."

"You made her happy. And the camera was stolen anyway. It's not as if the person you took it from really owned it."

"Anything for art, eh, Paul?"

"I wouldn't say that. But at least you've put the camera to good use."

"And now you've got your Christmas story, don't you?"

"Yes," I said, "I suppose I do."

I paused for a moment, studying Auggie as a wicked grin spread across his face. I couldn't be sure, but the look in his eyes at that moment was so mysterious, so fraught with the glow of some inner delight, that it suddenly occurred to me that he had made the whole thing up. I was about to ask him if he'd been putting me on, but then I realized he would never tell. I had been tricked into believing him, and that was the only thing that mattered. As long as there's one person to believe it, there's no story that can't be true.

"You're an ace, Auggie," I said. "Thanks for being so helpful."

"Any time," he answered, still looking at me with that maniacal light in his eyes. "After all, if you can't share your secrets with your friends, what kind of a friend are you?"

"I guess I owe you one."

"No you don't. Just put it down the way I told you, and you don't owe me a thing."

"Except the lunch."

"That's right. Except the lunch."

I returned Auggie's smile with a smile of my own, and then I called out to the waiter and asked for the check.

CHRISTMAS GIFT

Robert Turner

There was no snow and the temperature was a mild sixty-eight degrees and in some of the yards nearby the shrubbery was green, along with the palm trees, but still you knew it was Christmas Eve. Doors on the houses along the street held wreaths, some of them lighted. A lot of windows were lighted with red, green, and blue lights. Through some of them you could see the lighted glitter of Christmas trees. Then, of course, there was the music, which you could hear coming from some of the houses, the old familiar songs, "White Christmas," "Ave Maria," "Silent Night."

All of that should have been fine because Christmas in a Florida city is like Christmas any place else, a good time, a tender time. Even if you're a cop. Even if you pulled duty Christmas Eve and can't be home with your own wife and kid. But not necessarily if you're a cop on duty with four others and you're going to have to grab an escaped con and send him back, or more probably have to kill him because he was a lifer and just won't *go* back.

In the car with me was McKee, a Third-Grade, only away from a beat a few months. Young, clear-eyed, rosy-cheeked All-American-boy type, and very, very serious about his work. Which was fine; which was the way you should be. We were parked about four houses down from the rented house where Mrs. Bogen and her three children were living.

At the same distance the other side of the house was a sedan in which sat Lieutenant Mortell and

Detective First-Grade Thrasher. Mortell was a bitter-mouthed, needle-thin man, middle-aged and with very little human expression left in his eyes. He was in charge. Thrasher was a plumpish, ordinary guy, an ordinary cop.

On the street behind the Bogen house was another precinct car with two other Firsts in it, a couple of guys named Dodey and Fischman. They were back there in case Earl Bogen got away from us and took off through some yards to that other block. I didn't much think he'd get to do that.

After a while McKee said: "I wonder if it's snowing up north. I'll bet the hell it is." He shifted his position. "It don't really seem like Christmas, no snow. Christmas with palm trees, what a deal!"

"That's the way it was with the first one," I reminded him.

He thought about that. Then he said: "Yeah. Yeah. That's right. But I still don't like it."

I started to ask him why he stayed down here, then I remembered about his mother. She needed the climate; it was all that kept her alive.

"Y'know," McKee said then, "sarge, I been thinking; this guy Bogen must be nuts."

"You mean because he's human? Because he wants to see his wife and kids on Christmas?"

"Well, he must know there's a *chance* he'll be caught. If he is, it'll be worse for his wife and kids, won't it? Why the hell couldn't he just have *sent* them presents or something and then called them on the phone? Huh?"

"You're not married, are you, McKee?"

"No."

"And you don't have kids of your own. So I can't answer that question for you."

"I still think he's nuts."

I didn't answer. I was thinking how I could hound the stinking stoolie who had tipped us about Earl Bogen's visit home for Christmas, all next year, without getting into trouble. There was a real rat in my book, a guy who would stool on something like that, I was going to give him a bad time if it broke me.

Then I thought about what Lieutenant Mortell had told me an hour ago. "Tim," he said. "I'm afraid you're not a very good cop. You're too sentimental. You ought to know by now a cop can't be sentimental. Was Bogen sentimental when he crippled for life that manager of the finance company he stuck up on his last hit? Did he worry about *that* guy's wife and kids? Stop being a damned fool, will you, Tim?"

That was the answer I got to my suggestion that we let Earl Bogen get in and see his family and have his Christmas and catch him on the way out. What was there to lose, I'd said. Give the guy a break, I'd said. I'd known, of course, that Mortell wouldn't have any part of that, but I'd had to try anyhow. Even though I knew the lieutenant would think of the same thing I had—that when it came time to go, Bogen might be twice as hard to take.

McKee's bored young voice cut into my thoughts: "You think he'll really be armed? Bogen, I mean."

"I think so."

"I'm glad Mortell told us not to take any chances with him, that if he even makes a move that looks like he's going for a piece, we give it to him. He's a smart old cop, Mortell."

"That's what they say. But did you ever look at his eyes?"

"What's the matter with his eyes?" McKee said.

"Skip it," I said. "A bus has stopped."

We knew Earl Bogen had no car; we doubted he'd rent one or take a cab. He was supposed to be short of dough. A city bus from town stopped up at the corner. When he came he'd be on that, most likely. But he wasn't on this one. A lone woman got off and turned up the avenue. I let out a slight sigh and looked at the radium dial of my watch. Ten fifty. Another hour and ten minutes and we'd be relieved; it wouldn't happen on our tour. I hoped that was the way it would be. It was possible. The stoolie could have been wrong about the whole thing. Or something could have happened to change Bogen's plans, or at least to postpone his visit to the next day. I settled back to wait for the next bus.

McKee said: "Have you ever killed a guy, sarge?"

"No," I said. "I've never had to. But I've been there when someone else did."

"Yeah? What's it like?" McKee's voice took on an edge of excitement. "I mean for the guy who did the shooting? How'd he feel about it?"

"I don't know. I didn't ask him. But I'll tell you how he looked. He looked as though he was going to be sick to his stomach, as though he should've been but couldn't be."

"Oh," McKee said. He sounded disappointed. "How about the guy that was shot? What'd he do? I've never seen a guy shot."

"Him?" I said. "Oh, he screamed."

"Screamed?"

"Yeah. Did you ever hear a child scream when it's had a door slammed on its fingers? That's how he screamed. He got shot in the groin."

"Oh, I see," McKee said, but he didn't sound as though he really did. I thought that McKee was going to be what they called a good cop—a nice, sane, completely insensitive type guy. For the millionth time I told myself that I ought to get out. Not after tonight's tour, not next month, next week, tomorrow, but right now. It would be the best Christmas present in the world I could give myself and my family. And at the same time I knew I never would do that. I didn't know exactly why. Fear of not being able to make a living outside; fear of winding up a burden to everybody in my old age the way my father was—those were some reasons but not the whole thing. If I talk about how after being a cop so long it gets in your blood no matter how you hate it, that sounds phony. And it would sound even worse if I said one reason I stuck was in hopes that I could make up for some of the others, that I could do some good sometimes.

"If I get to shoot Bogen," McKee said, "he won't scream."

"Why not?"

"You know how I shoot. At close range like that, I'll put one right through his eyes."

"Sure, you will," I told him. "Except that you won't have the chance. We'll get him, quietly. We don't want any shooting in a neighborhood like this on Christmas Eve."

Then we saw the lights of the next bus stop up at the corner. A man and a woman got off. The woman turned up the avenue. The man, medium height but very thin, and his arms loaded with packages, started up the street.

"Here he comes," I said. "Get out of the car, McKee."

We both got out, one on each side. The man walking toward us from the corner couldn't see us. The street was heavily shaded by strings of Australian pine planted along the walk.

"McKee," I said. "You know what the orders are. When we get up to him, Thrasher will reach him first and shove his gun into Bogen's back. Then you grab his hands and get the cuffs on him fast. I'll be back a few steps covering you. Mortell will be behind Thrasher, covering him. You got it?"

"Right," McKee said.

We kept walking, first hurrying a little, then slowing down some, so that we'd come up to Bogen, who was walking toward us, just right, before he reached the house where his family were but not before he'd passed Mortell and Thrasher's car.

When we were only a few yards from Bogen, he passed through an open space, where the thin slice of moon filtered down through tree branches. Bogen wore no hat, just a sport jacket and shirt and slacks. He was carrying about six packages, none of them very large but all of them wrapped with gaudily colored paper, foil, and ribbon. Bogen's hair was crew cut instead of long the way it was in police pictures and he'd grown a mustache; but none of that was much of a disguise.

Just then he saw us and hesitated in his stride. Then

he stopped. Thrasher, right behind him, almost bumped into him. I heard Thrasher's bull-froggy voice say: "Drop those packages and put your hands up, Bogen. Right now!"

He dropped the packages. They tumbled about his feet on the sidewalk and two of them split open. A toy racing car was in one of them. It must have been still slightly wound up because when it broke out of the package, the little motor whirred and the tiny toy car spurted across the sidewalk two or three feet. From the other package, a small doll fell and lay on its back on the sidewalk, its big, painted eyes staring upward. It was what they call a picture doll, I think; anyhow, it was dressed like a bride. From one of the other packages a liquid began to trickle out onto the sidewalk and I figured that had been a bottle of Christmas wine for Bogen and his wife.

But when Bogen dropped the packages he didn't raise his hands. He spun around and the sound of his elbow hitting Thrasher's face was a sickening one. Then I heard Thrasher's gun go off as he squeezed the trigger in a reflex action, but the flash from his gun was pointed at the sky.

I raised my own gun just as Bogen reached inside his jacket but I never got to use it. McKee used his. Bogen's head went back as though somebody had jolted him under the chin with the heel of a hand. He staggered backward, twisted, and fell.

I went up to Bogen with my flash, The bullet from McKee's gun had entered Bogen's right eye and there was nothing there now but a horrible hole. I moved the flash beam just for a moment, I couldn't resist it, to McKee's face. The kid looked very white but his eyes were bright with excitement and he didn't look sick at all. He kept licking his lips, nervously. He kept saying: "He's dead. You don't have to be worrying about him, now. He's dead."

Front door lights began to go on then in nearby houses and people began coming out of them. Mortell shouted to them: "Go on back inside. There's nothing to see. Police business. Go on back inside."

Of course, most of them didn't do that. They came and looked, although we didn't let them get near the body. Thrasher radioed back to headquarters. Mortell told me: "Tim, go tell his wife. And tell her she'll have to come down and make final identification for us."

"Me?" I said. "Why don't you send McKee? He's not the sensitive type. Or why don't you go? This whole cute little bit was your idea, anyhow, lieutenant, remember?"

"Are you disobeying an order?"

Then I thought of something. "No," I told him. "It's all right. I'll go."

I left them and went to the house where Bogen's wife and kids lived. When she opened the door, I could see past her into the cheaply, plainly furnished living room that somehow didn't look that way now, in the glow from the decorated tree. I could see the presents placed neatly around the tree. And peering around a corner of a bedroom, I saw the eyes, big with awe, of a little girl about six and a boy about two years older.

Mrs. Bogen saw me standing there and looked a little frightened. "Yes?" she said. "What is it?"

I thought about the newspapers, then. I thought: "What's the use? It'll be in the newspapers tomorrow, anyhow." Then I remembered that it would be Christmas Day; there wouldn't *be* any newspapers published tomorrow, and few people would bother about turning on radios or television sets.

"Don't be alarmed," I told her, then. "I'm just letting the people in the neighborhood know what happened. We surprised a burglar at work, ma'am, and he ran down this street. We caught up with him here and had to shoot him. But it's all over now. We don't want anyone coming out, creating any more disturbance, so just go back to bed, will you please?"

Her mouth and eyes opened very wide. "Who— who was it?" she said in a small, hollow voice.

"Nobody important," I said. "Some young hood."

"Oh," she said then and I could see the relief come

over her face and I knew then that my hunch had been right and Bogen hadn't let her know he was coming; he'd wanted to surprise her. Otherwise she would have put two and two together.

I told her good night and turned away and heard her shut the door softly behind me.

When I went back to Mortel I said: "Poor Bogen. He walked into the trap for nothing. His folks aren't even home. I asked one of the neighbors and she said they'd gone to Mrs. Bogen's mother's and wouldn't be back until the day after Christmas."

"Well, I'll be damned," Mortell said, watching the men from the morgue wagon loading Bogen onto a basket.

"Yes," I said. I wondered what Mortell would do to me when he learned what I'd done and he undoubtedly would, eventually. Right then I didn't much care. The big thing was that Mrs. Bogen and those kids were going to have their Christmas as scheduled. Even when I came back and told her what had happened, the day after tomorrow, it wouldn't take away the other.

Maybe it wasn't very much that I'd given them but it was something and I felt a little better. Not much, but a little.

RUMPOLE AND THE CHAMBERS PARTY

John Mortimer

Christmas comes but once a year. Once a year I receive a gift of socks from She Who Must Be Obeyed; each year I add to her cellar of bottles of lavender water, which she now seems to use mainly for the purpose of "laying down" in the bedroom cupboard (I suspect she has only just started on the 1980 vintage).

Tinseled cards and sprigs of holly appear at the entrance to the cells under the Old Bailey and a constantly repeated tape of "God Rest Ye Merry Gentlemen" adds little zest to my two eggs, bacon, and sausage on a fried slice in the Taste-Ee-Bite, Fleet Street; and once a year the Great Debate takes place at our December meeting. Should we invite solicitors to our Chambers party?

"No doubt at the season of our Savior's birth we should offer hospitality to all sorts and conditions of men," "Soapy" Sam Ballard, Q.C., our devout Head of Chambers, opened the proceedings in his usual manner, that of a somewhat backward bishop addressing Synod on the wisdom of offering the rites of baptism to non-practicing, gay Anglican converts of riper years.

"All conditions of men and *women*." Phillida Erskine-Brown, Q.C., nee Trant, the Portia of our Chambers, was looking particularly fetching in a well fitting black jacket and an only slightly flippant version of a male collar and tie. As she looked doe-eyed at him, Ballard, who hides a ridiculously susceptible heart beneath his monkish exterior, conceded her point.

"The question before us is, does all sorts and conditions of men, and women, too, of course, include members of the junior branch of the legal profession?"

"I'm against it!" Claude Erskine-Brown had remained an aging junior whilst his wife Phillida fluttered into silk, and he was never in favor of radical change. "The party is very much a family thing for the chaps in Chambers, and the clerk's room, of course. If we ask solicitors, it looks very much as though we're touting for briefs."

"I'm very much in favor of touting for briefs." Up spake the somewhat grey barrister, Hoskins. "Speaking as a man with four daughters to educate. For heaven's sake, let's ask as many solicitors as we know, which, in my case, I'm afraid, is not many."

"Do you have a view, Rumpole?" Ballard felt bound to ask me, just as a formality.

"Well, yes, nothing wrong with a bit of touting, I agree with Hoskins. But I'm in favor of asking the people who really provide us with work."

"You mean solicitors?"

"I mean the criminals of England. Fine conservative fellows who should appeal to you, Ballard. Greatly in favor of free enterprise and against the closed shop. I propose we invite a few of the better-class crooks who have no previous engagements as guests of Her Majesty, and show our gratitude."

A somewhat glazed look came over the assembly at this suggestion and then Mrs. Erskine-Brown broke the silence with: "Claude's really being awfully stuffy and old-fashioned about this. I propose we invite a smattering of solicitors, from the better-class firms."

Our Portia's proposal was carried *nem con*, such was the disarming nature of her sudden smile on everyone, including her husband, who may have had some reason to fear it. Rumpole's suggestion, to nobody's surprise, received no support whatsoever.

Our clerk, Henry, invariably arranged the Chambers party for the night on which his wife put on the

Nativity play in the Bexley Heath Comprehensive at which she was a teacher. This gave him more scope for kissing Dianne, our plucky but somewhat hit-and-miss typist, beneath the mistletoe which swung from the dim, religious light in the entrance hall of number three Equity Court.

Paper streamers dangled from the bookcase full of All England Law Reports in Ballard's room and were hooked up to his views of the major English cathedrals. Barristers' wives were invited, and Mrs. Hilda Rumpole, known to me only as She Who Must Be Obeyed, was downing sherry and telling Soapy Sam all about the golden days when her daddy, C. H. Wystan, ran Chambers. There were also six or seven solicitors among those present.

One, however, seemed superior to all the rest, a solicitor of the class we seldom see around Equity Court. He had come in with one hand outstretched to Ballard, saying, "Daintry Naismith, happy Christmas. Awfully kind of you fellows to invite one of the junior branch." Now he stood propped up against the mantelpiece, warming his undoubtedly Savile Row trousers at Ballard's gas fire and receiving the homage of barristers in urgent need of briefs.

He appeared to be in his well preserved fifties, with grey wings of hair above his ears and a clean-shaven, pink, and still single chin poised above what I took to be an old Etonian tie. Whatever he might have on offer, it wouldn't, I was sure, be a charge of nicking a frozen chicken from Safeways. Even his murders, I thought, as he sized us up from over the top of his gold-rimmed half glasses, would take place among the landed gentry.

He accepted a measure of Pommeroy's very ordinary white plonk from Portia and drank it bravely, as though he hadn't been used to sipping Chassagne-Montrachet all his adult life.

"Mrs. Erskine-Brown," he purred at her, "I'm looking for a hard-hitting silk to brief in the Family Division. I suppose you're tremendously booked up."

"The pressure of my work," Phillida said modestly, "is enormous."

"I've got the Geoffrey Twyford divorce coming. Pretty hairy bit of in-fighting over the estate and the custody of young Lord Shiplake. I thought you'd be just right for it."

"Is that the Duke of Twyford?" Claude Erskine-Brown looked suitably awestruck. In spite of his other affectations, Erskine-Brown's snobbery is completely genuine.

"Well, if you have a word with Henry, my clerk"—Mrs. Erskine-Brown gave the solicitor a look of cool availability—"he might find a few spare dates."

"Well, that is good of you. And you, Mr. Erskine-Brown, mainly civil work now, I suppose?"

"Oh, yes. Mainly civil." Erskine-Brown lied cheerfully; he's not above taking on the odd indecent assault when tort gets a little thin on the ground. "I do find crime so sordid."

"Oh, I agree. Look here. I'm stumped for a man to take on our insurance business, but I suppose you'd be far too busy."

"Oh, no. I've got plenty of time." Erskine-Brown lacked his wife's laid-back approach to solicitors. "That is to say, I'm sure I could make time. One gets used to extremely long hours, you know." I thought that the longest hours Erskine-Brown put in were when he sat, in grim earnest, through the *Ring* at Covent Garden, being a man who submits himself to Wagner rather as others enjoy walking from Land's End to John O'Groats.

And then I saw Naismith staring at me and waited for him to announce that the Marquess of Something or Other had stabbed his butler in the library and could I possibly make myself available for the trial. Instead he muttered, "Frightfully good party," and wandered off in the general direction of Soapy Sam Ballard.

"What's the matter with you, Rumpole?" She Who Must Be Obeyed was at my elbow and not sounding best pleased. "Why didn't you push yourself forward?" Erskine-Brown had also moved off by this time to join the throng.

"I don't care for divorce," I told her. "It's too bloodthirsty for me. Now if he'd offered me a nice gentle murder—"

"Go after him, Rumpole," she urged me, "and make yourself known. I'll go and ask Phillida what her plans are for the Harrods sale."

Perhaps it was the mention of the sale which spurred me toward that undoubted source of income, Mr. Daintry Naismith. I found him talking to Ballard in a way which showed, in my view, a gross overestimation of that old darling's forensic powers. "Of course the client would have to understand that the golden tongue of Samuel Ballard, Q.C., can't be hired on the cheap," Naismith was saying. I thought that to refer to our Head of Chambers, whose voice in Court could best be compared to a rusty saw, as golden-tongued was a bit of an exaggeration.

"I'll have to think it over." Ballard was flattered but cautious. "One does have certain principles about"—he gulped, rather in the manner of a fish struggling with its conscience—"encouraging the publication of explicitly sexual material."

"Think it over, Mr. Ballard. I'll be in touch with your clerk." And then, as Naismith saw me approach, he said, "Perhaps I'll have a word with him now." So this legal Santa Claus moved away in the general direction of Henry and once more Rumpole was left with nothing in his stocking.

"By the way," I asked Ballard, "did *you* invite that extremely smooth solicitor?"

"No, I think Henry did." Our Head of Chambers spoke as a man whose thoughts are on knottier problems. "Charming chap, though, isn't he?"

Later in the course of the party I found myself next to Henry. "Good work inviting Mr. Daintry Naismith," I said to our clerk. "He seems set on providing briefs for everyone except me."

"I don't really know the gentleman," Henry admitted. "I think he must be a friend of Mr. Ballard's. Of course, we hope to see a lot of him in the future."

Much later, in search of a small cigar, I remembered the box, still in its special Christmas reindeer-patterned wrapping, that I had left in my brief tray. I opened the door of the clerk's room and found the lights off and Henry's desk palely lit by the old gas lamp outside in Equity Court.

There was a dark-suited figure standing beside the desk who seemed to be trying the locked drawers rather in the casual way that suspicious-looking youths test car handles. I switched on the light and found myself staring at our star solicitor guest. And as I looked at him, the years rolled away and I was in Court defending a bent house agent. Beside him in the dock had been an equally curved solicitor's clerk who had joined my client as a guest of Her Majesty.

"Derek Newton," I said, "Inner London Sessions. Raising mortgages on deserted houses that you didn't own. Two years."

"I knew you'd recognize me, Mr. Rumpole. Sooner or later."

"What the hell do you think you are doing?"

"I'm afraid—well, barristers' chambers are about the only place where you can find a bit of petty cash lying about at Christmas." The man seemed resolved to have no secrets from Rumpole.

"You admit it?"

"Things aren't too easy when you're knocking sixty, and the business world's full of wide boys up to all the tricks. You can't get far on one good suit and the Old Etonian tie nowadays. You always defend, don't you, Rumpole? That's what I've heard. Well, I can only appeal to you for leniency."

"But coming to our party," I said, staggered by this most confident of tricksters, "promising briefs to all the learned friends—"

"I always wanted to be admitted as a solicitor." He smiled a little wistfully. "I usually walk through the Temple at Christmastime. Sometimes I drop in to the parties. And I always make a point of offering work.

It's a pleasure to see so many grateful faces. This is, after all, Mr. Rumpole, the season of giving."

What could I do? All he had got out of us, after all, was a couple of glasses of Pommeroy's Fleet Street white; that and the five-pound note he "borrowed" from me for his cab fare home. I went back to the party and explained to Ballard that Mr. Daintry Naismith had made a phone call and had to leave on urgent business.

"He's offered me a highly remunerative brief, Rumpole, defending a publisher of dubious books. It's against my principles, but even the greatest sinner has a right to have his case put before the Court."

"And put by your golden tongue, old darling," I flattered him. "If you take my advice, you'll go for it."

It was, after all, the season of goodwill, and I couldn't find it in my heart to spoil Soapy Sam Ballard's Christmas.

MURDER AT CHRISTMAS

C. M. Chan

There were eight days till Christmas. That meant there were six days till Phillip Bethancourt would be called to gather round the family hearth and join in the exchanging of good cheer and discussions of the principle that, although one might be independently wealthy, this did not eliminate the need for doing something useful with one's life and why couldn't he have become a barrister like his cousin Robert? Or head up a charity like his sister? If he was so interested in criminal investigation, why didn't he get a job with the CID? Bethancourt always smiled and said he wanted to be a writer, a notion that was just barely borne out by the publishing of three or four of his articles.

Eight days till Christmas also meant five days till he would be required to place before Marla, his girlfriend, a present both expensive and spectacular. This was only their second Christmas together, but Marla's attitude toward presents was clear to anyone who had known her a week, and Bethancourt knew better than to disappoint her.

Bethancourt, proceeding down Bond Street towards Asprey's, caught sight of a stocky figure in a tweed overcoat just crossing the street. This bore a strong resemblance to Detective Sergeant Jack Gibbons, a great friend of Bethancourt's and his chief source for the practicing of his amateur detective hobby. Bethancourt sprinted forward to catch him up at the corner.

"Phillip!" grinned Gibbons. "I was going to call you when I got back to the office."

"Christmas shopping, I see," said Bethancourt, eyeing the three bulging shopping bags in Gibbons' chapped red hand.

Gibbons made a face. "It may be the last chance I'll get," he said. "There's been a murder off in Dorset. I was sent back this morning to get the postmortem and interview one or two people, but I thought I'd better get some Christmas shopping done while I was still in town."

Bethancourt's eyes brightened behind his glasses. "Were you going to call me just to say happy holidays, or is the murder particularly interesting?"

Gibbons laughed. "Well, it's an odd one, certainly." He shifted the packages in his hands. "There's an elderly widow, quite well off, living alone now in a huge Victorian monstrosity where she brought up five children."

"Sounds normal so far," observed Bethancourt. "Children, I take it, live in London or other equally faraway places."

"Yes, yes," said Gibbons. "I haven't come to the odd bit yet. It's the murder itself that's so bizarre."

"Well, who was murdered?"

"We don't know."

"You don't?"

"No. If you'd just be quiet for a bit, I could tell this in an orderly fashion."

"Very well."

"Mrs. Bainbridge got a Christmas tree in a couple of days ago and went up to the attic to bring down the ornaments. Well, she opens the attic door and a truly awful stench greets her. It's so dreadful, she's nearly sick on the spot—"

"Jack, you can't mean—"

"Oh, yes, I can. Her Christmas ornaments were scattered all over the place and in the old steamer trunk where she usually stores them, there was a dead man—several months gone, we think."

"My God," said Bethancourt, fascinated. "What a shock for the old girl."

"Oh, she didn't discover the body herself," said

Gibbons. "The smell alarmed her enough so that she went back downstairs and called a neighbor. He and his wife came over, and he was the one who went up and opened the trunk—and he *was* sick. It was rather a pity that he'd just finished lunch," added Gibbons reflectively.

"You can't blame him," said Bethancourt with feeling. "It must have been perfectly foul."

"Oh, certainly," agreed Gibbons cheerfully. "Well, it's all quite a mystery at the moment. Mrs. Bainbridge hadn't been up in the attic since she put the ornaments away last Christmas, and she doesn't think anyone else has been, but the place has been simply overrun by children and grandchildren. Once we find out who the dead man was and when he was killed, it may all become a lot clearer."

"It's a lovely puzzle as it stands," said Bethancourt, an eager look in his eyes. "I say, Jack, you wouldn't want a lift back to Dorset tomorrow or anything, would you?"

Gibbons laughed at him. "Well, I don't know if tomorrow will suit," he said slyly. "I've got to interview two grandchildren first, and if I don't find them in this afternoon—"

"You devil," said Bethancourt. "I will pay for the taxis and even carry one of your bags if you will let me come with you."

"*And* drive me to Dorset tomorrow?"

"Yes, damn you."

"Very well," said Gibbons, holding out a shopping bag. "I knew you'd find this one interesting, Phillip."

The postmortem was waiting for Gibbons when they returned to New Scotland Yard to drop off the packages.

"Well," said Gibbons, frowning at it, "he apparently met his fate sometime in August, or possibly early September."

"Lord," said Bethancourt, pushing his glasses more firmly onto his nose and peering over Gibbons' shoulder. "You'd think the whole house would have smelt of it by now."

"The third story did a bit," said Gibbons. "But that's the old servants' quarters, and of course nobody goes up there nowadays. Mrs. Bainbridge's daily goes up to clean once a year in the spring, but that's all."

"Stabbed, eh?"

"So they think, but you can see how vague they are. A stiletto or a whacking great kitchen knife: it could have been anything. There were bloodstains in the trunk, but the scene-of-the-crime men didn't find them anywhere else. So it's likely he was killed elsewhere."

"Well, of course. You don't lure people to attics to kill them."

"You could," said Gibbons. "I don't see why not. No, don't start, Phillip—we've got to get over to the university and find Mrs. Bainbridge's granddaughter."

Maureen Bainbridge, emerging from a chemistry class, was a truly lovely creature of about twenty. There was something kittenlike about her, how she held her head and brushed her dark hair aside, and it made a fascinating contrast to her open, straightforward manner. She was tall and slender, with the famous English peaches and cream complexion.

Even Bethancourt, who had a high standard of female beauty, gave a low whistle when the student they approached pointed her out. They extracted her from her classmates, introduced themselves and explained their presence, and then followed her to an empty classroom where they could talk.

"It's incredible, isn't it?" she said, sitting down on one of the desks. "I really can't quite believe it."

"I'm sure it's a shock," said Gibbons. "Can you tell us, please: when was the last time you were at your grandmother's house?"

"In the summer," she replied promptly. "We were all there during the Bank Holiday."

"All of you?"

"The whole family," she said expansively, and then

hastily amended, "All my aunts and uncles, I mean. Only one of my cousins showed up. Oh, and Dad brought one of his business partner's sons. Grandmother was annoyed about that because it meant an extra bedroom, but there he was, you know."

Gibbons pulled a notebook from his pocket and consulted a page. "That would be Renaud Fibrier," he said.

"Yes," she nodded. "He was just a little older than me, so my cousin Daniel and I did our best to entertain him. But, of course, there were a lot of family demands, and I'm afraid Renaud must have gotten bored. He left Monday morning, at any rate, instead of staying on till Tuesday."

"He sounds a rather tedious houseguest," said Gibbons.

"I didn't mean that," Maureen said. "Renaud was really rather charming. I only thought he must have been bored because he left early."

"I see," said Gibbons. "We haven't spoken with Mr. Fibrier yet; your grandmother didn't have his address."

"Neither do I," she replied promptly, "but Dad should know."

"Yes, we should be speaking to him soon," said Gibbons. He glanced down at his notebook again. "So the houseparty consisted of Paul and Clarissa North, Bill and Bernice Clayton, Michael and—"

"Oh, no," she interrupted. "Uncle Michael wasn't there; he lives in America. But Aunt Cathy was visiting from Australia. None of us had seen her in years, so there was a sort of family reunion. Most of them were only there for the weekend. My parents and I stayed for a week—we always do during the summer. Oh!" She put a hand to her mouth in what Bethancourt could not help but feel was a very becoming gesture.

"What is it?" asked Gibbons.

"I've just remembered. I was at Grandmother's house for a weekend in November. I was a bit behind here and I just wanted a quiet place to study and Grandmother said I was welcome. She always does."

"Did you go up to the attic or the third floor while you were there?" asked Gibbons.

"No. The last time I was in the attic was last year when I helped Grandmother with the Christmas things."

"Do you remember whether anyone else went up there during the August visit?"

Maureen wrinkled her brow thoughtfully. "I don't know," she said after a moment. "I don't remember anything like that, but there were so many people . . . it was awfully busy."

"That's understandable," said Gibbons. "Now, can you tell me when you were last at the house before the August visit?"

She paused again. "I think in April," she said at last. "There was the vacation and I went up then, I know. I don't think I was there again until August."

"You were alone with your grandmother in April?"

"Yes—no, Aunt Clarissa came up and spent a night, I think."

"Don't you have brothers or sisters?" asked Bethancourt. "Or did they not go to your grandmother's in August?"

She grinned at him. "I'm an only child," she said, "and the youngest of my cousins. Dad married late."

"Really?" said Bethancourt. "Did you know that only children are often very high achievers?"

"Great," she answered. "Maybe I'll win the Nobel prize someday, then. I'm studying physics."

"Well," said Gibbons, rising, "you've been very helpful, Miss Bainbridge. Here's my card; please call me if you think of anything else. Right now, we have an appointment to keep with Daniel North. I believe he was the cousin you mentioned who was also at the August reunion?"

"That's right. Say hello to him for me."

"We will," promised Bethancourt. Outside, he added, "Quite something, isn't she?"

"She's too young for you, Phillip."

"Much too young," Bethancourt agreed. "But I could always wait for her to grow up."

"Incorrigible," muttered Gibbons.

Daniel North was a goodlooking man of about thirty, conservatively dressed as befitted a junior member of a prominent solicitor's office. He received them with a quick smile and asked them to be seated. He denied having been in his grandmother's attic since he was a child, and he had certainly not gone up there in August, which was the last time he had been at the house. Asked who else had been there at that time, his list tallied with Maureen's, with one exception.

"I thought," said Gibbons, "that Maureen's father had brought a business associate?"

"Oh, him," said North. "I'd forgotten. Yes, he was there. I can't think why Uncle David brought him—I never cared for the fellow myself. Unsavory type, if you ask me. Anyway, if you want someone who's been in the attic recently, you should talk to my mother."

Gibbons looked up. "She's been up there?"

"I don't know," answered North, "but she often visits my grandmother—much more frequently than the rest of us. If anyone's been in the attic, it would be she. In fact, I think she's in Dorset now."

"Yes," said Gibbons. "The chief inspector was going to see her this morning. Well, thank you very much for your time, Mr. North."

North ushered them to the door, where the clerk appeared to escort them from the premises.

"Well," said Gibbons, shrugging into his coat in the vestibule, "that's done with."

"It hasn't got you much further."

"No one really thought it would. But you never can tell," added Gibbons cheerfully. "One of them might have been up there near the crucial times."

"Look here," said Bethancourt, leading the way out into the street, "why don't you come round to dinner tonight and we can go over it?"

"Where are you dining?" asked Gibbons suspiciously. He had previously accepted dinner invitations from Bethancourt and found himself eating in restaurants that he could ill afford on his salary.

"I'm meeting Marla at eight thirty at Joe's Cafe," answered Bethancourt, confirming Gibbons' worst fears.

"Well, I don't know, Phillip—"

"Don't be a spoilsport, Jack. I'm sure there's heaps of things about this case you haven't told me yet."

Gibbons had an inspiration. "How would it be if I met you there for a drink before dinner?"

"If that's the best you can do, I suppose I'll have to be happy with it. Eight thirty, then, in the bar."

"We could make it earlier, so that when Marla comes—"

"She'll be late."

"So will you."

Bethancourt assumed a solemn expression. "I give you my word, Jack, tonight I shall be punctual."

"Oh, very well. Half eight then."

The bar at Joe's Cafe was crowded. Gibbons ordered a whisky and positioned himself in view of the door. He did not bother to search for Bethancourt among the other patrons, having less than no faith in his friend's promise to be on time.

He was pleasantly surprised, therefore, when Bethancourt made his way through the door at eight thirty-five, beaming triumphantly.

"I told you I'd be here," he said happily. "Here, let's move down a bit. We can just fit in over there. Now then, Jack," said Bethancourt, having obtained a drink and wedged himself firmly between Gibbons and a rather large man in evening dress, "let's start from the beginning."

"And what do you mean by the beginning?"

"The murdered man, of course," replied Bethancourt promptly.

"You saw the p.m.," said Gibbons, shrugging and sipping his drink.

"Yes. A man of about thirty, stabbed in the back sometime in August or early September and considerably decomposed. But what was he wearing? Was he dark or light?"

"Dark hair," answered Gibbons. "Open-necked shirt and linen pants and black loafers. And if that tells you anything—"

"It tells me he wasn't chopping wood when he was killed," retorted Bethancourt.

"Yes, but what we really need to know is who he was. And that will have to wait until we've finished comparing his description with the missing persons list. Until we find out who knew him, and where he might have been, we're working in a void. He might have been killed anywhere, anytime, by anybody, and put into the attic anytime subsequently."

"He didn't belong to the village, I suppose?"

"No. That was the first thing we checked. None of the villagers in the immediate area is missing anyone. But one of the villagers, or else one of Mrs. Bainbridge's family, must be the murderer."

"Because, you mean, of knowing Mrs. Bainbridge's habits. You don't suspect her?"

Gibbons shrugged. "She's a very elderly woman. She hasn't been to the top of the house in a year because it's hard for her to climb the stairs. I really can't imagine her carting a man's body up three flights."

"No, I suppose not."

There was a slight disturbance in the bar. The various conversations paused momentarily as people's attentions were caught. In a moment the cause of this became evident as several gentlemen shifted their position to allow a spectacularly beautiful woman to pass through. She walked down the aisle they made for her as if it were her right, head crowned with copper hair held high, jade green eyes passing them over until she found the one for whom she searched. And then she smiled, and her slender figure moved quickly forward.

"Marla!" said Bethancourt, glancing hastily at his watch. "It's not even nine o'clock yet."

"You said half eight," she reminded him, kissing

him lightly. "Hello, Jack. Phillip didn't tell me you were joining us."

"I'm not really," denied Gibbons hastily. "Just a drink."

"Come now," said Bethancourt firmly: "You simply can't refuse to join us. Now that Marla's come, we can get a table and be comfortable. I'll just speak to the maitre d'."

And he moved off while Gibbons was explaining that he really couldn't.

"Why not?" asked Marla, smiling. "Have another date?"

"No," said Gibbons uncomfortably. "It's just that, well, I did all my Christmas shopping today and I'm feeling a little low on funds."

"That is not a good excuse," said Marla firmly. "Besides, I expect Phillip will pay."

"I expect so, but I don't like him to."

"That's just one of those male things," replied Marla, hunting in her bag for a cigarette. "If you were a woman, you wouldn't mind at all." Gibbons was spared from answering by the return of Bethancourt, who herded them without further ado towards the dining room. He sighed resignedly.

When they had put the menus aside and had ordered the wine, Bethancourt said casually, "I'll have to get up early tomorrow, Marla. I told Jack I'd drive him back to Dorset."

"Dorset?" asked Marla. "Whatever are you doing out there? I thought your people lived in Suffolk?"

"They do," answered Gibbons. "I'm working in Dorset."

"Oh, God," said Marla. "Not another murder investigation." She glared accusingly at Bethancourt.

Marla did not like her boyfriend's hobby. She found murders an unpleasant and unhealthy topic and, moreover, felt that investigating them took an inordinate amount of time and thought. Time and thought which could far more pleasantly be devoted to herself.

"Well, yes," admitted Bethancourt. "But it's only

a little one, Marla, and will probably be cleared up by the time we get there."

"Hmpf," said Marla, or something very much like it.

"Actually," went on Bethancourt, unperturbed, "it's a rather unusual case."

"Is it?" she asked frostily.

"Yes," said Bethancourt firmly. "There's this old woman, you see, a widow—"

"Excuse me," said Marla, rising. "I have to go to the w.c."

This was a tactical error on her part. By the time she returned, Bethancourt and Gibbons were deep in a discussion of Mrs. Bainbridge's progeny and the possibility of their having visited the attic.

"Chris O'Leary is interviewing the ones in Northants," Gibbons was saying. "That's Bill and Bernice Clayton."

"Bernice is Mrs. Bainbridge's second daughter?" asked Bethancourt.

"That's right. Clarissa North, Daniel's mother, is the eldest. Next is Bernice Clayton, and after her is Maureen's father, David. There's another son living in America who hasn't been to England in some time, and then the youngest is Cathy Dresler, who now lives in Australia and was the cause of the August reunion."

"I suppose none of them is missing?"

"No. No, I'm afraid not."

Bethancourt filled Marla's wine glass, lit her cigarette, and considered.

"And has Mrs. Bainbridge had any visitors other than her children and grandchildren?"

"She says not."

"What on earth does it matter whether she has or not?" asked Marla impatiently.

"Because, my love, the murdered man was a stranger to the village. Either one of Mrs. Bainbridge's family ran into him unexpectedly in August, when most of them were there, killed him, and hid him in the attic, or else they killed him somewhere else, at some other time, and transported the body to

Dorset, thinking that the best hiding place. Incidentally, Jack, it would be interesting to find out which of Mrs. Bainbridge's relatives visited her by car."

"It sounds very farfetched to me," said Marla.

"True," agreed Bethancourt. "Which is why it is more likely to be one of the villagers. One of them either has a visitor or goes to meet the victim. In a moment of passion, he kills him. He's left with the body, all in a panic, when suddenly he remembers Mrs. Bainbridge, all alone in a huge house and slightly deaf. It's late at night and he knows she doesn't lock her doors. So he pushes the body along and carries it up to the attic."

"Lovely," said Gibbons dryly, "but Mrs. Bainbridge is *not* slightly deaf. And how do you know he was killed late at night?"

"This theory," went on Bethancourt, unheeding, "also explains why the body was never moved. One of the family would most likely not desire their mother or grandmother to discover a rotting corpse in her attic. Moreover, they will naturally fall under some suspicion, as they are connected with the house. Whereas one of the villagers has no real connection to the house and may be less considerate of Mrs. Bainbridge's feelings."

"It's possible," allowed Gibbons. "But it is also very possible that Cathy Dresler is the murderess and did not have the opportunity to retrieve the body before she had to leave for Australia."

"Anything's possible," said Marla. "It's quite possible that Phillip killed this man himself, just to give himself something foolproof to investigate."

"Now, Marla—"

"Here come the starters," she said sweetly. "Shall I stay and eat them with you, or go elsewhere?"

"Sorry, darling," said Bethancourt. "Jack and I will keep off murder while we're eating."

"Of course," agreed Gibbons hastily, knowing Marla to be perfectly capable of dumping the starters over their heads if they did not desist. "Not an appropriate dinner topic in any case."

This rule was adhered to during the rest of the meal, for which Bethancourt insisted on paying. Gibbons excused himself soon afterward, saying he still had his notes to put in order before returning to Dorset the next day.

"All right," said Bethancourt. "I'll see you in the morning, then."

"Nine o'clock, don't forget," said Gibbons.

"I won't. Goodnight, Jack."

"Goodnight," chimed in Marla, and, just to show there were no hard feelings, kissed his cheek.

Chief Inspector Wallace Carmichael made his way down the stairs from his room and stood in the doorway, surveying the clientele of the Lion's Head pub in Dorset. He was a tall, ruddy-faced man with bristling brown mustaches and sharp blue eyes. He glanced at his watch, swore vehemently under his breath, and marched to a corner table from which he could keep the door in view. Where the hell was Gibbons, anyway? He had rung up last night to say he would be back this morning and here it was, wanting only a few minutes to twelve, and no Gibbons. Carmichael felt himself to be a lenient man with his subordinates; he gave them every opportunity to follow up their own leads and express their opinions. After all, he wasn't going to be at the Yard forever, and there were the chief inspectors of tomorrow to think of. But he didn't think much of sleeping in when there was a job to be done, and young Gibbons was going to get a piece of his mind on the subject. If he ever showed up.

Carmichael had procured himself a pint of bitter and a ploughman's lunch and was just sitting down to it when Gibbons entered, closely followed by a tall, slender young man with fair hair, horn-rimmed glasses, and a large Russian wolfhound, Carmichael heaved a great sigh.

"I have only one thing to say," he pronounced when Gibbons reached the table. "I am always pleased to have Bethancourt here give us any help he likes, but

he is not a member of the force, he therefore cannot
be disciplined by us, and if he can't get up in the
morning, *do not,* in future, accept rides with him."

"I really am most awfully sorry, chief inspector,"
said Bethancourt while Gibbons murmured, "Yes,
sir," and glared at his friend.

Carmichael held up a hand. "No more to be said.
Just bear it in mind next time. Now, get yourselves
some food and drink and make a report."

"I'll get everything," offered Bethancourt. "You sit
down, Jack, and don't waste any more time."

Gibbons shot him another glare, sat down, and
began digging in his briefcase for the postmortem
report.

Carmichael looked it over and listened to Gibbons'
recitation of the two interviews he had conducted.
Bethancourt, having procured the viands, sat silent
and alert, giving his best impression of the good
schoolboy.

"Nothing yet on his clothes or from missing persons?" asked Carmichael when Gibbons was gone.

"No, sir. Not yet."

"Well, there's been a development or two here."
Carmichael sipped his beer and wiped his mustache
carefully. "I've spoken to Mrs. Dresler in Australia.
She says she was in the attic sometime at the beginning of her visit here. She can't pin it down exactly,
but it was certainly prior to the Bank Holiday weekend. Nothing was out of place when she was there—at
any rate, the Christmas ornaments were not scattered
about."

"Does Mrs. Bainbridge corroborate her statement?"

Carmichael shrugged. "She's not sure. Mrs. Dresler
says she was looking for an old book of her father's.
A first edition of Dickens it was. Mrs. Bainbridge
remembers her daughter asking after it and later finding it. She herself was under the impression the book
was still in the library, although she admits that she
did pack up some of her husband's books at one time,
and moved some others to different parts of the

house. There is a box of books in the attic, so Mrs. Dresler's story may be quite true."

"What about fingerprints?"

"The attic's filled with them. The Australian police are taking a copy of Mrs. Dresler's and sending them along." Carmichael pulled a cigar from his breast pocket and lit it carefully.

"O'Leary's rung up from Northants," he went on, puffing, "but he hasn't got much more than you, Gibbons. In fact, we've got just about the whole family covered, but no one's been in the attic in donkey's years, or so they claim."

"Who haven't we talked to, sir?"

"David Bainbridge—he's on business over in France and his wife doesn't know when he'll be returning. He was called there rather unexpectedly, I gather. And we haven't talked to Renaud Fibrier."

"That was David Bainbridge's business partner?" asked Bethancourt.

"Actually, his partner's son. I haven't really made much of an attempt to get hold of him yet—it seems unlikely he would have gone to the attic unless he accompanied one of the others. In any case, it may be a bit of a job finding him, since we don't know whether he lives here or in France. Mrs. Bainbridge— David's wife, not the old lady—says she was under the impression that he was living in England in August but had no idea if that was a permanent or temporary situation."

"Probably Mr. Bainbridge will know, when he gets back," said Gibbons.

"That's what I've been counting on." Carmichael drained the last of his pint. "Well, if you're finished, boys, we best get on with it. There's a whole village out there that may know something. I assume you're coming with us, Bethancourt?"

"Actually, I think I'd better beg off," said that young man. "Since you two are occupying the only two rooms this pub has to offer, I have to find someplace to stay. And somewhere to leave Cerberus." He indicated the dog at his feet. "But I'll catch you up later, if I may."

"Certainly, certainly," answered Carmichael heartily. He was a broadminded man, and even if Bethancourt's father had not been thick as thieves with the chief commissioner of New Scotland Yard, well, he had to say Bethancourt had never gotten in the way yet. And he could be very helpful when he chose, although Carmichael couldn't help thinking that if Phillip was so interested in detection, he should get himself a proper job doing it.

Bethancourt, once they had gone, moved over to the bar and ordered another pint. Cerberus came and lay patiently at his feet. From his overcoat pocket, he produced a book entitled *Where to Stay in England,* and began leafing through the Dorset section.

"Sorry I can't put you up," said the publican, noticing this.

"That's all right," replied Bethancourt amiably. "If you've only got two guest rooms, well, there it is."

"That's a fact, sir. Or should I say inspector?"

"No, no," said Bethancourt, sampling his beer. "I'm not a policeman."

"Oh," said the publican, taken aback. "Excuse me, sir, but I saw you with the chief inspector and the sergeant there, and I just assumed. . . ."

"I'm just a friend," explained Bethancourt. "I sometimes push round and give the police a hand, if I'm wanted. My name's Bethancourt."

"Sam Heathcote, at your service, Mr. Bethancourt."

The two men shook hands.

"Perhaps you could help me," said Bethancourt, referring to his book. "Do you happen to know a Mrs. Tyzack?"

Heathcote chuckled. "There's not many folk I don't know hereabouts. Mrs. Tyzack's place is just outside the village, on the same road as Mrs. Bainbridge, and she'll do you proud. Nice rooms she has, and a good cook into the bargain. If you don't mind a bit of chat, her place is as good as they come."

"A bit of a talker, is she?"

"Lor', sir. To be frank, she'd talk the hind leg off a donkey. But she's a good sort—don't misunderstand me."

"Lived here long?"

"Ever since she was married. She started the bed and breakfast after old Tyzack passed on. Just between you and me, he left her decently provided for—she just likes the company."

"I see," said Bethancourt. "Just one more thing—what about the dog?" He indicated Cerberus, who had apparently fallen asleep.

"That's a fine animal, sir. Well, Mrs. Tyzack has a dog of her own—a Yorkshire terrier, he is. If you think your dog wouldn't mind that. . . ."

"Oh, Cerberus is a friendly sort," Bethancourt assured him. "So long as the terrier is friendly, too, there shouldn't be a problem. Perhaps I might use your phone to see if Mrs. Tyzack has a room free?"

"You can take it from me she does. There's not much call for that sort of thing at this time of year. She doesn't have a guest in the place."

"Well, then," said Bethancourt, finishing his beer, "I'll just pop round and fix it up with her. Thank you very much, Mr. Heathcote."

Mrs. Tyzack was a short, plump woman of sixty who was delighted to give Bethancourt a room and thought Cerberus a lovely dog. This opinion was given after Cerberus had put down his nose to sniff at the terrier doubtfully, and then proceeded to ignore him. The terrier, puzzled by this attitude, butted him playfully; Cerberus looked round dispassionately, carefully moved his hindquarters out of the terrier's reach, and then turned back with the air of having settled something. This did not deter the terrier, however, and the performance was repeated several times on the way upstairs.

"This is the nicest room," said Mrs. Tyzack, opening a door. "Looks down on the garden, as you can see, and, being on the corner of the house, it has an extra window. Makes it ever so airy, I always think.

Oh, yes, thank you, I did do it up myself, although I had someone in to help with the wallpaper. I'm glad you like it. There's the bathroom just down the hall on the right—it's the second door down, you can't miss it. And your towels are here, as you can see. There's no one else in the house at the moment, so you can leave them in the bathroom if you'd rather. Well, I suppose I'd best let you get settled. Would you like some tea or anything?"

"That would be lovely," said Bethancourt. "I'll be down in a few minutes."

"Take your time," she replied cheerfully. "Oh, and when you do come down, Mr. Bethancourt, would you sign the register for me? I always like to have a little record of the people who visit. It's fun to look through and see where they all come from."

Bethancourt promised to sign the register, and with that she left him.

He was not very long in following her down, and the tea had not yet appeared in the sitting room. He went back to the entrance hall and found the register spread open on a little table. He wrote his name and address beneath a signature dated in late November, and then turned back the pages to the August entries. These were plentiful; apparently Mrs. Tyzack did brisk business during the summer months. Unfortunately, it was impossible to tell who had been traveling alone and who had not, since everyone except the married couples signed their names on a separate line. Still, if Carmichael was looking for strangers to the village, here was a large list of them. Bethancourt wondered if Mrs. Tyzack had seen all of them leave, luggage in hand.

"There you are, Mr. Bethancourt. I've got the tea all set up now."

"I'm just coming, Mrs. Tyzack."

"You've been signing the book, I see," she went on, leading the way back to the sitting room.

"Yes. You haven't had anybody in lately."

"No, it's not the season for it, you see. People mostly come in the summer—by the end of October we're down to a trickle. And it's *very* unusual to get anyone this close to Christmas." She looked at him curiously.

"I'm here to work with the police," supplied Bethancourt.

"Oh, about poor Mrs. Bainbridge's body," said Mrs. Tyzack with eager interest. She seated herself and began to pour out the tea. "Wasn't it just awful? Who would have left it there for the poor woman to find I just can't imagine. People have no consideration for the elderly these days at all."

"I suppose you know her quite well?"

"Oh, yes. The family was living here when I married George. Louisa Bainbridge is older than I am, but she had her Cathy just about the same time I had my Ken, and we got quite chummy over the baby prams. She's not had a very easy time of it, poor woman, and now to have this happen in her old age—well, it's just too bad."

"Not an easy time?" asked Bethancourt cautiously, hoping this was not a reference to childbirth. "But I understood she was in easy circumstances, and her family seems to be very close."

"They are now," said Mrs. Tyzack with emphasis. "But it was a long time coming, I can tell you. It was her husband, you see. Very strict he was, with a nasty temper, *and* an awful snob. I'm afraid they didn't get on very well, though she never complained except to say once she'd been married too young. I know you won't believe this, but when the third child died—just a baby, it was, and born before its time, too—and Mrs. Connelly said to him how sorry she was, he said it didn't matter much, it had only been another girl, anyhow."

"That," said Bethancourt with distaste, "is unpardonable."

"Just so," said Mrs. Tyzack, nodding. "Although he changed his mind in the end, when he found out what a bother boys can be. Louisa had two boys in a row after that, but it was the last child, Cathy, who

was always his favorite. Not that he didn't end by
alienating her, just as he had all the rest."

"He didn't get on with his children, then?"

"Far from it," said Mrs. Tyzack. "Everything was
more or less fine when they were little, but when they
began to grow up! Well, there were fireworks. He
positively tormented the oldest boy, David. Nothing
the child did was good enough. He's been a sore trial
to his mother over the years, and it's my belief that
it was all his father's doing. He wouldn't let the boy
marry the girl he wanted to—threatened to cut him
off without a penny if he went ahead with the wed-
ding. Didn't think she was good enough for his son,
although she was a decent, well-brought-up girl even
if she wasn't no more than the baker's daughter. He
forced David to join the navy, though he didn't want
to and didn't stick it for very long. He tried to make
his second son, Michael, join too, but Michael always
had more spirit than David and he flat refused. Ran
off to America, he did. But poor David was so muddled, he didn't know what to do. He was very devoted
to little Cathy, too, and it's my belief he stuck it out
so's not to be separated from her."

"He must have been sad when she married and
moved to Australia," said Bethancourt, pouring more
tea for them both.

"Why, thank you, dear, that's kind of you. David
wasn't just sad when she went, he nearly went out of
his mind. He accused his father of driving her away,
which was true enough. I'm not saying she doesn't
have a happy marriage, because to the best of my
knowledge she does, but she told her mother at the
time that she was going to get away from her father.
And then she slipped off one night, without him
knowing. And they weren't married until they got to
Melbourne. Mr. Bainbridge had old fashioned ideas
about that sort of thing, and he refused ever to speak
to her or have her in his house again. He said he
would disinherit David for accusing him of driving her
away, but he never did. I expect it was because David
was the only one left, really. The two older girls were

married and didn't come home much, and if they wrote, it was to their mother. Michael was off in America, and Cathy in Australia. Anyway, they had a lot of trouble with David from then on. He started drinking too much and lost a couple of jobs because of it. Was taken up for being drunk and disorderly, and for fighting once, too. It went on for years. Then all at once he ran off—no news of him at all for more than a year—and when he turned up again, he was sober, hardly drinking at all, and had married a French girl. Mr. Bainbridge didn't take to that much, but there wasn't a thing he could do. David's wife was already pregnant, and once the baby was born, David never looked back. He dotes on that child to this day, and so did his father."

"That's a very interesting history," said Bethancourt. "When did Mr. Bainbridge die?"

"Oh, about ten years back. And things have been fine ever since. All the children come to visit their mother now, and she is so pleased to see them. They'll be here for Christmas—all except for Michael and Cathy—and all the grandchildren, too. That's why it's such a pity their nice time has to be ruined by this dreadful body."

"It is indeed," agreed Bethancourt. "Do your children come to you, too?"

"No, no. I go up to Ken's home in Bristol, ever since they had the baby."

Mrs. Tyzack chatted on about her grandchild for a few minutes, and then Bethancourt excused himself, saying he had better get back to the police.

Bethancourt found Scotland Yard back at the pub, having a well-deserved pint before proceeding to Mrs. Bainbridge's.

"I want to get that in before supper," said Carmichael, "because most of the old lady's family hasn't been here since August and if we can get their movements over that weekend clear, we may be able to eliminate the whole lot."

But the interview with Mrs. Bainbridge and her

daughter, Clarissa North, was uncomfortable and unprofitable. Both women were alarmed, despite Carmichael's reassurances, at having their family's movements investigated, nor could they remember very accurately what had occurred. Gibbons took notes furiously, occasionally getting muddled among the different names and relationships. It seemed, once they had at last finished, that it would have been virtually impossible for anyone to sneak a body up to the attic at any time except at night when everyone was asleep. At night, it was perfectly possible since everyone had slept on the second floor, with the exception of the French boy, who had slept in a little room off the kitchen. Unfortunately, both Mrs. Bainbridge and her daughter were early risers and could shed no light on how late the others might have stayed up on any given night. They suggested that Maureen Bainbridge or her cousin Daniel North might know better.

"And night is about the only time any of them could have committed the murder," said Gibbons afterward in the pub, with his notes strewn about him. "None of them seems to have been alone for any appreciable time over the entire weekend. Although," he added apologetically, "it was awfully hard to keep track."

"I can see that it was," said Carmichael. "I've a large family myself, but at least they don't all mill about together over weekends, killing people. Well, never mind. We'll just have to interview the family members to see if their accounts tally with what we've got here."

"It *would* be useful to know at what time people were getting to bed," said Bethancourt. "If Mrs. Bainbridge and Mrs. North were rising between seven and eight every morning, and the younger members of the family were going to bed at four in the morning, well, it doesn't leave much time."

"On the other hand," put in Gibbons, "if they were going to bed virtuously before midnight, eight hours is plenty of time for any killer."

"It'll have to be checked into," sighed Carmichael. "And may have no bearing on the case at all, once we find out who the dead man was. Well, I'm for bed and start again tomorrow."

"Wake up, Phillip."

Bethancourt opened a bleary eye and reached for his glasses. "What time is it?"

"Quarter past eight," replied Gibbons.

Bethancourt groaned and sat up slowly. "Why don't you start without me?"

"I couldn't possibly. You're driving me to Brighton. Here." Gibbons picked up the dressing gown from the foot of the bed and threw it at his friend. "Mrs. Tyzack is bringing up early tea—you'd better put something on." He grinned. "I gathered you'd told her to give breakfast a miss."

"Yes, I did," said Bethancourt, flinging on his robe. "I loathe food first thing in the morning. Good morning, Cerberus."

Cerberus thumped his tail on the carpet, and Gibbons knelt to rub his chest.

"I am going to brush my teeth," announced Bethancourt. "When I return, I hope you will have devised a suitable explanation for your ill-considered phrase, 'driving to Brighton.' "

Bethancourt took some time in the bathroom, and the tea had arrived by the time he emerged. He took the cup Gibbons poured for him and sipped cautiously at it. "Now then, Jack," he said.

"We are going to Brighton because we've had word that David Bainbridge has returned from France and I've been told to see him."

"When you put it like that," said Bethancourt, "it seems more reasonable. I don't suppose it's more than a couple of hours anyway."

"That's right," said Gibbons. "I will even volunteer to drive there, if you will drive back. Now, do put on your clothes, there's a good chap."

They arrived at the offices of David Bainbridge's import-export business shortly before lunchtime and were shown into his office by a youthful, if severe, secretary. Bainbridge himself was a sober-faced man with dark circles beneath his eyes, dressed conservatively in a blue suit and unobtrusive tie. He greeted them quietly and offered them seats and coffee.

"My wife told me the news last night," he said. "It's an appalling thing for my mother."

"It is indeed," agreed Gibbons, "but she seems to be bearing up well. Your sister, Mrs. North, is with her."

"That's good," he said. "One can always count on Clarissa. Well, how may I help you gentlemen?"

"First of all, Mr. Bainbridge, we'd like to know of any visit you've made to your mother's house since August."

Bainbridge grimaced. "Only one," he answered. "I usually go up more frequently, but various business emergencies have prevented me this fall. In fact, I planned to be there a week ago, to help with Christmas things, but just when I was ready to go, I got another call from France." He sighed. "Well, let me see. I was there for the Bank Holiday in August, and then again about a month later."

"Were your family with you in September?"

"No. No, I was alone that weekend."

"Did you go up to the third floor or attic on either of those occasions?"

"Oh, I see," said Bainbridge. "No, I'm afraid I didn't. I can't remember the last time I was up there, in fact."

"That's all right, sir, no one else can either. Now, if you'd be so good as to go over with us how you spent the holiday weekend."

Bainbridge looked startled. "The holiday weekend?" he repeated. "Was that when—"

"We're not certain, sir," replied Gibbons implacably, "but it is a possibility at this time."

Bainbridge's account of the weekend did not measurably differ from his mother's.

"One last thing," said Gibbons when he had done, "we'd appreciate it if you could give us Renaud Fibrier's address."

"I'm afraid I can't do that, sergeant. I don't know it."

"Well then, the name and address of your partner."

"That I can give you, but I'm afraid he'll be no help. You see, Renaud and his family are estranged."

Gibbons was surprised. "And yet you took him to your family reunion?" he said.

"Oh, yes. I can explain that. You see, Renaud is his father's eldest son, but I'm afraid they've never got on very well together. I've always found the boy most charming myself. Very polite and so on. Anyway, about a year or more ago, Renaud got himself into some scrape or another, and his father absolutely refused to help him again. Renaud ran off and ceased to communicate with his family at all. His father was very upset. Then last August I was in London and happened to run into him. It wasn't the most congenial meeting—he wasn't disposed to trust me at first, even though I had some sympathy for him." Bainbridge smiled. "I had some differences with my own father in my youth, so I wasn't prepared to lay quite *all* the blame at Renaud's door. At any rate, I managed to make sure he was all right for money and to get his phone number, although he wouldn't tell me where he was staying. I called his father, and it was he who suggested I invite Renaud to our family gathering. He hoped, I suppose, that seeing how happily my own situation had turned out would influence Renaud. But I'm afraid it didn't."

"It was not a success?"

Bainbridge sighed and rubbed his chin. "No," he answered. "Family life bored Renaud. He was very pleasant, but he insisted on taking the first train on Monday morning, even though I had understood that he would stay until Tuesday. I had to get up to drive him, at some inconvenience to myself—no one else was even up yet. Still, I thought it better that he leave if he wished to. You can't force family feeling on people."

"That's true, sir." Gibbons nodded and slowly closed his notebook. "Well, thank you very much, sir.

That's quite clear. We may call on you again once we discover who this unfortunate man was."

"Certainly, sergeant. I hope you clear it up quickly."

They took their leave and made their way back to the car where Cerberus waited for them with a doleful look on his face.

"It's all right, boy," murmured Bethancourt a little absently.

"Well," said Gibbons, settling himself into his seat while Bethancourt maneuvered out of the parking space, "that was a fat lot of help. I wish to God they'd hurry up and identify the body. At this rate, I'm going to miss my Christmas Holidays altogether."

"There's still a week to go, Jack. Who knows? Maybe there'll be good news waiting for us when we get back to Dorset."

Gibbons grunted disconsolately, and they drove on in silence. In a few minutes, Gibbons roused himself to point out that Bethancourt had made a wrong turn.

"You should have stayed on the A27," he said.

"Actually," said Bethancourt, "I thought we'd run up to London."

"What on earth for?"

"I thought we'd see Maureen again. David Bainbridge was no help at all as to when they all went to bed over the weekend."

"Phillip, it's perfectly likely that the body was put there after the weekend."

"If it was, that exonerates the family."

"Except for Cathy Dresler in Australia. We've only her word for it that there was no body there before the weekend."

"Yes, but it seems unlikely that she would have any motive. She's been living in Australia for years. Why should she go around murdering people in England?"

"Maybe our corpse was Australian."

They wrangled comfortably over this point as the car shot northward to London.

*   *   *

When they arrived, Maureen Bainbridge, to Bethancourt's disappointment, had just begun a two hour lecture, so they sought out Daniel North instead. He seemed pleased at this distraction from his normal duties and insisted on giving them tea. Then he leaned his elbows on his desk and frowned in an effort to recall the Bank Holiday weekend.

"Well, let's see," he said. "I went down on Friday with Dad—Mother was already there. We got a late start and were the last to arrive. There was dinner, of course . . . yes, and we all went up early, except for Maureen and Renaud. They stayed up talking for a bit, but it couldn't have been long because I heard her come up just as I was turning out my light."

"They got on well, then?" asked Gibbons.

North looked offended. "Renaud is certainly the type that women are attracted to," he said, "but Maureen is hardly that superficial. She wouldn't take up with someone like him."

"Perhaps," suggested Bethancourt tactfully, "their late chat was rather onesided?"

North smiled, appeased. "I expect so," he said.

"You seem to have known Renaud prior to that weekend," said Gibbons, "but the rest of the family had never met him before. How is that?"

"Met him one evening at a club," North said. "A friend of mine knew someone in his party, and after some talk, Renaud and I discovered our connection. He seemed quite pleasant at first, but I didn't care for the whole crowd. I'm sure they were doing drugs, and their behavior, well, it left much to be desired."

"Then you wouldn't know anything about his present whereabouts?"

"Certainly not." North was affronted again. "Uncle David should know, if that's what you want."

"Unfortunately," said Gibbons, "he doesn't."

"Oh." North paused thoughtfully. "Wait a moment," he said slowly, "I believe Renaud did say something about where he was staying. Yes, Camden Town, I think it was. North London, anyhow."

Gibbons jotted "Camden?" in his notebook. "Thank

you," he said, "that may be helpful. Now, sir, if you could go on with your description of the weekend?"

"Yes, of course. Where was I up to? Saturday? Everyone was up quite late that night. It was well past two by the time the last of us went to bed. I think the last up were Uncle David, Aunt Cathy, Maureen, Renaud, and myself."

"That brings us to Sunday."

"Yes, let's see. Oh, Sunday was the night we went to the pub. Just Maureen, Renaud, and I. We ran into a couple there that Renaud knew from London." A look of distaste came over North's face. "Not the sort of people I usually associate with."

"Of course not," said Bethancourt, his voice full of false sympathy. He was beginning to think North was a bit of a prig.

"Could you describe them for us, sir?" asked Gibbons, ignoring his friend.

"Well, the man—Dick was his name—was all right. He was about my age, I suppose, dark-haired and wearing a leather jacket. I think he said he was a mechanic. The girl was called Penny. Bleached hair and too much eye makeup, and wearing a dress that kept slipping off her shoulder. Way off."

Bethancourt made a "tsk-tsk" sound, and Gibbons glared at him.

"You stayed at the pub how long?" he asked.

"Maureen and I left first," said North. "Renaud was behaving quite badly. He'd spent most of the weekend chatting up Maureen, but now he'd switched to Penny. Naturally I didn't mind that, and Maureen didn't seem to care, but after all, Penny was with another man. I didn't think Penny was very happy with his attentions, but when I got up to go to the men's room, I saw his hand on her leg. No," he corrected himself, "not on her leg. He'd pushed her dress up and had his hand on the inside of her thigh."

"No!" exclaimed Bethancourt, feigning shock. Gibbons kicked him surreptitiously.

"I can quite see how you felt," he said.

"Yes," said North, gratified by this display of sympathy. "Well, you can imagine that I came back from the w.c. and took Maureen right off."

"Of course," said Gibbons. "Was everyone else still up when you got back?"

North took a moment to put aside righteous indignation. "No," he said. "Not everyone. Just, let's see, Aunt Cathy, and my father and Aunt Bernice. But they went off to bed twenty minutes or so after we got back. Maureen and I stayed up a bit. It must have been about midnight—perhaps a little after—when I said goodnight and Maureen went to get a glass of milk to take to bed with her."

"And Renaud hadn't yet returned?"

"No. Well, if he had, he didn't come into the living room." He paused and scratched his chin. "That brings us to Monday. Most of us left that evening so as to be at work on Tuesday. Mother stayed on, and so did Maureen and her parents—they always take a week in the summer to visit Grandmother."

"Yes," said Gibbons, consulting his notes. "They all stayed until Thursday, except for David Bainbridge, who was called away on business Tuesday." He looked up. "Well, that's very clear, Mr. North, thank you. You heard nothing, I suppose, during any of the nights you spent there?"

"Not me," replied North. "I'm a heavy sleeper."

Gibbons thanked him and rose to leave.

Outside, Bethancourt walked Cerberus round the block while Gibbons phoned Carmichael in Dorset to say they were starting back. Having supplied themselves with sandwiches and coffee for the drive back, they threaded their way out of London and were soon spinning along the M3 under heavy skies.

"It's going to rain," observed Gibbons.

"Or snow," said Bethancourt. "Dorset should look very pretty in the snow. Very Christmaslike and all that."

"Don't be silly," answered Gibbons. "It's not cold enough to snow." Then he went on, rather abruptly, "I wonder if we shouldn't make more of an effort to find Renaud Fibrier than we have been doing. The only members of the family who knew anything about him confirm the bad reputation his own father gave him. Supposing he and that other chap fought over the girl after North and Maureen had left. Fibrier might have killed him and put the body in the attic after everyone else was in bed. It certainly fits with his wanting to leave first thing in the morning."

Bethancourt nodded. "That's true, Jack. I think it would be very interesting to find out what sort of trouble he was in in France."

"Very interesting," agreed Gibbons. "We'll run it by Carmichael and see if he doesn't want to put in a call to France this afternoon."

Chief Inspector Carmichael did. They found him at the local police station, where he informed them that missing persons was no further along with connecting the body to anyone on their lists. He was considerably cheered, however, by the thought of Renaud Fibrier as murderer and Dick the mechanic as victim.

"We'll have to check all the hotels and B&B's in the area," he said. "If we can find their last names, it should be easy enough to trace them in London. If we start now," he added wistfully, "we might even be able to go back to town tonight. I'll just ring the Sûreté and then we can have some supper and get on with it."

"I'll meet you at the pub," said Bethancourt. "I want a change of clothes. It won't take me long."

Mrs. Tyzack's house was quiet as Bethancourt let himself in. There was a light burning in the front hall, and he paused by the registry book lying open on the hall table. Pulling off his gloves, he turned the pages back once again to the late August entries and was pleased to find that Dick Tottle and Penny Cranston had conformed to custom and inscribed their names and addresses.

Turning away, he had another thought and, bypassing the stairs, headed for the back of the house and the sitting room, where Cerberus was greeted with joyful barks by the terrier.

"Hello," said Mrs. Tyzack. "I didn't hear you come in. Can I get you anything?"

Bethancourt smiled and dropped into the easy chair opposite her. "What I really need is information," he said. "Can you think back to the August Bank Holiday weekend and a couple of guests you had then?"

The names meant nothing to her, but once he had described the couple and placed the weekend in her mind by mentioning the Bainbridge reunion, she began to remember.

"Yes," she said slowly. "Yes, I think they came on the Saturday. Here, let me just fetch the reservation book—"

Bethancourt politely performed this service for her. She pored over the entries for a moment and then looked up and beamed at him.

"Here it is," she said. "They came on the Saturday evening, booked through till Monday. I remember them now—they had the room across the hall from yours and were rather quiet. Spent a lot of time at the pub, I believe."

"That's splendid," said Bethancourt warmly. "Now, what I really need to know is: did you see them returning from the pub on Sunday or leaving Monday morning?"

She thought for a moment. "No," she said at last. "No, I shouldn't have seen them Sunday night—oh, yes, of course. Look, it's here in the book as well. They paid up on Sunday afternoon, saying they'd be off on the first train on Monday. Yes, the girl explained she had to work Monday, although I don't remember now what she said she did. I asked if they'd want breakfast, but they said no, it would be too early, they'd just get up and leave. So I had a nice lie-in because the other guests didn't want breakfast till nine. They were gone by the time I got up—I remember I checked their room to make sure."

She smiled up at him, pleased with her success. "Is that what you wanted?" she asked. "Is it important?"

"It's very important," answered Bethancourt, beaming back at her. "Mrs. Tyzack, you're a marvel."

* * *

Carmichael and Gibbons were equally pleased when Bethancourt joined them at the Lion's Head.

"That's pure jam," said Carmichael with satisfaction. "We might as well start back directly after supper then. Thank you, Bethancourt." He fished in his pocket for a train schedule, pulling out a whole sheaf of papers in the process.

"I can drive you back, sir," offered Bethancourt.

"Why, thank you again," responded the chief inspector. "I—oh, damme." He was gazing at a slip of paper in dismay. "Bethancourt, I forgot. When I talked to the Yard earlier, they said several urgent messages had been left for you. I do apologize for not telling you sooner."

"Urgent?" asked Gibbons, startled.

"From a young lady. Name of Marla Tate."

Gibbons laughed heartily while Bethancourt said, "Oh, my God," and Carmichael raised a bushy eyebrow.

"It's Phillip's girlfriend," explained Gibbons. "And it's hardly likely to be urgent."

"To Marla it is," said Bethancourt glumly. "I'd better go outside and ring her before I eat."

He returned while the others were in the midst of their meal and breathed a sigh of relief as he sat down.

"Disaster has been averted," he announced. "There's a Christmas party tonight that I forgot, but I promised her I'd be back in time for it." He looked at his watch. "Can we be ready to leave in forty-five minutes?"

"Yes, by all means," answered Carmichael. "Mustn't keep a pretty young lady waiting," he added with a wink. "I assume she is pretty, Bethancourt?"

Gibbons guffawed, thinking of Marla's flawless beauty, while Bethancourt replied modestly that he found her so.

"Hello, Phillip," said Gibbons cheerfully. "Did I wake you?"

"Yes," answered Bethancourt tartly, shifting the

phone to light a cigarette. "It's only nine thirty, and that party went on till all hours."

"I thought you'd want to hear the latest."

Bethancourt sighed. "I suppose I do," he answered. "I take it by the tone of your voice it's good news?"

"It is," Gibbons assured him. "Dick Tottle's no longer at that address you got from Mrs. Tyzack—in fact, no one is. The building was razed to make way for a new block of flats last October. But Penny Cranston is listed in the phone directory. We haven't talked to her yet—she's out, but it's only a matter of time. Best of all, Carmichael heard from the Sûreté this morning. Renaud Fibrier was involved in several brawls, was convicted of petty larceny, and was involved in another brawl just before he disappeared. Unofficially, the police in his hometown say that he was once accused of rape but no charges were ever brought, and that he stole from his parents as well, who naturally never pressed charges. They're sure the latter is true, but unsure about the first, the source of the accusation being somewhat unreliable."

Bethancourt gave a low whistle. "Not a very good record," he observed. "I wonder how much of that David Bainbridge knew."

"Probably not very much," said Gibbons cheerfully. "He was likely just told that Renaud was 'in trouble' from time to time. I believe that's the usual conversational refuge of parents with problem children. Anyway, Fibrier could well be our man, Phillip. We're trying to track him down. Carmichael's sent out a bulletin on him, and I'm to start trying to find out where he was staying in London."

"Starting in Camden?"

"Starting in Camden. Do you want to come?"

"And spend all day knocking on one door after another? No, thank you. I'm going back to my nice warm bed with my nice warm girlfriend."

"Fine. You'll be sorry when I find the place myself."

"I'll join you tomorrow. Plenty of doors left for then."

"Ha! You don't know how lucky I'm feeling."

"Well, I'm not feeling lucky at all, and I wouldn't want to ruin your day," retorted Bethancourt. "Call me when you get back to the Yard."

"Very well," said Gibbons. "But you'll be sorry." He rang off and contemplated the long list in front of him. It consisted of all the hotels and bed and breakfasts in Camden and had been compiled by himself with the help of the London telephone directory. Bethancourt was right, of course: he couldn't possibly get through all of them in one day. Moreover, there was no guarantee that Fibrier hadn't been staying with friends. But that line of inquiry would have to wait until the Sûreté had done their best to find some of Fibrier's acquaintances and had discovered, if they could, any English connections.

He sighed, wishing he had been able to persuade Bethancourt to accompany him, and went forth to do his job.

His feeling of luck soon evaporated in the cold, damp day and, indeed, he met with no success. It was well after dark and he was chilled to the bone when he decided to stop for the day. He found a public call box and rang Penny Cranston's number as he had at intervals throughout the day, but once again there was no answer. Sighing, he turned away toward the underground to return to the Yard and report to Chief Inspector Carmichael.

The next morning Bethancourt consented to accompany his friend on his cheerless rounds of lodgings in Camden Town, with the proviso that they stop at Bond Street first.

"What on earth for?" asked Gibbons.

"Marla's Christmas present, of course," replied Bethancourt. "She is furious with me for letting this investigation interfere with the holiday festivities, and she will get still angrier before we're done."

"Oh, very well," said Gibbons. "But it had better not take long."

"It won't," Bethancourt assured him. "It need only be handsome, very extravagant, and green."

Indeed, Bethancourt accomplished his goal as swiftly as the Christmas crowds permitted, but Gibbons was horrified at the cost of the emerald and diamond bracelet.

"Surely that's a bit much," he said in a low voice.

"You forget how annoyed she is with me," replied Bethancourt. "This will put her right in a minute."

"It bloody well ought to," muttered Gibbons.

From Asprey's, they proceeded to Camden Town, but success did not crown their efforts. Moreover, it was a slow, painstaking business, asking people to remember a young Frenchman who might have stayed with them last August and then to look up past records. It was the kind of thing Bethancourt hated, and Gibbons soon found him more hindrance than help, for he amused himself by trying to charm the innkeepers senseless or, when that palled, by poking about shamelessly in everything he could find while Gibbons conducted the interview.

They lunched solidly at a pub, Bethancourt drinking several pints of Old Peculiar to fortify himself, and then went back to it under increasingly threatening skies.

"It's going to rain again," said Bethancourt at about four o'clock as they tramped down Anson Road.

"Probably," agreed Gibbons.

"Must we do very many more? In all probability he was staying with friends."

"We'll stop at five," said Gibbons consolingly.

"And get caught in rush hour? Thanks very much."

"Here's the next," said Gibbons. "And do try to behave, Phillip."

A middle-aged woman greeted them pleasantly and announced that she wasn't taking any boarders over the holidays.

"Goodness!" she said once Gibbons had explained their purpose. "Last August, you say? Now that's difficult to remember. I'll have to pull out the books for that."

"We are fairly certain he would have checked out in late August," said Bethancourt with a smile. "But unfortunately, we're not at all sure when he would have arrived. We're working on the assumption at the moment that he arrived no earlier than the beginning of July."

"Well," she answered, setting a heavy book down on the counter with a thump, "I haven't had anyone staying that long. A two month stay I would have remembered. There was that American family—they stayed three weeks." She opened the book and began flipping through the pages. "And I did have a whole group of Frenchmen in, but they only stayed a day or two. And that was earlier on, I think. Half a mo'!" She looked up at them suddenly. "There *was* a young man that stayed a fortnight or so. Only I thought he was Swiss."

"Swiss?" asked Gibbons.

"Yes," she answered, going back to the book and rapidly turning the leaves. "There was a group—I'm sure the couple were Swiss. There was another man, too, I think. They all stayed a few days and then, when the others left, one stayed on and I switched him to a single." She bent over the book, running her finger down the page. "I *think* it was August," she muttered. "Yes, here we are: 11 August, two doubles. The others left on the sixteenth, and the one that was left changed rooms. Here he is: Renaud Fibrier. Wasn't that the name you mentioned?"

Bethancourt gave a loud whoop of triumph and, leaning over the counter, kissed her soundly on the cheek. "That's it, adorable woman," he said, "that's it! We've found him, Jack!"

Gibbons was grinning broadly. "When did he check out?"

"On the twenty-ninth," she answered, consulting the book. "The Tuesday after Bank Holiday."

"That fits," said Gibbons to Bethancourt. "He returns from the murder, packs up, and clears off. He's probably been back on the Continent for months."

They thanked her for her help and left, well pleased with themselves.

There was a call box on the corner and here Gibbons stopped, fishing in his pocket for change.

"I'm going to try Penny Cranston again," he said.

Bethancourt looked surprised. "You did that half an hour ago," he said mildly.

Gibbons grinned at him. "I'm feeling lucky," he said.

His luck held true. In a moment he emerged, his grin broader than ever.

"She's home," he announced. "We can go straight over. Let's grab a taxi—it's not far."

Penny Cranston's bedsitter was small and rather dirty. There was a pile of clothes on the single armchair, the carpet had seen better days and had faded to a pinky-brown, and the kitchen sink was crowded with unwashed dishes.

Penny herself had a slatternly appearance; her hair was bleached an incredible shade of yellow, revealing almost an inch of dark brown at the roots. She was thin, but not elegantly so; rather, she gave the impression of being scrawny except for her breasts, which were large and swung freely beneath a shiny purple shirt. She seemed suspicious of them, despite Gibbons' reassurances and Bethancourt's scrupulous politeness. Indeed, the latter appeared to make her uneasy and, as if in reaction, she did not offer them seats, but only leaned against the little breakfast table, planted squarely in the center of the worn carpet.

However, she was willing enough, once their mission was explained, to discuss Renaud Fibrier.

"That one," she said, and snorted to show her opinion of him. "I haven't seen him in months, nor want to, neither."

"We're particularly interested in the August Bank Holiday weekend," said Gibbons, and waited, a little anxiously, for her reaction.

But the mention of it did not appear to stir any deep feelings. "That was when I gave him the shove-off," she nodded. "Down in that nowhere place in the country."

"Just so," said Gibbons, a little disappointed, but

still hoping. "You went down with your boyfriend?" She looked blank, so he added, "Dick Tottle?"

"Oh." She giggled. "Dick's not my boyfriend. He's just a friend."

Gibbons apologized for misunderstanding. "Anyway, you ran into Renaud Fibrier?"

"Not exactly ran into. We were supposed to meet him there."

"I see."

Bit by bit the story emerged. She had met Renaud Fibrier in a nightclub a fortnight or so before that weekend and they had had, she stated defiantly, a good time. Then he had told her he was going to Dorset for the holiday weekend and suggested she come along. It would be awfully dull, he said, but between the two of them, they might liven it up a bit and he could use the free meal ticket. He couldn't invite her to stay with him, but she could stay cheaply in a B&B. They could appear to run into each other by accident.

"I couldn't get away till Saturday evening," she said. "I was scheduled to work the restaurant, see? So we fixed up to meet at the village pub on Saturday night. Renaud said he might have to wait until after dinner to slip out, but I should just sit tight at the pub. Only then I didn't fancy the idea of waiting for hours in some dead and gone pub, and besides, when I rung the B&B, it was more than we'd thought. So I asked Dick if he'd like to come with me. I told him what was up," she added. "He knew it was Renaud I was going to see."

"So you met Renaud on Saturday?"

Her eyes flashed. "That's just what we didn't do," she said. "We went to the pub for dinner and stayed till closing, but he never showed. I was mad, I can tell you. I wanted to go straight to London, but Dick pointed out that we'd reserved the room for Sunday and the B&B lady would probably make us pay for it anyway. So we stayed. I was sure glad I'd thought of asking Dick along—I'd've gone out of my mind in that place otherwise. We went back to the pub the next night—there wasn't no place else—and lo and behold, in comes Renaud. And then I see why he didn't show the night before because he's got a real snooty looker on his arm. So I says to Dick, 'Let's get out of here,' only before we get the chance, Renaud comes over and is introducing us, and everybody's sitting down. I didn't want to make a fuss in front of that girl, so I sat tight for a bit. And you know what that nogooder does next?"

"He—er—started chatting you up?" ventured Bethancourt.

"Chatting up's not the half of it," she replied fiercely. "He started feeling my leg underneath the table, just as if everything was fine. I tried to brush him off, but he was back in a flash. Like I said, I didn't want to make a fuss, but was I ever glad when that girl and her cousin took off. I gave him a piece of my mind then, I did."

"And well-deserved, too."

"I told him just what I thought of him and his fancy bit, and then I said he could just tear up my phone number because I wouldn't be answering calls from him no more. And then I took Dick and left."

"Did he follow you?"

She sniffed. "Not him. I meant what I said and he knew it."

Gibbons and Bethancourt exchanged glances, hope waning. If Dick Tottle had left Dorset hale and hearty . . .

"And you and Dick left by the first train on Monday?"

"That's right. I had early shift at the restaurant, you see."

"Yes," said Gibbons, disappointed. "I take it, in view of what you've said, that Renaud didn't ride back to town with you?"

"Of course not," she replied, amazed at his stupidity.

"You didn't see him on the station platform?" asked Bethancourt.

"No. There wasn't anybody there. Dick and I were

early and had to wait a bit and we didn't see a soul
except for one man who drove into the car park right
when the train arrived."

"He didn't let anybody off?"

"We didn't see. We were busy boarding. A blue
Ford Escort, it was. I remember because Dick's a
mechanic and he was laughing at me trying to make
out the makes of cars, but I knew that one because
my sister's got an Escort." She looked curious. "Did
you think Renaud had taken the same train as us?"

"Yes," answered Gibbons, dispiritedly. "We did."

"Well, maybe he did come on at the last minute.
We were waiting, like I said, and got on right away."

"That's certainly possible," said Bethancourt.
"Thank you very much, Miss Cranston. You've been
an enormous help."

Gibbons paused in the act of picking up his coat.
"I expect you still keep in touch with Dick Tottle?"
he asked.

"Oh, yes. Saw him last night, in fact."

"Could you let us have his address and phone
number?"

She gave them the information from memory and
they bade her goodbye, making their way down the
narrow stairs in silence.

"You don't think she was lying?" asked Gibbons
hopelessly.

"No," answered Bethancourt. "Anyway, if she was,
you'll soon know when you see Tottle."

"Aren't you coming with me?" asked Gibbons in
surprise.

Bethancourt shook his head. "Another Christmas
party," he said. "I've got to dress and meet Marla.
It's getting late."

He swung open the front door, and they stepped
out into the chill drizzle.

"I'll call you tomorrow. Don't look so down, Jack.
We were wrong, that's all. Tomorrow we'll come up
with a better theory."

"Yes, all right. Tomorrow, then, Phillip."

Gibbons turned away from his friend, in search of

a call box and Dick Tottle, desperately wishing he was the one going to a Christmas party. Then it occurred to him that there was no reason he should not partake of some holiday cheer himself, at least after he had interviewed Tottle. Accordingly, he put through two calls instead of one and, with his plans for the evening made, went off to see Dick Tottle in a better frame of mind.

Marla was annoyed with him again, but Bethancourt would hardly have noticed if she hadn't announced the fact. He had, she said, been preoccupied during the whole of the cocktail party they had attended, and he was to stop thinking of his silly case and rouse himself for dinner, which was to be eaten with two other couples. Bethancourt meekly agreed to this on the condition that he could phone Gibbons from the restaurant. Gibbons was not home, however, and it was not long before Bethancourt dropped out of the conversation and began to smoke abstractedly. Marla nudged him with a steely look in her green eyes.

"Darling," she said, "do you want any more of those escargots or can the waiter clear?"

"What?" Bethancourt became aware that everyone else had long since finished their first course. "Oh, no, have him take them away."

He lit another cigarette and leaned back out of the waiter's way. Something had occurred to him during the cocktail party, triggered by a chance remark, and he was desperate to get hold of Gibbons and check it out. It was such a simple solution that he couldn't help but feel that there must be something against it or they would have thought of it earlier.

"You're not very lively tonight, Phillip," said Shelley.

"Late party last night," he replied absently. Then he stubbed out his cigarette and rose. "Will you excuse me a minute? I've just remembered something."

Marla looked daggers at him, but the others all murmured politely and went on with their conversation.

Gibbons was still not home. Annoyed, Bethancourt

tapped his fingers impatiently against the receiver. He
felt it was quite unreasonable of his friend to be out
on the town just when he was wanted.

Bethancourt returned to the table and, after being
kicked sharply on the ankle by Marla, managed to
enter into the conversation with some animation. He
was halfway through his entree when another thought
struck him. He turned it over in his mind for a few
minutes, and then bolted the rest of his dinner and
asked to be excused again.

Once more there was no answer at Gibbons', but
with this new idea in his brain, Bethancourt was in no
mood to sit through the rest of dinner. Returning to
the dining room, he announced he had been called
away and dashed off, thinking to himself it was lucky
he had come up to scratch on Marla's Christmas present because otherwise she would never forgive him.

Outside, it was beginning to rain again. Bethancourt
hailed a taxi and gave Gibbons' address. He was
determined to plant himself on the doorstep and wait
even if Gibbons stayed out until three in the morning.
In reality, however, he soon grew cold and went round
the corner to wait in the nearest pub. Bursting with
his news, the minutes dragged by like hours until at
last Gibbons answered his call—the fifth in half an
hour.

"I'm round the corner," announced Bethancourt.
"I'll be up directly." And he rang off before Gibbons
could protest.

Gibbons had not yet undressed. He felt it was
unreasonable of Bethancourt to desert him for the
evening and then to come tramping up to his flat at a
quarter past eleven when he was trying to have an
early night. Resignedly, he poured himself a scotch.

"I've got the answer!" Bethancourt announced dra-
matically as soon as Gibbons opened the door.

Gibbons eyed him as he stood flushed with the cold,
eyes bright behind his glasses, grinning happily.

"You've been drinking," he said.

"Of course I've been drinking," replied Bethancourt, pushing past him and shedding his overcoat.

"I've just come from cocktails and dinner. At least I'm not still drinking," he added, seeing the glass in Gibbons' hand. Then he rounded on his friend and asked abruptly, "Did Dick Tottle confirm Penny's story?"

"In every particular," answered Gibbons, getting another glass and filling it. He handed the drink to Bethancourt who took it mechanically and sat down. "Now, what's this idea of yours?"

"It's not an idea," retorted Bethancourt, "it's the solution to the whole puzzle. Who the dead man is and who killed him."

"Well, who?"

"The dead man was Renaud Fibrier."

"I thought we'd just decided he was the murderer."

"We were wrong. Think about it, Jack—he's everything we want in a victim. The right age, the right looks, and he disappeared late on Sunday night or early Monday morning."

Gibbons thought about it. "So you're casting David Bainbridge as the murderer?"

"Why not? After all, Renaud spent the weekend chatting up his daughter, on whom he dotes. Who knows, maybe she even succumbed. Or maybe Renaud was blackmailing him—he sounds the sort of chap who wouldn't balk at a little extortion. And we've only Bainbridge's word for it that Fibrier left for London early Monday. Penny and Dick never saw him."

"Well, yes," said Gibbons reflectively, "but wait a minute, Phillip. We know Renaud checked out of his lodgings on Tuesday. He could hardly do that if he was murdered on Sunday night."

Bethancourt waved a hand airily. "That's because when we talked to Mrs. Whatsis at his lodgings, we were expecting to hear that he had checked out on Monday or Tuesday. We didn't ask her the right questions. If I hadn't pressed Mrs. Tyzack when I was inquiring after Penny and Dick, she would just have said that they left on Monday, not that they paid up on Sunday afternoon and she hadn't seen them since."

"That's true," said Gibbons.

"And, Jack, I've remembered something else. You know what Penny said about a Ford Escort? Well, there was a blue one parked outside Bainbridge's office when we went to see him."

"Was there?" said Gibbons, more confused by this piece of information than enlightened.

"Yes!" said Bethancourt triumphantly. "If Bainbridge killed Renaud during the night, then he had to substantiate his story about taking him to the train in the morning, you know."

"Of course," said Gibbons, the light dawning. "He had his wife with him. He'd have to get up early and what better way to lend verisimilitude to an otherwise—"

"Just so."

"That's more promising," said Gibbons. "You could be right, Phillip. Look here, we'll go round to Fibrier's lodgings again first thing in the morning, and if that turns out right, I'll put it up to Carmichael. If the dead man *is* Fibrier, it should be easy enough to confirm through the Sûreté. Then we can go on from there. It's going to be tricky, though, getting evidence."

"Bah!" said Bethancourt, finishing off his drink. "His own words damn him. If Fibrier was dead in the attic on Monday morning, the best barrister in the world is going to find it difficult to explain why Bainbridge claims to have driven him to the station."

"Well, perhaps," said Gibbons, grinning. He raised his glass. "You may well have it, Phillip. Congratulations."

They interrupted Renaud's landlady during her first cup of coffee the next morning. She poured coffee for them while they explained what they wanted and then went to consult her registration book.

"Look here," she said, returning with the book. "I remember now. I've even made a note in the book, but I missed it yesterday somehow." She set the volume down and took up her coffee. "Renaud came to me," she said slowly, as if trying to get the memory clear in her head, "and said he'd been invited to the country for the weekend but would be back on the Monday night. I said I could probably rent the room for the weekend, it being the holiday and all, but if I didn't he'd have to pay for it. So he moved his things out and I put them in the closet. I did rent the room for the weekend, you can see by the book, but he never came back."

"So his things are still here?"

She shook her head. "No. On the Tuesday another man came and said Renaud had to leave in a hurry— his father had fallen ill, I think. Anyway, he paid me up to Tuesday and returned the key Renaud had gone off with and took his things away."

"Would you recognize this man again?" asked Gibbons eagerly.

She looked doubtful. "I might," she said, "and then again I might not. He was older, I remember, and looked respectable."

Gibbons described David Bainbridge. "Could that have been the man?" he asked.

"It could be," she agreed, "there's nothing against it to my recollection. But I wouldn't know until I saw him, and even then I'm not sure I'd recognize him."

They thanked her profusely for her help, warned her they might call again, and left on swift, jubilant feet for Scotland Yard.

Carmichael was enormously pleased with both of them. He put through a call to the Sûreté and then sat puffing out his mustaches at them.

"Well done," he said several times. "That's a champion bit of work, lads."

In an hour or two, the copy of Renaud Fibrier's dental records arrived and were matched by forensics with those of the previously unidentified body. An air of satisfaction pervaded Carmichael's office.

"I'll just ring down to Brighton and have Bainbridge detained," he said. "Then we'd better drive down ourselves. Bethancourt, would you care to accompany us?"

Bethancourt accepted this offer, and Carmichael

smiled and nodded while he dialed the Brighton station. He made his request, and in seconds all the light had gone out of the room. The two young men watched Carmichael anxiously, but they could make little of the few monosyllables he spoke. At last he rang off and sighed.

"We're too late," he announced. "Bainbridge committed suicide yesterday."

"What?" exclaimed Gibbons.

"He must have realized," said Bethancourt, "that it was only a matter of time before we identified the body."

"Did he leave a note?"

"Yes," answered Carmichael, "but it's hardly a confession. It asks his wife to forgive him and says it will be better this way. Then he says she knows he's always been a weak man, and that he's glad to have found the strength to do this."

"Well," said Gibbons dully, "that's that."

It was raining again and the evening air was chill. Bethancourt paused for a moment in the vestibule while Cerberus shook himself dry. Then he firmly pressed the bell.

She was surprised to see him. Her eyes were red with weeping and she looked tired, but she invited him in politely.

"I didn't expect the police again," she said.

"I'm not the police, Maureen," said Bethancourt gently, divesting himself of his overcoat. "I came to satisfy a personal curiosity. There is no reason for you to talk to me if you don't want to. But if you do, it will be between you and me."

"I don't mind," she said. "But I don't know if I can tell you anything more."

"Your father either wrote or called you before he died," said Bethancourt simply.

Her eyes widened a little. "How do you know that?" she asked.

"The note that he left was addressed only to your mother, yet you were very dear to him. I've been thinking it all over, and my guess is that you know what happened that night, the night Renaud Fibrier died, that you knew before you heard from your father. You know because you were there."

She did not look at him, nor did she speak.

"Did Renaud rape you?" Bethancourt asked softly.

She flung her head up in surprise and pain, and tears started in her eyes. "Yes!" she said, almost defiantly. "'If that's what you came to find out: yes, he did. He held a knife to my throat and threatened to kill me if I didn't do what he said. I was terrified. . . ."

"I'm sorry," said Bethancourt. "I'm truly sorry."

She had begun to cry again, and she wiped the tears furiously from her face. "How did you know?"

"He raped another girl once, in France," answered Bethancourt. "I couldn't think why your father would have killed him. After all, he knew he was a bad sort long before that weekend. But it wasn't until tonight, when I realized your father had communicated with you separately, that I thought of the answer." He paused. "Your father must have come down to the kitchen for something and found you."

"Yes. He couldn't sleep and came down for some milk."

"There was the knife," continued Bethancourt, "the one Renaud had used to threaten you, still lying where he cast it aside afterward. Anyway, when your father came down, you were in shock. He must have taken you upstairs and then come back down. The attic must have seemed a good temporary hiding place. What I can't understand is why he didn't remove the body later."

"He tried," she answered, "when he went back in September. But he couldn't bring himself to do it. I expect it was pretty awful by then, and he lost his nerve. That's what he said, anyway. He knew he'd have to do it before Christmas, but then he was called away, and Grandmother went up to the attic early. . . ."

"I see," said Bethancourt. "Of course, you knew nothing of that. He would have been careful to keep it from you."

She nodded slowly. "He wrote me about it before he—before he killed himself."

Bethancourt sighed. "Then there's only one thing more," he said. "That night, after your father took you upstairs and then came back down, what did he do?"

She stared at him uncomprehendingly.

"Did he confront Renaud and stab him? Or did he merely remove the knife that was already there and hide the body, so that no one would ever know what his beloved daughter had done or what had happened to her to make her do it."

There was a long pause. Maureen raised her eyes to gaze at him levelly, the tears still wet on her face. Then she lifted her chin, and said, "I loved my father very much. He died so that this murder would never be connected with me. I will not make his sacrifice useless. He killed Renaud Fibrier. Renaud raped me, and my father killed him for it. That is what happened."

"I understand," said Bethancourt. "Thank you for talking with me." He rose and reached for his overcoat. In silence, she accompanied him to the door. He paused there for a moment, thoughtfully drawing on his gloves.

"Does your mother know you were raped?" he asked.

She shook her head violently. "No one knows."

"It's a horrible thing," he said. "Sometimes it can be very difficult to deal with. If you ever need to talk about it, well, my number's in the phone directory."

"Thank you," she said. "Thank you very much."

Outside it was still raining. Cerberus stepped over a puddle and bent to sniff the base of the lamp post. Bethancourt stood for a moment, watching the rainfall in the light from the street lamp. Then he sighed and looked at his watch.

"A bad business, old thing," he said to the dog. "Sometimes I wonder what I do it for. Come on then, Cerberus, it's time to meet Marla and give her Christmas present to her."

FATHER CRUMLISH
CELEBRATES
CHRISTMAS

Alice Scanlan Reach

"Eat that and you'll be up all night with one of your stomach gas attacks." Emma Catt's voice boomed out from the doorway of what she considered to be her personal sanctuary—the kitchen of St. Brigid's rectory.

Caught in the act of his surreptitious mission, Father Francis Xavier Crumlish hastily withdrew the arthritic fingers of his right hand which had been poised to enfold one of several dozen cookies cooling on the wide, old-fashioned table.

"I—I was just thinking to myself that a crumb or two would do no harm," he murmured, conscious of the guilty flush seeping into the seams, tucks, and gussets of his face.

"It would seem to me that a man of the cloth would be the first to put temptation behind him," Emma observed tartly as she strode across the worn linoleum flooring. "Particularly a man of your age," she added, giving him a meaningful look.

The pastor swallowed a heavy sigh. After Emma had arrived to take charge of St. Brigid's household chores some 22 years ago, he had soon learned to his sorrow that her culinary feats were largely confined to bland puddings, poached prunes, and a concoction which she called "Irish Stew" and which was no more

than a feeble attempt to disguise the past week's
leftovers.

So he was most agreeably surprised one day when
Emma miraculously produced a batch of cookies of
such flavorful taste and texture that the priest mentally
forgave her all her venial sins. And since it was Father
Crumlish's nature to share his few simple pleasures
with others, he promptly issued instructions that, once
a year, Emma should bake as many of the cookies as
the parish's meager budget would allow. As a result,
although St. Brigid's pastor and his housekeeper were
on extra-short rations from Thanksgiving until Christmas Eve, many a parishioner's otherwise cheerless
Christmas Day was brightened by a bag of the sugar-
and-spice delicacies.

Now, today, as the priest quickly left the kitchen
area to avoid any further allusions to his ailments and
his advancing years, the ringing of the telephone was
entirely welcome. He hurried down the hallway to his
office and picked up the receiver.

"St. Brigid's."

"It's Tom, Father."

Father Crumlish recognized the voice of Lieutenant
Thomas Patrick "Big Tom" Madigan of Lake City's
police force and realized, from the urgency in the
policeman's tone, that his call was not a social one.

"I'm at the Liberty Office Building," Madigan said
in a rush. "A guy's sitting on a ledge outside the top-
story window. Says he's going to jump. If I send a car
for you—"

"I'll be waiting at the curb, Tom," Father interrupted and hung up the phone.

"Big Tom" Madigan was waiting outside the elderly
office building when Father Crumlish arrived some
minutes later. Quickly he ushered the priest through
the emergency police and fire details and the crowd
of curious onlookers who were gazing in awe at the
scarecrow figure perched on a ledge high above the
street.

"Do you know the man, Tom?" Father asked. He followed the broad-shouldered policeman into the building lobby and, together, they entered a self-service elevator.

"And so do you, Father," Madigan said as he pressed the elevator button. "He's one of your people. Charley Abbott."

"God bless us!" the pastor exclaimed. "What do you suppose set Charley off this time?" He sighed. "The poor lad's been in and out of sanitariums half a dozen times in his thirty years. But this is the first time he's ever tried to do away with himself."

"This may not be just one of Abbott's loony notions," Madigan replied grimly. "Maybe he's got a good reason for wanting to jump off that ledge."

"What do you mean, Tom?"

"Last week a man named John Everett was found murdered in his old farmhouse out in Lake City Heights. He was a bachelor, lived alone, no relative—"

"I read about it," Father interrupted impatiently. "What's that got to do—"

"We haven't been able to come up with a single clue," Madigan broke in, "until half an hour ago. One of my detectives, Dennis Casey, took an anonymous phone call from a man who said that if we wanted to nab Everett's murderer we should pick up the daytime porter at the Liberty Office Building."

"That's Charley," Father nodded, frowning. "I myself put in a good word for him for the job."

"Casey came over here on a routine check," Madigan went on as the elevator came to a halt and he and the priest stepped out into the corridor. "He showed Abbott his badge, said he was investigating Everett's murder, and wanted to ask a few questions. Abbott turned pale—looked as if he was going to faint, Casey says. Then he made a dash for the elevator, rode it up to the top floor, and climbed out the corridor window onto the ledge."

"But surely now, Tom," Father protested, "you can't be imagining that Charley Abbott had a hand in that killing? Why, you know as well as I that, for all his peculiar ways, Charley's gentle as a lamb."

"All I know," Madigan replied harshly, "is that when we tried to ask him a few questions, he bolted." He ran a hand over his crisp, curly brown hair. "And I know that innocent men don't run."

"Innocent or guilty," Father Crumlish said, "the man's in trouble. Take me to him, Tom."

When Father Crumlish entered the priesthood more than forty years before, he never imagined that he was destined to spend most of those years in St. Brigid's parish—that weary bedraggled section of Lake City's waterfront where destitution and despair, avarice and evil, walked hand in hand. And although, on the occasions when he lost a battle with the Devil, he too sometimes teetered on the brink of despair, he unfailingly rearmed himself with his intimate, hard-won knowledge of his people.

But now, as the old priest leaned out the window and caught sight of the man seated on the building's ledge, his confidence was momentarily shaken. Charley Abbott had the appearance and demeanor of a stranger. The man's usually slumped, flaccid shoulders were rigid with purpose; his slack mouth and chin were set in taut hard lines; and in place of his normal attitude of wavering indecision, there was an aura about him of implacable determination.

There was not a doubt in Father Crumlish's mind that Abbott intended to take the fatal plunge into eternity. The priest took a deep breath and silently said a prayer.

"Charley," he then called out mildly, "it's Father Crumlish. I'm right here close to you, lad. At the window."

Abbott gave no indication that he'd heard his pastor's voice.

"Can you hear me, Charley?"

No response.

"I came up here to remind you that we have been through a lot of bad times together," Father continued conversationally. "And together we'll get through whatever it is that's troubling you now."

The priest waited for a moment, hoping to elicit some indication that Abbott was aware of his presence. But the man remained silent and motionless, staring into space. Father decided to try another approach.

"I've always been proud of you, Charley," Father said. "And never more so than when you were just a tyke and ran in the fifty-yard dash in our Annual Field Day Festival." He sighed audibly. "Ah, but that's so many years ago, and my memory plays leprechaun's tricks. I can't recall for the life of me, lad—did you come in second or third?"

Again Father waited, holding his breath. Actually he remembered the occasion clearly. The outcome had been a major triumph in his attempts to bring a small spark of reality into his young parishioner's dreamy, listless life.

Suddenly Abbott's long legs, which were dangling aimlessly over the perilous ledge, stiffened, twitched. Slowly he turned his head and focused his bleak eyes on the priest.

"I—I won!" he said, in the reproachful, defensive voice of a small child.

"I can't hear you, Charley," Father said untruthfully, striving to keep the tremor of relief from his voice. "Could you speak a little louder? Or come a bit closer?"

To Father Crumlish it seemed an eternity before Abbott's shoulders relaxed a trifle, before his death-like grip on the narrow slab of concrete and steel diminished, before slowly, ever so slowly, the man began to inch his way along the ledge until he came within an arm's reach of the window and the priest. Then he paused and leaned tiredly against the building's brick wall.

"I won," he repeated, this time in a louder and firmer tone.

"I remember now," Father said, never taking his dark blue eyes from his parishioner's pale, distraught face. "So can you tell me why a fellow like yourself, with a fine pair of racing legs, would be hanging them out there in the breeze?"

The knuckles of Charley's hands grasping the ledge whitened. "The cops are going to say I murdered Mr. Everett—" He broke off in agitation.

"Go on, Charley."

"They're going to arrest me. Put me away." Abbott's voice rose hysterically. "And this time it'll be forever. I can't stand that, Father." Abruptly he turned his head away from the priest and made a move as if to rise to his feet. "I'll kill myself first."

"Stay where you are!" Father Crumlish commanded. "You'll not take your life in the sight of God, with me standing by to have it on my conscience that I wasn't able to save you."

Cowed by Father's forcefulness, Abbott subsided and once more turned his stricken gaze on the pastor's face.

"I want you to look me straight in the eye, Charley," Father said, "and answer my question: as God is your Judge, did you kill the man?"

"No, Father. No!" The man's slight form swayed dangerously. "But nobody will believe me."

Father Crumlish stared fixedly into Abbott's pale blue eyes which were dazed now and dark with desperation. But the pastor also saw in them his parishioner's inherent bewilderment, fear—and his childlike innocence. Poor lad, he though compassionately. Poor befuddled lad.

"*I* believe you, Charley," he said in a strong voice. "And I give you my word that you'll not be punished for a crime you didn't commit." With an effort the priest leaned further out the window and extended his hand. "Now come with me."

Hesitatingly Abbott glanced down at the priest's outstretched, gnarled fingers.

"My word, Charley."

Abbott sat motionless, doubt and indecision etched on his thin face.

"Give me your hand, lad," Father said gently.

Once again the man raised his eyes until they met the priest's.

"Give me your hand!"

It was a long excruciating moment before Charley released his grip on the ledge, extended a nailbitten, trembling hand, and permitted the pastor's firm warm clasp to lead him to safety.

It was Father Crumlish's custom to read the *Lake City Times* sports page while consuming his usual breakfast of coddled egg, dry toast and tea. But this morning he delayed learning how his beloved Giants, and in particular Willie Mays, were faring until he'd read every word of the running story on John Everett's murder.

Considerable space had been devoted to the newest angle on the case—Charley Abbott's threatened suicide after the police had received an anonymous telephone tip and had sought to question him. Abbott, according to the story, had been taken to Lake City Hospital for observation. Meanwhile, the police were continuing their investigation, based on the few facts at their disposal.

To date, John Everett still remained a "mystery man." With the exception of his lawyer, banker, and the representative of a large real estate management concern—and his dealings with all three had been largely conducted by mail or telephone—apparently only a handful of people in Lake City were even aware of the man's existence. As a result, his murder might not have come to light for some time had it not been for two youngsters playing in the wooded area which surrounded Everett's isolated farmhouse. Prankishly peering in a window, they saw his body sprawled on the sparsely furnished living-room floor and notified the police. According to the Medical Examiner, Everett had been dead less than 24 hours. Death was the result of a bullet wound from .25 automatic.

Although from all appearances Everett was a man of modest means, the story continued, investigation showed that in fact he was extremely wealthy—the "hidden owner" of an impressive amount of real estate in Lake City. Included in his holdings was the Liberty Office Building where Charley Abbott had almost committed suicide.

Frowning, Father Crumlish put down the newspaper and was about to pour himself another cup of tea when the telephone rang. Once again it was Big Tom Madigan—and Father was not surprised. It was a rare day when Madigan failed to "check in" with his pastor—a habit formed years ago when he'd been one of the worst hooligans in the parish and the priest had intervened to save him from reform school. And in circumstances like the present, where one of St. Brigid's parishioners was involved in a crime, the policeman always made sure that Father Crumlish was acquainted with the latest developments.

"I've got bad news, Father," Madigan said, his voice heavy with fatigue.

The priest braced himself.

"Seems Everett decided to demolish quite a few old buildings that he owned. Turn the properties into parking lots. I've got a list of the ones that were going to be torn down and the Liberty is on it." Madigan paused a moment. "In other words, Charley Abbott was going to lose his job. Not for some months, of course, but—"

"Are you trying to tell me that any man would commit murder just because he was going to lose his job?" Father was incredulous.

"Not *any* man. *Charley*. You know that he didn't think his porter's job was menial. To him it was a 'position,' a Big Deal, the most important thing that ever happened to him."

Father Crumlish silently accepted the truth of what Big Tom had said. And yet . . . "But I still can't believe that Charley is capable of murder," he said firmly. "There's something more to all this, Tom."

"You're right, Father, there is," Madigan said. "Abbott lived in the rooming house run by his sister and brother-in-law, Annie and Steve Swanson."

"That I know."

"Casey—the detective who tried to question Charley yesterday—went over to the house to do a routine check on Charley's room. Hidden under the carpet, beneath the radiator, he found a recently fired .25 automatic."

The priest caught his breath.

"Casey also found a man's wallet. Empty—except for a driver's license issued to John Everett."

"What will happen to poor Charley now, Tom?" Father finally managed to ask.

"In view of the evidence I'll have to book him on suspicion of murder."

After hanging up the phone, the priest sat, disconsolate and staring into space, until Emma Catt burst into the room, interrupting his troubled thoughts.

"I just went over to church to put some fresh greens on the roof of the crib," Emma reported. "Some of the statuettes have been stolen again."

Wincing at her choice of the word, the pastor brushed at his still-thick, snow-white hair, leaned back in his desk chair, and closed his eyes.

In observance of the Christmas season St. Brigid's church traditionally displayed a miniature crib, or manger, simulating the scene of the Nativity. Statuettes representing the participants in the momentous event were grouped strategically in the stable. And to enhance the setting, boughs of fir, pine, and holly were placed around the simple structure.

So while Father Crumlish was please by Emma's attention to the crib's appearance, he also understood the full meaning of her report. It was sad but true that each year, on more than one occasion, some of the statuettes would be missing. But unlike Emma, Father refused to think of the deed as "stealing." From past experience (sometimes from a sobbing whisper in the Confessional), he knew that some curious child had knelt in front of the crib, stretched out an eager hand, perhaps to caress the Infant, and then . . .

"What's missing this time," the priest asked tiredly.

"The Infant, the First Wise Man, and a lamb."

"Well, no harm done. I'll step around to Herbie's and buy some more."

"It would be cheaper if you preached a sermon on stealing."

" 'They know not what they do'," the old priest murmured as he adjusted his collar and his bifocals, shrugged himself into his shabby overcoat, quietly closed the rectory door behind him, and walked out into the gently falling snow.

Minutes later he opened the door of Herbie's Doll House, a toy and novelty store which had occupied the street floor of an aged three-story frame building on Broad Street as long as the pastor could remember. As usual at this time of the year, the store was alive with the shrill voices of excited youngsters as they examined trains, wagons, flaxen-haired dolls, and every imaginable type of Christmas decoration. Presiding over the din was the proprietor, Herbie Morris, a shy, slight man in his late sixties.

Father Crumlish began to wend his way through the crowd, reflecting sadly that most of his young parishioners would be doomed to disappointment on Christmas Day. But in a moment Herbie Morris caught sight of the priest, quickly elbowed a path to his side, and eagerly shook Father's outstretched hand.

"I can see that the Christmas spirit has caught hold of you again this year," Father Crumlish said with a chuckle. "You're a changed man." It was quite true. Herbie Morris' normally pale cheeks were rosy with excitement and his usually dull eyes were shining.

"I know you and all the store-keepers in the parish think I'm a fool to let the kids take over in here like this every Christmas," Herbie said sheepishly but smiling broadly. "You think they rob me blind." He sighed. "You're right. But it's worth it just to see them enjoying themselves—" He broke off, and a momentary shadow crossed his face. "When you have no one—no real home to go to—it gets lonely—" his voice faltered. "Especially at Christmas."

Father Crumlish put an arm around the man's thin

shoulder. "It's time you had a paying customer," he said heartily. "I need a few replacements for the crib."

Nodding, Morris drew him aside to a counter filled with statuettes for the manger and Father quickly made his selections. The priest was about to leave when Herbie clasped his arm.

"Father," he said, "I've been hearing a lot about Charley Abbott's trouble. I room with the Swansons."

"I know you do," Father said, "I'm on my way now to see Annie and Steve."

"George says Charley had been acting funny lately."

"George?"

"George Floss. He rooms there too."

"The same fellow who's the superintendent of the Liberty Office Building?" Father was surprised.

"That's him. Charley's boss."

Thoughtfully the priest tucked the box of statuettes under his arm and departed. Although his destination was only a few minutes' walk, it was all of half an hour before he arrived. He'd been detained on the way in order to halt a fist fight or two, admire a new engagement ring, console a recently bereaved widow, and steer homeward a parishioner who'd been trying to drain dry the beer tap in McCaffery's Tavern. But finally he mounted the steps of a battered house with a sign on the door reading: *Rooms*.

He had little relish for his task. Annie and Steve were a disagreeable, quarrelsome pair, and the pastor knew very well that they considered his interest in Charley's welfare all through the years as "meddling." Therefore he wasn't surprised at the look of annoyance on Steve's face when he opened the door.

"Oh, it's you, Father," Steve said ungraciously. "C'mon in. Annie's in the kitchen."

Silently Father followed the short, barrel-chested man, who was clad in winter underwear and a pair of soiled trousers, down a musty hallway. Annie was seated at the kitchen table peeling potatoes. She was a scrawny, pallid-complexioned woman who, Father knew, was only in her mid-forties. But stringy gray hair and deep lines of discontent crisscrossing her face made her appear to be much older. Now, seeing her visitor, she started to wipe her hands on her stained apron and get to her feet. A word from the pastor deterred her.

"I suppose you've come about Charley," she said sulkily.

"Ain't nothing you can do for him this time, Father," Steve said with a smirk. "This time they got him for good—and good riddance."

"Shut up," Annie snapped, shooting her husband a baleful glance.

"First time the crazy fool ever had a decent-paying job," Steve continued, ignoring her. "And what does he do?" He cocked his thumb and forefinger. "Gets a gun and—"

"Shut up, I said!" Annie's face flamed angrily.

"Hiya, Father," a jovial voice interrupted from the doorway. "You here to referee?"

Father turned and saw that the tall burly man entering the kitchen was one of the stray lambs in his flock—George Floss. Murmuring a greeting, the priest noticed that Floss was attired in a bathrobe and slippers.

"It's my day off," George volunteered, aware of Father's scrutiny. He yawned widely before his heavy-jowled face settled into a grin. "So I went out on the town last night."

"That explains your high color," Father remarked dryly. He turned back to the table where Annie and Steve sat glowering at each other. "Now if you can spare a moment from your bickering," he suggested, "maybe you can tell me what happened to set Charley off again."

Steve pointed a finger at Floss. "He'll tell you."

"Charley was doing fine," George said as he poured a cup of coffee from a pot on the stove. "Didn't even seem to take it too hard—at least, not at first—when I told him he was going to be out of a job."

"*You* told him?" the priest said sharply.

"Why, sure," Floss replied with an important air. "I'm the Super at the Liberty building. Soon as I knew the old dump was going to be torn down, I told every-body on the maintenance crew that they'd be getting the ax. Me too." He scowled and his face darkened. "A stinking break. There aren't too many good Super jobs around town."

He gulped some coffee and then brightened. "Of course it won't be for some time yet. That's what I kept telling Charley. But I guess it didn't sink in. He started worrying and acting funny—" He broke off with a shrug.

"You haven't heard the latest, George," Steve said. "That cop—Casey—was here nosing around Charley's room. Found a gun and the Everett guy's wallet."

"No kidding!" Floss's eyes widened in surprise. He shook his head and whistled.

"Gun, wallet, no matter what that cop found," Annie shrilled, waving the paring knife in her hand for emphasis, "I don't believe it. Charley may be a little feeble-minded, but he's no murderer—"

The air was suddenly pierced by a loud and pene-trating wail. In an upstairs bedroom a child was crying.

"Now see what you've done," Steve said disgust-edly. "Started the brat bawling."

Annie gave a potato a vicious stab with her knife. "Go on up and quiet her."

"Not me," Steve retorted with a defiant shake of his balding head. "That's your job."

"I've got enough jobs, cooking and cleaning around here. It won't kill you to take care of the kid once in a while."

Father Crumlish had stood in shocked silence during the stormy scene. But now he found his tongue.

"It's ashamed you should be," he said harshly, turn-ing his indignant dark blue eyes first on Annie, then on Steve. "When I baptized your little Mary Ann four years ago, I told both of you that you were blessed to have a child at your age and after so many years. Is this disgraceful behavior the way you give thanks to the good Lord? And is this home life the best you can offer the poor innocent babe?"

He took a deep breath to cool his temper. Annie and Steve sat sullen and wordless. The only sound in the silence was the child's crying.

"I'll go and see what's eating her," George offered, obviously glad to escape from the scene.

"I've an errand to do," Father told the Swansons. "But mind you," he held up a warning finger, "I'll be back before long to have another word or two with you."

Turning on his heel, he crossed the kitchen floor, walked down the hallway, and let himself out the door. But before he was halfway down the steps to the street, he heard Annie's and Steve's strident voices raised in anger again. And above the din he was painfully aware of the plaintive, persistent sound of the crying child.

Lieutenant Madigan was seated at his desk engrossed in a sheaf of papers when Father Crumlish walked into headquarters.

"Sit down, Father," Big Tom said sympathetically. "You look tired. And worried."

Irritated, the pastor clicked his tongue against his upper plate. He disliked being told that he looked tired and worried; he knew very well that he *was* tired and worried, and that was trouble enough. He considered remaining on his feet, stating his business succinctly, and then being on his way. But the chair next to Madigan's desk looked too inviting. He eased himself into it, suppressing a sigh of relief.

"I know all this is rough on you, Father," Madigan continued in a kind tone. "But facts are facts." He paused, extracted one of the papers in front of him, and handed it to the priest.

Father Crumlish read it slowly. It was a report on the bullet which had killed John Everett; the bullet definitely had been fired from the gun found in Charley Abbott's room. Silently the pastor placed the report on Big Tom's desk.

"This is one of those cases that are cut and dried," the policeman said. "One obvious suspect, one obvious motive." He shifted his gaze away from the bleak look on Father's face. "But you know that with his mental record Charley will never go to prison."

Abruptly Father Crumlish got to his feet.

"Can you tell me where I'll find Detective Dennis Casey?" he asked.

Madigan stared in astonishment. "Third door down the hall. But why—?"

Father Crumlish had already slipped out the door, closed it behind him, and a moment later he was seated beside Detective Casey's desk. Then, in response to the priest's request, Casey selected a manila folder from his files.

"Here's my report on the anonymous phone call, Father," he said obligingly. "Not much to it, as you can see."

A glance at the typed form confirmed that the report contained little information that Father didn't already have.

"I was hoping there might be more," the pastor said disappointedly. "I know you've been on this case since the beginning and I thought to myself that maybe there was something that might have struck you about the phone call. Something odd in the man's words, perhaps." Father paused and sighed. "Well then, maybe you can tell me about your talk with Charley. Exactly what you said to him—"

"Wait a minute, Father," Casey interrupted. He ran a hand through his carrot-hued hair. "Now that you mention it, I *do* remember something odd about that call. I remember hearing a funny sound. Just before the guy hung up."

"Yes?" Father waited hopefully for the detective to continue.

Casey's brows drew together as he tried to recall.

"It was a sort of whining. A cry, maybe." Suddenly his eyes lit up. "Yeah, that's it! It sounded like a baby—a kid—crying."

As Father Crumlish wearily started up the steps to the rectory door, his left foot brushed against a small patch of ice buried beneath the new-fallen snow. He felt himself slipping, sliding, and he stretched out a hand to grasp the old wrought-iron railing and steady himself. As he did, the package of statuettes, which he'd been carrying all these long hours, fell from under his arm and tumbled to the sidewalk.

"Hellfire!"

Gingerly Father bent down to retrieve the package. At that moment St. Brigid's chimes rang out. Six o'clock! Only two hours before Evening Devotions, the priest realized in dismay as he straightened and stood erect. And in even less time his parishioners would be arriving at church to kneel down at the crib, light their candles, and say their prayers.

Well, Father thought, he would have to see to it that they wouldn't be disappointed, that there would be nothing amiss in the scene of the Nativity. Moments later he stood in front of the crib and unwrapped the package. To his chagrin he discovered that the tumble to the sidewalk had caused one of the lambs to lose its head and one leg. But Herbie Morris could easily repair it, Father told himself as he stuffed the broken lamb into his pocket and proceeded to put his replacements in position. First, in the center of the crib, the Infant. Next, to the left, the First Wise Man. And then, close to the Babe, another unbroken lamb that he'd purchased.

Satisfied with his handiwork, Father knelt down and gazed at the peaceful tableau before him. Ordinarily the scene would have evoked a sense of serenity. But the priest's heart was heavy. He couldn't help but think that it was going to be a sad Christmas for Charley Abbott. And that the man's prospects for the future were even worse. Moreover, Father couldn't erase the memory of what he'd seen and heard at the Swansons—the anger, bitterness, selfishness, and, yes, even the cruelty.

Hoping to dispel his disquieting thoughts, the pastor started to close his eyes. But a slight movement in the crib distracted him. He stared in astonishment as he saw that a drop of moisture had appeared on the face of the Infant and had begun to trickle slowly down the pink waxen cheeks.

Even as he watched, fascinated, another drop appeared—and then the priest quickly understood the reason for the seeming phenomenon. The greens that Emma had placed on the roof of the stable had begun to lose their resilience in the steam heat of the church. The fir, pine, and holly boughs were drooping, shedding moisture on the face of the Child . . .

In the flickering rosy glow of the nearby vigil lights it struck the priest that the scene seemed almost real— as if the Child were alive and crying. As if He were weeping for all the people in the world. All the poor, lonely, homeless—

Father Crumlish stiffened. A startled expression swept over his face. For some time he knelt, alert and deep in thought, while his expression changed from astonishment to realization and, finally, to sadness. Then he rose from his knees, made his way to the rectory office, and dialed police headquarters.

"Could you read me that list you have of the buildings that John Everett was going to have torn down?" Father said when Madigan's voice came on the wire. The policeman complied.

"That's enough, Tom," the priest interrupted after a moment. "Now tell me, lad, will you be coming to Devotions tonight? I've a call to make and I thought, with this snow, you might give me a lift."

"Glad to, Father." Suspicion crept into Madigan's voice. "But if you're up to something—"

The pastor brought the conversation to an abrupt end by hanging up.

Herbie Morris was on the verge of locking up The Doll House when Father Crumlish and Big Tom walked in.

"Can you give this a bit of glue, Herbie?" Father asked as he handed the storekeeper the broken lamb.

"Forget it, Father," Herbie said, shrugging. "Help yourself to a new one."

"No need. I'm sure you can fix this one and it'll do fine."

Then, as Herbie began to administer to the statuette, the pastor walked over to a display of flaxen-haired dolls and leaned across the counter to select one. But the doll eluded his grasp and toppled over. The motion caused it to close its eyes, open its mouth, and emit the realistic sound of a child crying.

"I see your telephone is close by," Father said, pointing to the instrument a counter across the aisle. "So it's little wonder that Detective Casey thought he heard a real child crying while you were on the phone with him at headquarters. One of these dolls must have fallen over just as you were telling him to arrest Charley Abbott for John Everett's murder."

The priest was aware of Madigan's startled exclamation and the sound of something splintering. Herbie stood staring down at his hands which had convulsively gripped the lamb he'd been holding and broken it beyond repair.

"I know that you were notified that this building is going to be torn down, Herbie," Father said, "and I know these four walls are your whole life. But were you so bitter that you were driven to commit murder to get revenge?"

"I didn't want revenge," Herbie burst our passionately. "I just wanted to keep my store. That's all!" He wrung his hands despairingly. "I pleaded with Everett for two months, but he wouldn't listen. Said he wanted this land for a parking lot." Morris' shoulders sagged and he began to weep.

Madigan moved to the man's side. "Go on," he said in a hard voice.

"When I went to his house that night, I took the gun just to frighten him. But he still wouldn't change his mind. I went crazy, I guess, and—" He halted and looked pleadingly at the priest. "I didn't really mean to kill him, Father. Honest!"

"What about his wallet?" Madigan prodded him.

"It fell out of his pocket. There was a lot of money in it—almost a thousand dollars. I—I just took it."

"And then hid it along with the gun in the room of a poor innocent man," Father Crumlish said, trying to contain his anger. "And to make sure that Charley would be charged with your crime, you called the police."

"But the police would have come after *me*," Herbie protested, as if to justify his actions. "I read in the papers that they were checking Everett's properties and all his tenants. I was afraid—" The look on Father's face caused Herbie's voice to trail away.

"Not half as afraid as Charley when you kept warning him that the police would accuse him because of his mental record, because he worked in the Liberty Building and was going to lose his job. That's what you did, didn't you?" Father asked in a voice like thunder. "You deliberately put fear into his befuddled mind, told him he'd be put away—"

The priest halted and gazed at the little storekeeper's bald bowed head. There were many more harsh words on the tip of his tongue that he might have said. But, as a priest, he knew that he must forego the saying of them.

Instead he murmured, "God have mercy on you."

Then he turned away and walked out into the night. It had begun to snow again—soft, gentle flakes. They fell on Father Crumlish's cheeks and mingled with a few drops of moisture that were already there.

It was almost midnight before Big Tom Madigan rang St. Brigid's doorbell. Under the circumstances Father wasn't surprised by the policeman's late visit.

"How did you know, Father?" Madigan asked as he sank into a chair.

Wearily Father related the incident at the crib. "After what I heard at the Swansons and what Casey told me, a crying child was on my mind. And then, when I saw what looked like tears on the Infant's face, I got to thinking about all the homeless—" He paused for a long moment.

"Only a few hours before, Herbie had told me how hard it was, particularly at Christmas, to be lonely and without a real home. Charley was suspected of murder because he was going to lose his job. But wasn't it more reasonable to suspect a man who was going to lose his life's work? His whole world?" Father sighed. "I knew Herbie never could have opened another store in a new location. He would have had to pay much higher rent, and he was barely making ends meet where he was."

It was some moments before Father spoke again.

"Tom," he said brightly, sitting upright in his chair. "I happen to know that the kitchen table is loaded down with Christmas cookies."

The policeman chuckled. "And I happen to know that Emma Catt counts every one of 'em. So don't think you can sneak a few."

"Follow me, lad," Father said confidently as he got to his feet. "You're on the list for a dozen for Christmas. Is there any law against my giving you your present now?"

"Not that I know of, Father," Madigan replied, grinning.

"And in the true Christmas spirit, Tom," Father Crumlish's eyes twinkled merrily, "I'm sure you'll want to share and share alike."

Father Crumlish's Christmas Cookies

3 tablespoons butter
½ cup sugar
½ cup heavy cream
⅓ cup sifted flour
1¼ cup very finely chopped blanched almonds
¾ cup very finely chopped candied fruit and peels
¼ teaspoon ground cloves
¼ teaspoon ground nutmeg
¼ teaspoon ground cinnamon

(1) Preheat oven to 350 degrees.
(2) Combine butter, sugar, and cream in a saucepan and bring to a boil. Remove from the heat.
(3) Stir in other ingredients to form a batter.

(4) Drop batter by spoonfuls onto a greased baking sheet, spacing them about three inches apart.

(5) Bake ten minutes or until cookies begin to brown around the edges. Cool and then remove to a flat surface. If desired, while cookies are still warm, drizzle melted chocolate over tops.

YIELD: About 24 cookies

—Courtesy of the author

A MATTER OF LIFE
AND DEATH

Georges Simenon

"At home we always used to go to Midnight Mass. I can't remember a Christmas when we missed it, though it meant a good half hour's drive from the farm to the village."

The speaker, Sommer, was making some coffee on a little electric stove.

"There were five of us," he went on. "Five boys, that is. The winters were colder in those days. Sometimes we had to go by sledge."

Lecœur, on the switchboard, had taken off his earphones to listen. "In what part of the country was that?"

"Lorraine."

"The winters in Lorraine were no colder thirty or forty years ago than they are now—only, of course, in those days the peasant had no cars. How many times did you go to Midnight Mass by sledge?"

"Couldn't say, exactly."

"Three times? Twice? Perhaps no more than once. Only it made a great impression on you, as you were a child."

"Anyhow, when we got back, we'd all have black pudding, and I'm not exaggerating when I tell you I've never had anything like it since. I don't know what my mother used to put in them, but her *boudins* were quite different from anyone else's. My wife's tried, but it wasn't the same thing, though she had the exact recipe from my eldest sister—at least, my sister swore it was."

He walked over to one of the huge, uncurtained

windows, through which was nothing but blackness, and scratched the pane with a fingernail.

"Hallo, there's frost forming. That again reminds me of when I was little. The water used to freeze in our rooms and we'd have to break the ice in the morning when we wanted to wash."

"People didn't have central heating in those days," answered Lecœur coolly.

There were three of them on night duty. *Les nuiteux*, they were called. They had been in that vast room since eleven o'clock, and now, at six on that Christmas morning, all three were looking a bit jaded. Three or four empty bottles were lying about, with the remains of the sandwiches they had brought with them.

A lamp no bigger than an aspirin tablet lit up on one of the walls. Its position told Lecœur at once where the call came from.

"Thirteenth Arrondissement, Croulebarbe," he murmured, replacing his earphones. He seized a plug and pushed it into a hole.

"Croulebarbe? Your car's been called out—what for?"

"A call from the Boulevard Masséna. Two drunks fighting."

Lecœur carefully made a little cross in one of the columns of his notebook.

"How are you getting on down your way?"

"There are only four of us here. Two are playing dominoes."

"Had any *boudin* tonight?"

"No. Why?"

"Never mind. I must ring off now. There's a call from the Sixteenth."

A gigantic map of Paris was drawn on the wall in front of him and on it each police station was represented by a little lamp. As soon as anything happened anywhere, a lamp would light up and Lecœur would plug into the appropriate socket.

"Chaillot? Hallo! Your car's out?"

In front of each police station throughout the twenty

arrondissements of Paris, one or more cars stood waiting, ready to dash off the moment an alarm was raised.

"What with?"

"Veronal."

That would be a woman. It was the third suicide that night, the second in the smart district of Passy.

Another little cross was entered in the appropriate column of Lecœr's notebook. Mambret, the third member of the watch, was sitting at a desk filling out forms.

"Hallo! Odéon? What's going on? Oh, a car stolen."

That was for Mambret, who took down the particulars, then phoned them through to Piedbœuf in the room above. Piedbœuf, the teleprinter operator, had such a resounding voice that the others could hear it through the ceiling. This was the forty-eighth car whose details he had circulated that night.

An ordinary night, in fact—for them. Not so for the world outside. For this was the great night, *la nuit de Noël*. Not only was there the Midnight Mass, but all the theaters and cinemas were crammed, and at the big stores, which stayed open till twelve, a crowd of people jostled each other in a last-minute scramble to finish off their Christmas shopping.

Indoors were family gatherings feasting on roast turkey and perhaps also on *boudins* made, like the ones Sommer had been talking about, from a secret recipe handed down from mother to daughter.

There were children sleeping restlessly while their parents crept about playing the part of Santa Claus, arranging the presents they would find on waking.

At the restaurants and cabarets every table had been booked at least a week in advance. In the Salvation Army barge on the Seine, tramps and paupers queued up for an extra special.

Sommer had a wife and five children. Piedbœuf, the teleprinter operator upstairs, was a father of one week's standing. Without the frost on the windowpanes, they wouldn't have known it was freezing outside, In that vast, dingy room they were in a world apart, surrounded on all sides by the empty offices of the Préfecture de Police, which stood facing the Palais de Justice. It wasn't till the following day that those offices would once again be teeming with people in search of passport visas, driving licenses, and permits of every description.

In the courtyard below, cars stood waiting for emergency calls, the men of the flying squad dozing on the seats. Nothing, however, had happened that night of sufficient importance to justify their being called out. You could see that from the little crosses in Lecœur's notebook. He didn't bother to count them, but he could tell at a glance that there were something like two hundred in the drunks' column.

No doubt there'd have been a lot more if it hadn't been that this was a night for indulgence. In most cases the police were able to persuade those who had had too much to go home and keep out of trouble. Those arrested were the ones in whom drink raised the devil, those who smashed windows or molested other people.

Two hundred of that sort—a handful of women among them—were now out of harm's way, sleeping heavily on the wooden benches in the lockups.

There'd been five knifings. Two near the Porte d'Italie. Three in the remoter part of Montmartre, not in the Montmartre of the Moulin Rouge and the Lapin Agile but in the Zone, beyond where the Fortifs used to be, whose population included over 100,000 Arabs living in huts made of old packing cases and roofing-felt.

A few children had been lost in the exodus from the churches, but they were soon returned to their anxious parents.

"Hallo! Chaillot? How's your veronal case getting on?"

She wasn't dead. Of course not! Few went as far as that. Suicide is all very well as a gesture—indeed, it can be a very effective one. But there's no need to go and kill yourself!

"Talking of *boudin*," said Mambret, who was smok-

ing an enormous meerschaum pipe, "that reminds me
of—"

They were never to know what he was reminded of.
There were steps in the corridor, then the handle of
the door was turned. All three looked round at once,
wondering who could be coming to see them at ten
past six in the morning.

"*Salut!*" said the man who entered, throwing his hat
down on a chair.

"Whatever brings you here, Janvier?"

It was a detective of the Brigade des Homicides,
who walked straight to the stove to warm his hands.

"I got pretty bored sitting all by myself and I
thought I might as well come over here. After all, if
the killer's going to do his stuff I'd hear about it
quicker here than anywhere."

He, too, had been on duty all night, but round the
corner, in the Police Judiciaire.

"You don't mind, do you?" he asked, picking up
the coffeepot. "There's a bitter wind blowing."

It had made his ears red.

"I don't suppose we'll hear till eight, probably
later," said Lecœur.

For the last fifteen years, he had spent his nights in
that room, sitting at the switchboard, keeping an eye
on the big map with the little lamps. He knew half
the police in Paris by name, or, at any rate, those who
did night duty. Of many he knew even their private
affairs, as, when things were quiet, he would have
long chats with them over the telephone to pass the
time away. "Oh, it's you, Dumas. How are things at
home?"

But though there were many whose voices were
familiar, there were hardly any of them he knew by
sight.

Nor was his acquaintance confined to the police.
He was on equally familiar terms with many of the
hospitals.

"Hallo! Bichat? What about the chap who was
brought in half an hour ago? Is he dead yet?"

He was dead, and another little cross went into the

notebook. The latter was, in its unpretentious way, quite a mine of information. If you asked Lecœur how many murders in the last twelve months had been done for the sake of money, he'd give the answer in a moment—sixty-seven.

"How many murders committed by foreigners?"

"Forty-two."

You could go on like that for hours without being able to trip him up. And yet he trotted out his figures without a trace of swank. It was his hobby, that was all

For he wasn't obliged to make those crosses. It was his own idea. Like the chats over the telephone lines, they helped to pass the time away, and the result gave him much the same satisfaction that others derive from a collection of stamps.

He was unmarried. Few knew where he lived or what sort of a life he led outside that room. It was difficult to picture him anywhere else, even to think of him walking along the street like an ordinary person. He turned to Janvier to say: "For your cases, we generally have to wait till people are up and about. It's when a concierge goes up with the post or when a maid takes her mistress's breakfast into the bedroom that things like that come to light."

He claimed no special merit in knowing a thing like that. It was just a fact. A bit earlier in summer, of course, and later in winter. On Christmas Day probably later still, as a considerable part of the population hadn't gotten to bed until two or even later, to say nothing of their having to sleep off a good many glasses of champagne.

Before then, still more water would have gone under the bridge—a few more stolen cars, a few belated drunks.

"Hallo! Saint-Gervais?"

His Paris was not the one known to the rest of us— the Eiffel Tower, the Louvre, the Opéra—but one of somber, massive buildings with a police car waiting under the blue lamp and the bicycles of the *agents cyclistes* leaning against the wall.

"The chief is convinced the chap'll have another go tonight," said Janvier. "It's just the night for people of that sort. Seems to excite them."

No name was mentioned, for none was known. Nor could he be described as the man in the fawn raincoat or the man in the grey hat, since no one had ever seen him. For a while the papers had referred to him as Monsieur Dimanche, as his first three murders had been on Sunday, but since then five others had been on weekdays, at the rate of about one a week, though not quite regularly.

"It's because of him you've been on all night, is it?" asked Mambret.

Janvier wasn't the only one. All over Paris extra men were on duty, watching or waiting.

"You'll see," put in Sommer, "when you do get him you'll find he's only a loony."

"Loony or not, he's killed eight people," sighed Janvier, sipping his coffee. "Look, Lecœur—there's one of your lamps burning."

"Hallo! Your car's out? What's that? Just a moment."

They could see Lecœur hesitate, not knowing in which column to put a cross. There was one for hangings, one for those who jumped out of the window, another for—

"Here, listen to this. On the Pont d'Austerlitz, a chap climbed up onto the parapet. He had his legs tied together and a cord round his neck with the end made fast to a lamppost, and as he threw himself over he fired a shot into his head!"

"Taking no risks, what? And which column does that one go into?"

"There's one for neurasthenics. We may as well call it that."

Those who hadn't been to Midnight Mass were now on their way to early service. With hands thrust deep in their pockets and drops on the ends of their noses, they walked bent forward into the cutting wind, which seemed to blow up a fine, icy dust from the pavements. It would soon be time for the children to be waking up, jumping out of bed, and gathering barefoot around lighted Christmas trees.

"But it's not at all sure the fellow's mad. In fact, the experts say that if he was he'd always do it the same way. If it was a knife, then it would always be a knife."

"What did he use this time?"

"A hammer."

"And the time before?"

"A dagger."

"What makes you think it's the same chap?"

"First of all, the fact that there've been eight murders in quick succession. You don't get eight new murderers cropping up in Paris all at once." Belonging to the Police Judiciaire, Janvier had, of course, heard the subject discussed at length. "Besides, there's a sort of family likeness between them all. The victims are invariably solitary people, people who live alone, without any family or friends."

Sommer looked at Lecœur, whom he could never forgive for not being a family man. Not only had he five children himself, but a sixth was already on the way. "You'd better look out, Lecœur—you see the kind of thing it leads to!"

"Then, not one of the crimes has been committed in one of the wealthier districts."

"Yet he steals, doesn't he?"

"He does, but not much. The little hoards hidden under the mattress—that's his mark. He doesn't break in. In fact, apart from the murder and the money missing, he leaves no trace at all."

Another lamp burning. A stolen car found abandoned in a little side street near the Place des Ternes.

"All the same, I can't help laughing over the people who had to walk home."

Another hour or more and they would be relieved, except Lecœur, who had promised to do the first day shift as well so that his opposite number could join in a family Christmas party somewhere near Rouen.

It was a thing he often did, so much so that he had

come to be regarded as an ever-ready substitute for anybody who wanted a day off.

"I say, Lecœur, do you think you could look out for me on Friday?"

At first the request was proffered with a suitable excuse—a sick mother, a funeral, or a First Communion, and he was generally rewarded with a bottle of wine. But now it was taken for granted and treated quite casually.

To tell the truth, had it been possible, Lecœur would have been only too glad to spend his whole life in that room, snatching a few hours' sleep on a camp bed and picnicking as best he could with the aid of the little electric stove. It was a funny thing—although he was as careful as any of the others about his personal appearance, and much more so than Sommer, who always looked a bit tousled, there was something a bit drab about him which betrayed the bachelor.

He wore strong glasses, which gave him big, globular eyes, and it came as a surprise to everyone when he took them off to wipe them with the bit of chamois leather he always carried about to see the transformation. Without them, his eyes were gentle, rather shy, and inclined to look away quickly when anyone looked his way.

"Hallo! Javel?"

Another lamp. One near the Quai de Javel in the 15th Arrondissement, a district full of factories.

"Votre car est sorti?"

"We don't know yet what it is. Someone's broken the glass of the alarm in the Rue Leblanc."

"Wasn't there a message?"

"No. We've sent our car to investigate. I'll ring you again later."

Scattered here and there all over Paris are red-painted telephone pillars standing by the curb, and you have only to break the glass to be in direct telephone communication with the nearest police station. Had a passerby broken the glass accidentally? It looked like it, for a couple of minutes later Javel rang up again.

"Hallo! Central? Our car's just got back. Nobody about. The whole district seems quiet as the grave. All the same, we've sent out a patrol."

How was Lecœur to classify that one? Unwilling to admit defeat, he put a little cross in the column on the extreme right headed "Miscellaneous."

"Is there any coffee left?" he asked.

"I'll make some more."

The same lamp lit up again, barely ten minutes after the first call.

"Javel? What's it this time?"

"Same again. Another glass broken."

"Nothing said?"

"Not a word. Must be some practical joker. Thinks it funny to keep us on the hop. When we catch him he'll find out whether it's funny or not!"

"Which one was it?"

"The one on the Pont Mirabeau."

"Seems to walk pretty quickly, your practical joker!"

There was indeed quite a good stretch between the two pillars.

So far, nobody was taking it very seriously. False alarms were not uncommon. Some people took advantage of these handy instruments to express their feelings about the police. *"Mort aux flics!"* was the favorite phrase.

With his feet on a radiator, Janvier was just dozing off when he heard Lecœur telephoning again. He half opened his eyes, saw which lamp was on, and muttered sleepily, "There he is again."

He was right. A glass broken at the top of the Avenue de Versailles.

"Silly ass," he grunted, settling down again.

It wouldn't be really light until half past seven or even eight. Sometimes they could hear a vague sound of church bells, but that was in another world. The wretched men of the flying squad waiting in the cars below must be half frozen.

"Talking of *boudin*—"

"What *boudin*?" murmured Janvier, whose cheeks were flushed with sleep.

"The one my mother used to—"

"Hallo! What? You're not going to tell me some-one's smashed the glass of one of your telephone pil-lars? Really? It must be the same chap. We've already had two reported from the Fifteenth. Yes, they tried to nab him but couldn't find a soul about. Gets about pretty fast, doesn't he? He crossed the river by the Pont Mirabeau. Seems to be heading in this direction. Yes, you may as well have a try."

Another little cross. By half past seven, with only half an hour of the night watch to go, there were five crosses in the Miscellaneous column.

Mad or sane, the person was a good walker. Per-haps the cold wind had something to do with it. It wasn't the weather for sauntering along.

For a time it had looked as though he was keeping to the right bank of the Seine, then he had sheered off into the wealthy Auteuil district, breaking a glass in the Rue la Fontaine.

"He's only five minutes' walk from the Bois de Bou-logne," Lecœur had said. "If he once gets there, they'll never pick him up."

But the fellow had turned round and made for the quays again, breaking a glass in the Rue Berton, just around the corner from the Quai de Passy.

The first calls had come from the poorer quarters of Grenelle, but the man had only to cross the river to find himself in entirely different surroundings—quiet, spacious, and deserted streets, where his footfalls must have rung out clearly on the frosty pavements.

Sixth call. Skirting the Place du Trocadéro, he was in the Rue de Longchamp.

"The chap seems to think he's on a paper chase," remarked Mambret. "Only he uses broken glass instead of paper."

Other calls came in in quick succession. Another stolen car, a revolver-shot in the Rue de Flandres, whose victim swore he didn't know who fired it, though he'd been seen all through the night drinking in company with another man.

"Hallo! Here's Javel again. Hallo! Javel? It can't be your practical joker this time: he must be somewhere near the Champs Elysées by now. Oh, yes. He's still at it. Well, what's your trouble? What? Spell it, will you? Rue Michat. Yes, I've got it. Between the Rue Lecourbe and the Boulevard Felix Faure. By the viaduct—yes, I know. Number 17. Who reported it? The concierge? She's just been up, I suppose. Oh, shut up, will you! No, I wasn't speaking to you. It's Sommer here, who can't stop talking about a *boudin* he ate thirty years ago!"

Sommer broke off and listened to the man on the switchboard.

"What were you saying? A shabby seven-story block of flats. Yes—"

There were plenty of buildings like that in the district, buildings that weren't really old, but of such poor construction that they were already dilapidated. Buildings that as often as not thrust themselves up bleakly in the middle of a bit of wasteland, towering over the little shacks and hovels around them, their blind walls plastered with advertisements.

"You say she heard someone running downstairs and then a door slam. The door of the house, I suppose. On which floor is the flat? The *entresol*. Which way does it face? Onto an inner courtyard— Just a moment, there's a call coming in from the Eighth. That must be our friend of the telephone pillars."

Lecœur asked the new caller to wait, then came back to Javel.

"An old woman, you say. Madame Fayet. Worked as charwoman. Dead? A blunt instrument. Is the doctor there? You're sure she's dead? What about her money? I suppose she had some tucked away somewhere. Right. Call me back. Or I'll ring you."

He turned to the detective, who was now sleeping soundly.

"Janvier! Hey, Janvier! This is for you."

"What? What is it?"

"The killer."

"Where?"

"Near the Rue Lecourbe. Here's the address. This time he's done in an old charwoman, a Madame Fayet."

Janvier put on his overcoat, looked round for his hat, and gulped down the remains of the coffee in his cup.

"Who's dealing with it?"

"Gonesse, of the Fifteenth."

"Ring up the P.J., will you, and tell them I've gone there."

A minute or two later, Lecœur was able to add another little cross to the six that were already in the column. Someone has smashed the glass of the pillar in the Avenue d'Iéna only one hundred and fifty yards from the Arc de Triomphe.

"Among the broken glass they found a handkerchief flecked with blood. It was a child's handkerchief."

"Has it got initials?"

"No. It's a blue-check handkerchief, rather dirty. The chap must have wrapped it round his knuckles for breaking the glass."

There were steps in the corridor. The day shift coming to take over. They looked very clean and close-shaven and the cold wind had whipped the blood into their cheeks.

"Happy Christmas!"

Sommer closed the tin in which he brought his sandwiches. Mambret knocked out his pipe. Only Lecœur remained in his seat, since there was no relief for him.

The fat Godin had been the first to arrive, promptly changing his jacket for the grey-linen coat in which he always worked, then putting some water on to boil for his grog. All through the winter he suffered from one never-ending cold which he combated, or perhaps nourished, by one hot grog after another.

"Hallo! Yes, I'm still here. I'm doing a shift for Potier, who's gone down to his family in Normandy. Yes. I want to hear all about it. Most particularly.

Janvier's gone, but I'll pass it on to the P.J. An invalid, you say? What invalid?"

One had to be patient on that job, as people always talked about their cases as though everyone else was in the picture.

"A low building behind, right. Not in the Rue Michat, then? Rue Vasco de Gama. Yes, yes. I know. The little house with a garden behind some railings. Only I didn't know he was an invalid. Right. He doesn't sleep much. Saw a young boy climbing up a drainpipe? How old? He couldn't say? Of course not, in the dark. How did he know it was a boy, then? Listen, ring me up again, will you? Oh, you're going off. Who's relieving you? Jules? Right. Well, ask him to keep me informed."

"What's going on?" asked Godin.

"An old woman who's been done in. Down by the Rue Lecourbe."

"Who did it?"

"There's an invalid opposite who says he saw a small boy climbing up a drainpipe and along the top of a wall."

"You mean to say it was a boy who killed the old woman?"

"We don't know yet."

No one was very interested. After all, murders were an everyday matter to these people. The lights were still on in the room, as it was still only a bleak, dull daylight that found its way through the frosty window panes. One of the new watch went and scratched a bit of the frost away. It was instinctive. A childish memory perhaps, like Sommer's *boudin*.

The latter had gone home. So had Mambret. The newcomers settled down to their work, turning over the papers on their desks.

A car stolen from the Square la Bruyère.

Lecœur looked pensively at his seven crosses. Then, with a sigh, he got up and stood gazing at the immense street plan on the wall.

"Brushing up on your Paris?"

"I think I know it pretty well already. Something's just struck me. There's a chap wandering about smashing the glass of telephone pillars. Seven in the last hour and a half. He hasn't been going in a straight line but zigzagging—first this way, then that."

"Perhaps he doesn't know Paris."

"Or knows it only too well! Not once has he ventured within sight of a police station. If he'd gone straight, he'd have passed two or three. What's more, he's skirted all the main crossroads where there'd be likely to be a man on duty." Lecœur pointed them out. "The only risk he took was in crossing the Pont Mirabeau, but if he wanted to cross the river he'd have run that risk at any of the bridges."

"I expect he's drunk," said Godin, sipping his rum.

"What I want to know is why he's stopped."

"Perhaps he's got home."

"A man who's down by the Quai de Javel at half past six in the morning isn't likely to live near the Etoile."

"Seems to interest you a lot."

"It's got me scared!"

"Go on."

It was strange to see the worried expression on Lecœur's face. He was notorious for his calmness and his most dramatic nights were coolly summarized by the little crosses in his notebook.

"Hallo! Javel? Is that Jules? Lecœur speaking. Look here, Jules, behind the flats in the Rue Michat is the little house where the invalid lives. Well, now, on one side of it is an apartment house, a red-brick building with a grocer's shop on the ground floor. You know it?

"Good. Has anything happened there? Nothing reported. No, we've heard nothing here. All the same, I can't explain why, but I think you ought to inquire."

He was hot all at once. He stubbed out a half finished cigarette.

"Hallo! Ternes? Any alarms gone off in your neighborhood? Nothing Only drunks? Is the *patrouille cycliste* out? Just leaving? Ask them to keep their eyes open for a young boy looking tired and very likely bleeding from the right hand. Lost? Not exactly that. I can't explain now."

His eyes went back to the street plan on the wall, in which no light went on for a good ten minutes, and then only for an accidental death in the Eighteenth Arrondissement, right up at the top of Montmartre, caused by an escape of gas.

Outside, in the cold streets of Paris, dark figures were hurrying home from the churches . . .

One of the sharpest impressions Andre Lecœur retained of his infancy was one of immobility. His world at that period was a large kitchen in Orleans, on the outskirts of the town. He must have spent his winters there, too, but he remembered it best flooded with sunlight, with the door wide open onto a little garden where hens clucked incessantly and rabbits nibbled lettuce leaves behind the wire netting of their hutches. But, if the door was open, its passage was barred to him by a little gate which his father had made one Sunday for that express purpose.

On weekdays, at half past eight, his father went off on his bicycle to the gas works at the other end of the town. His mother did the housework, doing the same things in the same order every day. Before making the beds, she put the bedclothes over the windowsill for an hour to air.

At ten o'clock, a little bell would ring in the street. That was the greengrocer, with his barrow, passing on his daily round. Twice a week at eleven, a bearded doctor came to see his little brother, who was constantly ill. Andre hardly ever saw the latter, as he wasn't allowed into his room.

That was all, or so it seemed in retrospect. He had just time to play a bit and drink his milk, and there was his father home again for the midday meal.

If nothing had happened at home, lots had happened to him. He had been to read the meters in any number of houses and chatted with all sorts of people, about whom he would talk during dinner.

As for the afternoon, it slipped away quicker still,

perhaps because he was made to sleep during the first part of it.

For his mother, apparently, the time passed just as quickly. Often had he heard her say with a sigh: "There, I've no sooner washed up after one meal than it's time to start making another!"

Perhaps it wasn't so very different now. Here in the Préfecture de Police the nights seemed long enough at the time, but at the end they seemed to have slipped by in no time, with nothing to show for them except for these columns of the little crosses in his notebook.

A few more lamps lit up. A few more incidents reported, including a collision between a car and a bus in the Rue de Clignancourt, and then once again it was Javel on the line.

It wasn't Jules, however, but Gonesse, the detective who'd been to the scene of the crime. While there he had received Lecœur's message suggesting something might have happened in the other house in the Rue Vasco de Gama. He had been to see.

"Is that you, Lecœur?" There was a queer note in his voice. Either irritation or suspicion.

"Look here, what made you think of that house? Do you know the old woman, Madame Fayet?"

"I've never seen her, but I know all about her."

What had finally come to pass that Christmas morning was something that Andre Lecœur had foreseen and perhaps dreaded for more than ten years. Again and again, as he stared at the huge plan of Paris, with its little lamps, he had said to himself, "It's only a question of time. Sooner or later, it'll be something that's happened to someone I know."

There'd been many a near miss, an accident in his own street or a crime in a house nearby. But, like thunder, it had approached only to recede once again into the distance.

This time it was a direct hit.

"Have you seen the concierge?" he asked. He could imagine the puzzled look on the detective's face as he went on: "Is the boy at home?"

And Gonesse muttered, "Oh? So you know him, too?"

"He's my nephew. Weren't you told his name was Lecœur?"

"Yes, but—"

"Never mind about that. Tell me what's happened."

"The boy's not there."

"What about his father?"

"He got home just after seven."

"As usual. He does night work, too."

"The concierge heard him go up to his flat—on the third floor at the back of the house."

"I know it."

"He came running down a minute or two later in a great state. To use her expression, he seemed out of his wits."

"The boy had disappeared?"

"Yes. His father wanted to know if she'd seen him leave the house. She hadn't. Then he asked if a telegram had been delivered."

"Was there a telegram?"

"No. Can you make head or tail of it? Since you're one of the family, you might be able to help us. Could you get someone to relieve you and come round here?"

"It wouldn't do any good. Where's Janvier?"

"In the old woman's room. The men of the Identité Judiciaire have already got to work. The first thing they found were some child's fingerprints on the handle of the door. Come on—jump into a taxi and come round."

"No. In any case, there's no one to take my place."

That was true enough up to a point. All the same, if he'd really got to work on the telephone he'd have found someone all right. The truth was he didn't want to go and didn't think it would do any good if he did.

"Listen, Gonesse, I've got to find that boy, and I can do it better from here than anywhere. You understand, don't you? Tell Janvier I'm staying here. And tell him old Madame Fayet had plenty of money, probably hidden away somewhere in the room."

A little feverish, Lecœur stuck his plug into one socket after another, calling up the various police stations of the Eighth Arrondissement.

"Keep a lookout for a boy of ten, rather poorly dressed. Keep all telephone pillars under observation."

His two fellow-watchkeepers looked at him with curiosity.

"Do you think it was the boy who did the job?"

Lecœur didn't bother to answer. The next moment he was through to the teleprinter room, where they also dealt with radio messages.

"Justin? Oh, you're on, are you? Here's something special. Will you send out a call to all cars on patrol anywhere near the Etoile to keep a lookout for—"

Once again the description of the boy, François Lecœur.

"No. I've no idea in which direction he'll be making. All I can tell you is that he seems to keep well clear of police stations, and as far as possible from any place where there's likely to be anyone on traffic duty."

He knew his brother's flat in the Rue Vasco de Gama. Two rather dark rooms and a tiny kitchen. The boy slept there alone while his father was at work. From the windows you could see the back of the house in the Rue Michat, across a courtyard generally hung with washing. On some of the windowsills were pots of geraniums, and through the windows, many of which were uncurtained, you could catch glimpses of a miscellaneous assortment of humanity.

As a matter of fact, there, too, the windowpanes ought to be covered with frost. He stored that idea up in a corner of his mind. It might be important.

"You think it's a boy who's been smashing the alarm glasses?"

"It was a child's handkerchief they found," said Lecœur curtly. He didn't want to be drawn into a discussion. He sat mutely at the switchboard, wondering what to do next.

*   *   *

In the Rue Michat, things seemed to be moving fast. The next time he got through it was to learn that a doctor was there as well as an examining magistrate who had most likely been dragged from his bed.

What help could Lecœur have given them? But if he wasn't there, he could see the place almost as clearly as those that were, the dismal houses and the grimy viaduct of the Métro which cut right across the landscape.

Nothing but poor people in that neighborhood. The younger generation's one hope was to escape from it. The middle-aged already doubted whether they ever would, while the old ones had already accepted their fate and tried to make the best of it.

He rang Javel once again.

"Is Gonesse still there?"

"He's writing up his report. Shall I call him?"

"Yes, please. Hallo, Gonesse, Lecœur speaking. Sorry to bother you, but did you go up to my brother's flat? Had the boy's bed been slept in? It had? Good. That makes it look a bit better. Another thing: were there any parcels there? Yes, parcels, Christmas presents. What? A small square radio. Hadn't been unpacked. Naturally. Anything else? A chicken, a *boudin*, a Saint-Honoré. I suppose Janvier's not with you? Still on the spot. Right. Has he rung up the P.J.? Good."

He was surprised to see it was already half past nine. It was no use now expecting anything from the neighborhood of the Etoile. If the boy had gone on walking as he had been earlier, he could be pretty well anywhere by this time.

"Hallo! Police Judiciaire? Is Inspector Saillard there?"

He was another whom the murder had dragged from his fireside. How many people were there whose Christmas was going to be spoiled by it?

"Excuse my troubling you, Monsieur le Commissaire. It's about that young boy, Francois Lecœur."

"Do you know anything? Is he a relation of yours?"

"He's my brother's son. And it looks as if he may

well be the person who's been smashing the glasses of the telephone pillars. Seven of them. I don't know whether they've had time to tell you about that. What I wanted to ask was whether I might put out a general call?"

"Could you nip over to see me?"

"There's no one here to take my place."

"Right. I'll come over myself. Meanwhile you can send out the call."

Lecœur kept calm, though his hand shook slightly as he plugged in once again to the room above.

"Justin? Lecœur again. Appel General. Yes. It's the same boy. Francois Lecœur. Ten and a half, rather tall for his age, thin. I don't know what he's wearing, probably a khaki jumper made from American battle-dress. No, no cap. He's always bare-headed, with plenty of hair flopping over his forehead. Perhaps it would be as well to send out a description of his father, too. That's not so easy. You know me, don't you? Well, Olivier Lecœur is rather like a paler version of me. He has a timid look about him and physically he's not robust. The sort that's never in the middle of the pavement but always dodging out of other people's way. He walks a bit queerly, owing to a wound he got in the first war. No, I haven't the least idea where they might be going, only I don't think they're together. To my mind, the boy is probably in danger. I can't explain why—it would take too long. Get the descriptions out as quickly as possible, will you? And let me know if there's any response."

By the time Lecœur had finished telephoning, Inspector Saillard was there, having only had to come round the corner from the Quai des Orfèvres. He was an imposing figure of a man, particularly in his bulky overcoat. With a comprehensive wave of the hand, he greeted the three men on watch, then, seizing a chair as though it were a wisp of straw, he swung it round towards him and sat down heavily. "The boy?" he inquired, looking keenly at Lecœur.

"I can't understand why he's stopped calling us up."

"Calling us up?"

"Attracting our attention, anyway."

"But why should he attract our attention and then not say anything?"

"Supposing he was followed. Or was following someone."

"I see what you mean. Look here, Lecœur, is your brother in financial straits?"

"He's a poor man, yes."

"Is that all?"

"He lost his job three months ago."

"What job?"

"He was linotype operator at *La Presse* in the Rue du Croissant. He was on the night shift. He always did night work. Runs in the family."

"How did he come to lose his job?"

"I suppose he fell out with somebody."

"Is that a failing of his?"

They were interrupted by an incoming call from the Eighteenth to say that a boy selling branches of holly had been picked up in the Rue Lepic. It turned out, however, to be a little Pole who couldn't speak any French.

"You were asking if my brother was in the habit of quarreling with people. I hardly know what to answer. He was never strong. Pretty well all his childhood he was ill on and off. He hardly ever went to school. But he read a great deal alone in his room."

"Is he married?"

"His wife died two years after they were married, leaving him with a baby ten months old."

"Did he bring it up himself?"

"Entirely. I can see him now bathing the little chap, changing his diapers, and warming the milk for his bottle."

"That doesn't explain why he quarrels with people."

Admittedly. But it was difficult to put it into words.

"Soured?"

"Not exactly. The thing is—"

"What?"

"That he's never lived like other people. Perhaps

Olivier isn't really very intelligent. Perhaps, from reading so much, he knows too much about some things and too little about others."

"Do you think him capable of killing the old woman?"

The Inspector puffed at his pipe. They could hear the people in the room above walking about. The two other men fiddled with their papers, pretending not to listen.

"She was his mother-in-law," sighed Lecœur. "You'd have found it out anyhow, sooner or later."

"They didn't hit it off?"

"She hated him."

"Why?"

"She considered him responsible for her daughter's death. It seems she could have been saved if the operation had been done in time. It wasn't my brother's fault. The people at the hospital refused to take her in. Some silly question of her papers not being in order. All the same, Madame Fayet held to it that Olivier was to blame."

"Did they see each other?"

"Not unless they passed each other in the street, and then they never spoke."

"Did the boy know?"

"That she was his grandmother? I don't think so."

"You think his father never told him?"

Never for more than a second or two did Lecœur's eyes leave the plan of Paris, but, besides being Christmas, it was the quiet time of the day, and the little lamps lit up rarely. Two or three street accidents, a lady's handbag snatched in the Métro, a suitcase pinched at the Gare de L'Est.

No sign of the boy. It was surprising considering how few people were about. In the poor quarters a few little children played on the pavements with their new toys, but on the whole the day was lived indoors. Nearly all the shops were shuttered and the cafes and the little bars were almost empty.

For a moment, the town came to life a bit when the

church bells started pealing and families in their Sunday best hurried to High Mass. But soon the streets were quiet again, though haunted here and there by the vague rumble of an organ or a sudden gust of singing.

The thought of churches gave Lecœur an idea. Might not the boy have tucked himself away in one of them? Would the police think of looking there? He spoke to Inspector Saillard about it and then got through to Justin for the third time.

"The churches. Ask them to have a look at the congregations. They'll be doing the stations, of course—that's most important."

He took off his glasses for a moment, showing eyelids that were red, probably from lack of sleep.

"Hallo! Yes. The Inspector's here. Hold on."

He held the receiver to Saillard. "It's Janvier."

The bitter wind was still driving through the streets. The light was harsh and bleak, though here and there among the closely packed clouds was a yellowy streak which could be taken as a faint promise of sunshine to come.

When the Inspector put down the receiver, he muttered, "Dr. Paul says the crime was committed between five and half past six this morning. The old woman wasn't killed by the first blow. Apparently she was in bed when she heard a noise and got up and faced the intruder. Indeed, it looks as though she tried to defend herself with the only weapon that came to hand—a shoe."

"Have they found the weapon she was killed with?"

"No. It might have been a hammer. More likely a bit of lead piping or something of that sort."

"Have they found her money?"

"Only her purse, with some small change in it and her identity card. Tell me, Lecœur, did you know she was a money-lender?"

"Yes. I knew."

"And didn't you tell me your brother's been out of work for three months?"

"He has."

"The concierge didn't know."

"Neither did the boy. It was for his sake he kept it dark."

The Inspector crossed and uncrossed his legs. He was uncomfortable. He glanced at the other two men who couldn't help hearing everything, then turned with a puzzled look to stare at Lecœur.

"Do you realize what all this is pointing to?"

"I do."

"You've thought of it yourself?"

"No."

"Because he's your brother?"

"No."

"How long is it that this killer's been at work? Nine weeks, isn't it?"

Without haste, Lecœur studied the columns of his notebook.

"Yes. Just over nine weeks. The first was on the twentieth of October, in the Epinettes district."

"You say your brother didn't tell his son he was out of a job. Do you mean to say he went on leaving home in the evening just as though he was going to work?"

"Yes. He couldn't face the idea of telling him. You see—it's difficult to explain. He was completely wrapped up in the boy. He was all he had to live for. He cooked and scrubbed for him, tucked him up in bed before going off, and woke him up in the morning."

"That doesn't explain why he couldn't tell him."

"He couldn't bear the thought of appearing to the kid as a failure, a man nobody wanted and who had doors slammed in his face."

"But what did he do with himself all night?"

"Odd jobs. When he could get them. For a fortnight, he was employed as night watchman in a factory in Billancourt, but that was only while the regular man was ill. Often he got a few hours' work washing down cars in one of the big garages. When that failed, he'd sometimes lend a hand at the market unloading vegetables. When he had one of his bouts—"

"Bouts of what?"

"Asthma. He had them from time to time. Then he'd lie down in a station waiting room. Once he spent a whole night here, chatting with me."

"Suppose the boy woke up early this morning and saw his father at Madame Fayet's?"

"There was frost on the windows."

"There wouldn't be if the window was open. Lots of people sleep with their windows open even in the coldest weather."

"It wasn't the case with my brother. He was always a chilly person. And he was much too poor to waste warmth."

"As far as his window was concerned, the boy had only to scratch away the frost with his fingernail. When I was a boy—"

"Yes. So did I. The thing is to find out whether the old woman's window was open."

"It was, and the light was switched on."

"I wonder where Francois can have got to."

"The boy?"

It was surprising and a little disconcerting the way he kept all the time reverting to him. The situation was certainly embarrassing, and somehow made all the more so by the calm way in which Andre Lecœur gave the Inspector the most damaging details about his brother.

"When he came in this morning," began Saillard again, "he was carrying a number of parcels. You realize—"

"It's Christmas."

"Yes. But he'd have needed quite a bit of money to buy a chicken, a cake, and that new radio. Has he borrowed any from you lately?"

"Not for a month. I haven't seen him for a month. I wish I had. I'd have told him that I was getting a radio for Francois myself. I've got it here. Downstairs, that is, in the cloakroom. I was going to take it straight round as soon as I was relieved."

"Would Madame Fayet have consented to lend him money?"

"It's unlikely. She was a queer lot. She must have had quite enough money to live on, yet she still went out to work, charring from morning to evening. Often she lent money to the people she worked for. At exorbitant interest, of course. All the neighborhood knew about it, and people always came to her when they needed something to tide them over till the end of the month."

Still embarrassed, the Inspector rose to his feet. "I'm going to have a look," he said.

"At Madame Fayet's?"

"There and in the Rue Vasco de Gama. If you get any news, let me know, will you?"

"You won't find any telephone there, but I can get a message to you through the Javel police station."

The Inspector's footsteps had hardly died away before the telephone bell rang. No lamp had lit up on the wall. This was an outside call, coming from the Gare d'Austerlitz.

"Lecœur? Station police speaking. We've got him."

"Who?"

"The man whose description was circulated. Lecœur. Same as you. Olivier Lecœur. No doubt about it, I've seen his identity card."

"Hold on, will you?"

Lecœur dashed out of the room and down the stairs just in time to catch the Inspector as he was getting into one of the cars belonging to the Prefecture.

"Inspector! The Gare d'Austerlitz is on the phone. They've found my brother."

Saillard was a stout man and he went up the stairs puffing and blowing. He took the receiver himself.

"Hallo! Yes. Where was he? What was he doing? What? No, there's no point in your questioning him now. You're sure he didn't know? Right. Go on looking out. It's quite possible. As for him, send him here straightaway. At the Prefecture, yes."

He hesitated for a second and glanced at Lecœur before saying finally, "Yes. Send someone with him. We can't take any risks."

*   *   *

The Inspector filled his pipe and lit it before explaining, and when he spoke he looked at nobody in particular.

"He was picked up after he'd been wandering about the station for over an hour. He seemed very jumpy. Said he was waiting there to meet his son, from whom he'd received a message."

"Did they tell him about the murder?"

"Yes. He appeared to be staggered by the news and terrified. I asked them to bring him along." Rather diffidently he added: "I asked them to bring him here. Considering your relationship, I didn't want you to think—"

Lecœur had been in that room since eleven o'clock the night before. It was rather like his early years when he spent his days in his mother's kitchen. Around him was an unchanging world. There were the little lamps, of course, that kept going on and off, but that's what they always did. They were part and parcel of the immutability of the place. Time flowed by without anyone noticing it.

Yet, outside, Paris was celebrating Christmas. Thousands of people had been to Midnight Mass, thousands more had spent the night roistering, and those who hadn't known where to draw the line had sobered down in the police station and were now being called upon to explain things they couldn't remember doing.

What had his brother Olivier been doing all through the night? An old woman had been found dead. A boy had started before dawn on a breathless race through the streets, breaking the glass of the telephone pillars as he passed them, having wrapped his handkerchief round his fist.

And what was Olivier waiting for at the Gare d'Austerlitz, sometimes in the overheated waiting rooms, sometimes on the windswept platforms, too nervous to settle down in any one place for long?

Less than ten minutes elapsed, just time enough for Godin, whose nose really was running, to make himself another glass of hot grog.

"Can I offer you one, Monsieur le Commissaire?"

"No, thanks."

Looking more embarrassed than ever, Saillard leaned over towards Lecœur to say in an undertone, "Would you like us to question him in another room?"

No. Lecœur wasn't going to leave his post for anything. He wanted to stay there, with his little lamps and his switchboard. Was it that he was thinking more of the boy than of his brother?

Olivier came in with a detective on either side, but they had spared him the handcuffs. He looked dreadful, like a bad photograph faded with age. At once he turned to Andre. "Where's Francois?"

"We don't know. We're hunting for him."

"Where?"

Andre Lecœur pointed to his plan of Paris and his switchboard of a thousand lines. "Everywhere."

The two detectives had already been sent away.

"Sit down," said the Inspector. "I believe you've been told of Madame Fayet's death."

Olivier didn't wear spectacles, but he had the same pale and rather fugitive eyes as his brother had when he took his glasses off. He glanced at the Inspector, by whom he didn't seem the least overawed, then turned back to Andre. "He left a note for me," he said, delving into one of the pockets of his grubby mackintosh. "Here. See if you can understand."

He held out a bit of paper torn out of a schoolboy's exercise book. The writing wasn't any too good. It didn't look as though Francois was the best of pupils. He had used an indelible pencil, wetting the end in his mouth, so that his lips were very likely stained with it.

"Uncle Gedeon arrives this morning Gare d'Austerlitz. Come as soon as you can and meet us there. Love. Bib."

Without a word, Andre Lecœur passed it on to the Inspector, who turned it over and over with his thick fingers. "What's Bib stand for?"

"It's his nickname. A baby name. I never use it when other people are about. It comes from *biberon*. When I used to give him his bottle—" He spoke in a toneless voice. He seemed to be in a fog and was probably only dimly conscious of where he was.

"Who's Uncle Gedeon?"

"There isn't any such person."

Did he realize he was talking to the head of the Brigade des Homicides, who was at the moment investigating a murder?

It was his brother who came to the rescue, explaining, "As a matter of fact, we had an Uncle Gedeon but he's been dead for some years. He was one of my mother's brothers who emigrated to America as a young man."

Olivier looked at his brother as much as to say: What's the point of going into that?

"We got into the habit, in the family, of speaking— jocularly, of course—of our rich American uncle and of the fortune he'd leave us one day."

"Was he rich?"

"We didn't know. We never heard from him except for a postcard once a year, signed Gedeon. Wishing us a happy New Year."

"He died?"

"When Francois was four."

"Really, Andre, do you think it's any use—"

"Let me go on. The Inspector wants to know every-thing. My brother carried on the family tradition, talk-ing to his son about our Uncle Gedeon, who had become by now quite a legendary figure. He provided a theme for bedtime stories, and all sorts of adven-tures were attributed to him. Naturally he was fabu-lously rich, and when one day he came back to France—"

"I understand. He died out there?"

"In a hospital in Cleveland. It was then we found out he had been really a porter in a restaurant. It would have been too cruel to tell the boy that, so the legend went on."

"Did he believe in it?"

It was Olivier who answered. "My brother thought he didn't, that he'd guessed the truth but wasn't going to spoil the game. But I always maintained the con-

trary and I'm still practically certain he took it all in.
He was like that. Long after his schoolfellows had
stopped believing in Father Christmas, he still went
on."

Talking about his son brought him back to life,
transfigured him.

"But as for this note he left, I don't know what to
make of it. I asked the concierge if a telegram had
come. For a moment I thought Andre might have
played us a practical joke, but I soon dismissed the
idea. It isn't much of a joke to get a boy dashing off
to a station on a freezing night. Naturally I dashed off
to the Gare d'Austerlitz as fast as I could. There I
hunted high and low, then wandered about, waiting
anxiously for him to turn up. Andre, you're sure he
hasn't been—"

He looked at the street plan on the wall and at the
switchboard. He knew very well that every accident
was reported.

"He hasn't been run over," said Andre. "At about
eight o'clock he was near the Etoile, but we've completely lost track of him since then."

"Near the Etoile? How do you know?"

"It's rather a long story, but it boils down to this—
that a whole series of alarms were set off by someone
smashing the glass. They followed a circuitous route
from your place to the Arc de Triomphe. At the foot
of the last one, they found a blue-check handerchief,
a boy's handkerchief, among the broken glass."

"He has handkerchiefs like that."

"From eight o'clock onward, not a sign of him."

"Then I'd better get back to the station. He's certain to go there, if he told me to meet him there."

He was surprised at the sudden silence with which
his last words were greeted. He looked from one to
the other, perplexed, then anxious.

"What is it?"

His brother looked down at the floor. Inspector
Saillard cleared his throat, hesitated, then asked, "Did
you go to see your mother-in-law last night?"

Perhaps, as his brother had suggested, Olivier was

rather lacking in intelligence. It took a long time for the words to sink in. You could follow their progress in his features.

He had been gazing rather blankly at the Inspector. Suddenly he swung around on his brother, his cheeks red, his eyes flashing. "Andre, you dare to suggest that I—"

Without the slightest transition, his indignation faded away. He leaned forward in his chair, took his head in his two hands, and burst into a fit of raucous weeping.

Ill at ease, Inspector Saillard looked at Andre Lecœur, surprised at the latter's calmness, and a little shocked, perhaps, by what he may well have taken for heartlessness. Perhaps Saillard had never had a brother of his own. Andre had known his since childhood. It wasn't the first time he had seen Olivier break down. Not by any means. And this time he was almost pleased, as it might have been a great deal worse. What he had dreaded was the moment of indignation, and he was relieved that it had passed so quickly. Had he continued on that tack, he'd have ended by putting everyone's back up, which would have done him no good at all.

Wasn't that how he'd lost one job after another? For weeks, for months, he would go meekly about his work, toeing the line and swallowing what he felt to be humiliations, till all at once he could hold no more, and for some trifle—a chance word, a smile, a harmless contradiction—he would flare up unexpectedly and make a nuisance of himself to everybody.

What do we do now? The Inspector's eyes were asking.

Andre Lecœur's eyes answered, Wait.

It didn't last very long. The emotional crisis waned, started again, then petered out altogether. Olivier shot a sulky look at the Inspector, then hid his face again.

Finally, with an air of bitter resignation, he sat up, and with even a touch of pride said: "Fire away. I'll answer."

"At what time last night did you go to Madame Fayet's? Wait a moment. First of all, when did you leave your flat?"

"At eight o'clock, as usual, after Francois was in bed."

"Nothing exceptional happened?"

"No. We'd had supper together. Then he'd helped me to wash up."

"Did you talk about Christmas?"

"Yes. I told him he'd be getting a surprise."

"The table radio. Was he expecting one?"

"He'd been longing for one for some time. You see, he doesn't play with the other boys in the street. Practically all his free time he spends at home."

"Did it ever occur to you that the boy might know you'd lost your job at the *Presse*? Did he ever ring you up there?"

"Never. When I'm at work, he's asleep."

"Could anyone have told him?"

"No one knew. Not in the neighborhood, that is."

"Is he observant?"

"Very. He notices everything."

"You saw him safely in bed and then you went off. Do you take anything with you—anything to eat, I mean?"

The Inspector suddenly thought of that, seeing Godin produce a ham sandwich. Olivier looked blankly at his empty hands.

"My tin."

"The tin in which you took your sandwiches?"

"Yes. I had it with me when I left. I'm sure of that. I can't think where I could have left it, unless it was at—"

"At Madame Fayet's?"

"Yes."

"Just a moment. Lecœur, get me Javel on the phone, will you? Hallo! Who's speaking? Is Janvier there? Good, ask him to speak to me. Hallo! Is that you, Janvier? Have you come across a tin box containing some sandwiches? Nothing of the sort. Really?

All the same, I'd like you to make sure. Ring me back. It's important."

And, turning again to Olivier: "Was Francois actually sleeping when you left?"

"No. But he'd snuggled down in bed and soon would be. Outside, I wandered about for a bit. I walked down to the Seine and waited on the embankment."

"Waited? What for?"

"For Francois to be fast asleep. From his room you can see Madame Fayet's windows."

"So you'd made up your mind to go and see her."

"It was the only way. I hadn't a bean left."

"What about your brother?"

Olivier and Andre looked at each other.

"He'd already given me so much. I felt I couldn't ask him again."

"You rang at the house door, I suppose. At what time?"

"A little after nine. The concierge saw me. I made no attempt to hide—except from Francois."

"Had your mother-in-law gone to bed?"

"No. She was fully dressed when she opened her door. She said, 'Oh, it's you, you wretch!' "

"After that beginning, did you still think she'd lend you money?"

"I was sure of it."

"Why?"

"It was her business. Perhaps also for the pleasure of squeezing me if I didn't pay her back. She lent me ten thousand francs, but made me sign an I.O.U. for twenty thousand."

"How soon had you to pay her back?"

"In a fortnight's time."

"How could you hope to?"

"I don't know. Somehow. The thing that mattered was for the boy to have a good Christmas."

Andre Lecœur was tempted to butt in to explain to the puzzled Inspector, "You see! He's always been like that!"

"Did you get the money easily?"

"Oh, no. We were at it for a long time."

"How long?"

"Half an hour, I daresay, and during most of that time she was calling me names, telling me I was no good to anyone and had ruined her daughter's life before I finally killed her. I didn't answer her back. I wanted the money too badly."

"You didn't threaten her?"

Olivier reddened. "Not exactly. I said if she didn't let me have it I'd kill myself."

"Would you have done it?"

"I don't think so. At least, I don't know. I was fed up, worn out."

"And when you got the money?"

"I walked to the nearest Metro station, Lourmel, and took the underground to Palais Royal. There I went into the Grands Magasins du Louvre. The place was crowded, with queues at many of the counters."

"What time was it?"

"It was after eleven before I left the place. I was in no hurry. I had a good look around. I stood a long time watching a toy electric train."

Andre couldn't help smiling at the Inspector. "You didn't miss your sandwich tin?"

"No. I was thinking about Francois and his present."

"And with money in your pocket you banished all your cares!"

The Inspector hadn't known Olivier Lecœur since childhood, but he had sized him up all right. He had hit the nail on the head. When things were black, Olivier would go about with drooping shoulders and a hangdog air, but no sooner had he a thousand-franc note in his pocket than he'd feel on top of the world.

"To come back to Madame Fayet, you say you gave her a receipt. What did she do with it?"

"She slipped it into an old wallet she always carried about with her in a pocket somewhere under her skirt."

"So you knew about the wallet?"

"Yes. Everybody did."

The Inspector turned towards Andre.

"It hasn't been found!"

Then to Olivier: "You bought some things. In the Louvre?"

"No. I bought the little radio in the Rue Montmartre."

"In which shop?"

"I don't know the name. It's next door to a shoe shop."

"And the other things?"

"A little farther on."

"What time was it when you'd finished shopping?"

"Close on midnight. People were coming out of the theaters and movies and crowding into the restaurants. Some of them were rather noisy."

His brother at that time was already here at his switchboard.

"What did you do during the rest of the night?"

"At the corner of the Boulevard des Italiens, there's a movie that stays open all night."

"You'd been there before?"

Avoiding his brother's eye, Andre answered rather sheepishly: "Two or three times. After all, it costs no more than going into a cafe and you can stay there as long as you like. It's nice and warm. Some people go there regularly to sleep."

"When was it you decided to go to the movies?"

"As soon as I left Madame Fayet's."

Andre Lecœur was tempted to intervene once again to say to the Inspector: "You see, these people who are down and out are not so utterly miserable after all. If they were, they'd never stick it out. They've got a world of their own, in odd corners of which they can take refuge and even amuse themselves."

It was all so like Olivier! With a few notes in his pocket—and Heaven only knew how he was ever going to pay them back—with a few notes in his pocket, his trials were forgotten. He had only one thought: to give his boy a good Christmas. With that secured, he was ready to stand himself a little treat.

So while other families were gathered at table or

knelt at Midnight Mass, Olivier went to the movies all by himself. It was the best he could do.

"When did you leave the movie?"

"A little before six."

"What was the film?"

"*Cœurs Ardents*. With a documentary on Eskimos."

"How many times did you see the program?"

"Twice right through, except for the news, which was just coming on again when I left."

Andre Lecœur knew that all this was going to be verified, if only as a matter of routine. It wasn't necessary, however. Diving into his pockets, Olivier produced the torn-off half of a movie ticket, then another ticket—a pink one. "Look at that. It's the Métro ticket I had coming home."

It bore the name of the station—Opéra—together with the date and the time.

Olivier had been telling the truth. He couldn't have been in Madame Fayet's flat any time between five and six-thirty.

There was a little spark of triumph in his eye, mixed with a touch of disdain. He seemed to be saying to them all, including his brother Andre: "Because I'm poor and unlucky I come under suspicion. I know—that's the way things are. I don't blame you."

And, funnily enough, it seemed as though all at once the room had grown colder. That was probably because, with Olivier Lecœur cleared of suspicion, everyone's thoughts reverted to the child. As though moved by one impulse, all eyes turned instinctively toward the huge plan on the wall.

Some time had elapsed since any of the lamps had lit up. Certainly it was a quiet morning. On any ordinary day there would be a street accident coming in every few minutes, particularly old women knocked down in the crowded thoroughfares of Montmartre and other overpopulated quarters.

Today the streets were almost empty—emptier than in August, when half Paris is away on holiday.

Half past eleven. For three and a half hours there'd been no sign of Francois Lecœur.

"Hallo! Yes, Saillard speaking. Is that Janvier? You say you couldn't find a tin anywhere? Except in her kitchen, of course. Now, look here, was it you who went through the old girl's clothes? Oh, Gonesse had already done it. There should have been an old wallet in a pocket under her skirt. You're sure there wasn't anything of that sort? That's what Gonesse told you, is it? What's that about the concierge? She saw someone go up a little after nine last night. I know. I know who it was. There were people coming in and out the best part of the night? Of course. I'd like you to go back to the house in the Rue Vasco de Gama. See what you can find out about the comings and goings there, particularly on the third floor. Yes. I'll still be here."

He turned back to the boy's father, who was now sitting humbly in his chair, looking as intimidated as a patient in a doctor's waiting room.

"You understand why I asked that, don't you? Does Francois often wake up in the course of the night?"

"He's been known to get up in his sleep."

"Does he walk about?"

"No. Generally he doesn't even get right out of bed—just sits up and calls out. It's always the same thing. He thinks the house is on fire. His eyes are open, but I don't think he sees anything. Then, little by little, he calms down and with a deep sigh lies down again. The next day he doesn't remember a thing."

"Is he always asleep when you get back in the morning?"

"Not always. But if he isn't, he always pretends to be so that I can wake him up as usual with a hug."

"The people in the house were probably making more noise than usual last night. Who have you got in the next flat?"

"A Czech who works at Renault's."

"Is he married?"

"I really don't know. There are so many people in the house and they change so often we don't know much about them. All I can tell you is that on Sundays other Czechs come there and they sing a lot of their own songs."

"Janvier will tell us whether there was a party there last night. If there was, they may well have awakened the boy. Besides, children are apt to sleep more lightly when they're excited about a present they're expecting. If he got out of bed, he might easily have looked out of the window, in which case he might have seen you at Madame Fayet's. He didn't know she was his grand-mother, did he?"

"No. He didn't like her. He sometimes passed her in the street and he used to say she smelled like a squashed bug."

The boy would probably know what he was talking about. A house like his was no doubt infested with vermin.

"He'd have been surprised to see you with her?"

"Certainly."

"Did he know she lent money?"

"Everyone knew."

"Would there be anybody working at the *Presse* on a day like this?"

"There's always somebody there."

The Inspector asked Andre to ring them up.

"See if anyone's ever been round to ask for your brother."

Olivier looked uncomfortable, but when his brother reached for the telephone directory, he gave him the number. Both he and the Inspector stared at Andre while he got through.

"It's very important, Mademoiselle. It may even be a matter of life and death. Yes, please. See if you can find out. Ask everybody who's in the building now. What? Yes, I know it's Christmas Day. It's Christmas Day here, too, but we have to carry on just the same."

Between his teeth he muttered, "Silly little bitch!"

He could hear the linotypes clicking as he held the line, waiting for her answer.

"Yes. What? Three weeks ago. A young boy—"

Olivier went pale in the face. His eyes dropped, and

during the rest of the conversation he stared obstinately at his hands.

"He didn't telephone? Came round himself. At what time? On a Thursday, you say. What did he want? Asked if Olivier Lecœur worked there? What? What was he told?"

Looking up, Olivier saw a flush spread over his brother's face before he banged down the receiver.

"Francois went there one Thursday afternoon. He must have suspected something. They told him you hadn't been working there for some time."

There was no point in repeating what he had heard. What they'd said to the boy was: "We chucked the old fool out weeks ago."

Perhaps not out of cruelty. They may not have thought it was the man's son they were speaking to.

"Do you begin to understand, Olivier?"

Did he realize that the situation was the reverse of what he had imagined? He had been going off at night, armed with his little box of sandwiches, keeping up an elaborate pretense. And in the end he had been the one to be taken in!

The boy had found him out. And wasn't it only fair to suppose that he had seen through the Uncle Gedeon story, too?

He hadn't said a word. He had simply fallen in with the game.

No one dared say anything for fear of saying too much, for fear of evoking images that would be heartrending.

A father and a son each lying to avoid hurting the other.

They had to look at it through the eyes of the child, with all childhood's tragic earnestness. His father kisses him good night and goes off to the job that doesn't really exist, saying: "Sleep well. There'll be a surprise for you in the morning."

A radio. It could only be that. And didn't he know that his father's pockets were empty? Did he try to go to sleep? Or did he get up as soon as his father had gone, to sit miserably staring out of the window

obsessed by one thought? *His father had no money—
yet he was going to buy him a radio!*

To the accompaniment, in all probability, of a full-
throated Czech choir singing their national songs on
the other side of the thin wall!

The Inspector sighed and knocked out his pipe on
his heel.

"It looks as though he saw you at Madame Fayet's."

Olivier nodded.

"We'll check up on this, but it seems likely that,
looking down from his window, he wouldn't see very
far into the room."

"That's quite right."

"Could he have seen you leave the room?"

"No. The door's on the opposite side from the
window."

"Do you remember going near the window?"

"At one time I was sitting on the windowsill."

"Was the window open then? We know it was
later."

"It was open a few inches. I'm sure of that, because
I moved away from it, as I felt an icy draught on my
back. She lived with us for a while, just after our
marriage, and I know she couldn't bear not to have
her window open all the year round. You see, she'd
been brought up in the country."

"So there'd be no frost on the panes. He'd certainly
have seen you if he was looking."

A call. Lecœur thrust his contact plug into one of
the sockets.

"Yes. What's that? A boy?"

The other two held their breath.

"Yes. Yes. What? Yes. Send out the *agents cyclistes*.
Comb the whole neighborhood. I'll see about the station. How long ago was it? Half an hour? Couldn't he
have let us know sooner?"

Without losing time over explanations, Lecœur
plugged in to the Gare du Nord.

"Hallo! Gare du Nord! Who's speaking? Ah, Lam-
bert. Listen, this is urgent. Have the station searched

from end to end. Ask everybody if they've seen a boy of ten wandering about. What? Alone? He may be. Or he may be accompanied. We don't know. Let me know what you find out. Yes, of course. Grab him at once if you set eyes on him."

"Did you say accompanied?" asked Olivier anxiously.

"Why not? It's possible. Anything's possible. Of course, it may not be him. If it is, we're half an hour late. It was a small grocer in the Rue de Maubeuge whose shopfront is open onto the street. He saw a boy snatch a couple of oranges and make off. He didn't run after him. Only later, when a policeman passed, he thought he might as well mention it."

"Had your son any money?" asked the Inspector.

"Not a sou."

"Hasn't he got a money-box?"

"Yes. But I borrowed what was in it two days ago, saying that I didn't want to change a banknote."

A pathetic little confession, but what did things like that matter now?

"Don't you think it would be better if I went to the Gare du Nord myself?"

"I doubt if it would help, and we may need you here."

They were almost prisoners in that room. With its direct links with every nerve center of Paris, that was the place where any news would first arrive. Even in his room in the Police Judiciaire, the Inspector would be less well placed. He had thought of going back there, but now at last took off his overcoat, deciding to see the job through where he was.

"If he had no money, he couldn't take a bus or the Métro. Nor could he go into a cafe or use a public telephone. He probably hasn't had anything to eat since his supper last night."

"But what can he be doing?" exclaimed Olivier, becoming more and more nervous. "And why should he have sent me to the Gare d'Austerlitz?"

"Perhaps to help you get away," grunted Saillard.

"Get away? Me?"

"Listen. The boy knows you're down and out. Yet

you're going to buy him a little radio. I'm not reproaching you. I'm just looking at the facts. He leans on the windowsill and sees you with the old woman he knows to be a money-lender. What does he conclude?"

"I see."

"That you've gone to her to borrow money. He may be touched by it, he may be saddened—we don't know. He goes back to bed and to sleep."

"You think so?"

"I'm pretty sure of it. Anyhow, we've no reason to think he left the house then."

"No. Of course not."

"Let's say he goes back to sleep, then. But he wakes up early, as children mostly do on Christmas Day. And the first thing he notices is the frost on the window. The first frost this winter, don't forget that. He wants to look at it, to touch it."

A faint smile flickered across Andre Lecœur's face. This massive Inspector hadn't forgotten what it was like to be a boy.

"He scratches a bit of it away with his nails. It won't be difficult to get confirmation, for once the frost is tampered with it can't form again in quite the same pattern. What does he notice then? That in the buildings opposite one window is lit up, and one only—the window of the room in which a few hours before he had seen his father. It's guesswork, of course, but I don't mind betting he saw the body, or part of it. If he'd merely seen a foot it would have been enough to startle him."

"You mean to say—" began Olivier, wide-eyed.

"That he thought you'd killed her. As I did myself—for a moment. And very likely not her only. Just think for a minute. The man who's been committing all these murders is a man, like you, who wanders about at night. His victims live in the poorer quarters of Paris, like Madame Fayet in the Rue Michat. Does the boy know anything of how you've been spending your nights since you lost your job? No. All that he has to go on is that he has seen you in the murdered woman's room. Would it be surprising if his imagination got to work?

"You said just now that you sat on the windowsill. Might it be there that you put down your box of sandwiches?"

"Now I come to think of it, yes. I'm practically sure."

"Then he saw it. And he's quite old enough to know what the police would think when they saw it lying there. Is your name on it?"

"Yes. Scratched on the lid."

"You see! He thought you'd be coming home as usual between seven and eight. The thing was to get you as quickly as possible out of the danger zone."

"You mean—by writing me that note?"

"Yes. He didn't know what to say. He couldn't refer to the murder without compromising you. Then he thought of Uncle Gedeon. Whether he believed in his existence or not doesn't matter. He knew you'd go to the Gare d'Austerlitz."

"But he's not yet eleven!"

"Boys of that age know a lot more than you think. Doesn't he read detective stories?"

"Yes."

"Of course he does. They all do. If they don't read them, they get them on the radio. Perhaps that's why he wanted a set of his own so badly."

"It's true."

"He couldn't stay in the flat to wait for you, for he had something more important to do. He had to get hold of that box. I suppose he knew the courtyard well. He'd played there, hadn't he?"

"At one time, yes. With the concierge's little girl."

"So he'd know about the rainwater pipes, may even have climbed up them for sport."

"Very well," said Olivier, suddenly calm, "let's say he gets into the room and takes the box. He wouldn't need to climb down the way he'd come. He could simply walk out of the flat and out of the house. You can open the house door from inside without knocking up the concierge. You say it was at about six o'clock, don't you?"

"I see what you're driving at," grunted the Inspector. "Even at a leisurely pace, it would hardly have taken him two hours to walk to the Gare d'Austerlitz. Yet he wasn't there."

Leaving them to thrash it out, Lecœur was busy telephoning.

"No news yet?"

And the man at the Gare du Nord answered, "Nothing so far. We've pounced on any number of boys, but none of them was Francois Lecœur."

Admittedly, any street boy could have pinched a couple of oranges and taken to his heels. The same couldn't be said for the broken glass of the telephone pillars, however. Andre Lecœur looked once again at the column with the seven crosses, as though some clue might suddenly emerge from them. He had never thought himself much cleverer than his brother. Where he scored was in patience and perseverance.

"If the box of sandwiches is ever found, it'll be at the bottom of the Seine near the Pont Mirabeau," he said.

Steps in the corridor. On an ordinary day they would not have been noticed, but in the stillness of a Christmas morning everyone listened.

It was an *agent cycliste*, who produced a blood-stained blue-check handkerchief, the one that had been found among the glass splinters at the seventh telephone pillar.

"That's his, all right," said the boy's father.

"He must have been followed," said the Inspector. "If he'd had time, he wouldn't merely have broken the glass. He'd have said something."

"Who by?" asked Olivier, who was the only one not to understand. "Who'd want to follow him?" he asked. "And why should he call the police?"

They hesitated to put him wise. In the end it was his brother who explained:

"When he went to the old woman's he thought you were the murderer. When he came away, he knew you weren't. He knew—"

"Knew what?"

"He knew who was. Do you understand now? He found out something, though we don't know what. He wants to tell us about it, but someone's stopping him."

"You mean?"

"I mean that Francois is after the murderer or the murderer is after him. One is following, one is followed—we don't know which. By the way, Inspector, is there a reward offered?"

"A handsome reward was offered after the third murder and it was doubled last week. It's been in all the papers."

"Then my guess," said Andre Lecœur, "is that it's the kid who's doing the following. Only in that case—"

It was twelve o'clock, four hours since they'd lost track of him. Unless, of course, it was he who had snaffled the oranges in the Rue Maubeuge.

Might not this be his great moment? Andre Lecœur had read somewhere that even to the dullest and most uneventful lives such a moment comes sooner or later.

He had never had a particularly high opinion of himself or of his abilities. When people asked him why he'd chosen so dreary and monotonous a job rather than one in, say, the Brigade des Homicides, he would answer: "I suppose I'm lazy."

Sometimes he would add:

"I'm scared of being knocked about."

As a matter of fact, he was neither lazy nor a coward. If he lacked anything it was brains.

He knew it. All he had learned at school had cost him a great effort. The police exams that others took so easily in their stride, he had only passed by dint of perseverance.

Was it a consciousness of his own shortcomings that had kept him single? Possibly. It seemed to him that the sort of woman he would want to marry would be his superior, and he didn't relish the idea of playing second fiddle in the home.

But he wasn't thinking of all this now. Indeed, if this was his moment of greatness, it was stealing upon him unawares.

Another team arrived, those of the second day shift looking very fresh and well groomed in their Sunday clothes. They had been celebrating Christmas with their families, and they brought in with them, as it were, a whiff of good viands and liqueurs.

Old Bedeau had taken his place at the switchboard, but Lecœur made no move to go.

"I'll stay on a bit," he said simply.

Inspector Saillard had gone for a quick lunch at the Brasserie Dauphine just around the corner, leaving strict injunctions that he was to be fetched at once if anything happened. Janvier was back at the Quai des Orfèvres, writing up his report.

If Lecœur was tired, he didn't notice it. He certainly wasn't sleepy and couldn't bear the thought of going home to bed. He had plenty of stamina. Once, when there were riots in the Place de la Concorde, he had done thirty-six hours nonstop, and on another occasion, during a general strike, they had all camped in the room for four days and nights.

His brother showed the strain more. He was getting jumpy again.

"I'm going," he announced suddenly.

"Where to?"

"To find Bib."

"Where?"

"I don't know exactly. I'll start round the Gare du Nord."

"How do you know it was Bib who stole the oranges? He may be at the other end of Paris. We might get news at any minute. You'd better stay."

"I can't stand this waiting."

He was nevertheless persuaded to. He was given a chair in a corner. He refused to lie down. His eyes were red with anxiety and fatigue. He sat fidgeting, looking rather as, when a boy, he had been put in the corner.

With more self-control, Andre forced himself to take some rest. Next to the big room was a little one with a wash-basin, where they hung their coats and which was provided with a couple of camp beds on which the *nuiteux* could lie down during a quiet hour.

He shut his eyes, but only for a moment. Then his hand felt for the little notebook with never left him, and lying on his back he began to turn over the pages.

There were nothing but crosses, columns of columns of tiny little crosses which, month after month, year after year, he had accumulated, Heaven knows why. Just to satisfy something inside him. After all, other people keep a diary—or the most meticulous household accounts, even when they don't need to economize at all.

Those crosses told the story of the night life of Paris.

"Some coffee, Lecœur?"

"Thanks."

Feeling rather out of touch where he was, he dragged his camp bed into the big room, placing it in a position from which he could see the wall-plan. There he sipped his coffee, after which he stretched himself out again, sometimes studying his notebook, sometimes lying with his eyes shut. Now and again he stole a glance at his brother, who sat hunched in his chair with drooping shoulders, the twitching of his long white fingers being the only sign of the torture he was enduring.

There were hundreds of men now, not only in Paris but in the suburbs, keeping their eyes skinned for the boy whose description had been circulated. Sometimes false hopes were raised, only to be dashed when the exact particulars were given.

Lecœur shut his eyes again, but opened them suddenly next moment, as though he had actually dozed off. He glanced at the clock, then looked round for the Inspector.

"Hasn't Saillard got back yet?" he asked, getting to his feet.

"I expect he's looked in at the Quai des Orfèvres."

Olivier stared at his brother, surprised to see him pacing up and down the room. The latter was so absorbed in his thoughts that he hardly noticed that the sun had broken through the clouds, bathing Paris on that Christmas afternoon in a glow of light more like that of spring.

While thinking, he listened, and it wasn't long before he heard Inspector Saillard's heavy tread outside.

"You'd better go and get some sandwiches," he said to his brother. "Get some for me, too."

"What kind?"

"Ham. Anything. Whatever you find."

Olivier went out, after a parting glance at the map, relieved, in spite of his anxiety, to be doing something.

The men of the afternoon shift knew little of what was afoot, except that the killer had done another job the previous night and that there was a general hunt for a small boy. For them, the case couldn't have the flavor it had for those who were involved. At the switchboard, Bedeau was doing a crossword with his earphones on his head, breaking off from time to time for the classic: "Hallo! Austerlitz. Your car's out."

A body fished out of the Seine. You couldn't have a Christmas without that!

"Could I have a word with you, Inspector?"

The camp bed was back in the cloakroom. It was there that Lecœur led the chief of the homicide squad.

"I hope you won't mind my butting in. I know it isn't for me to make suggestions. But, about the killer—"

He had his little notebook in his hand. He must have known its contents almost by heart.

"I've been doing a lot of thinking since this morning and—"

A little while ago, while he was lying down, it had

seemed so clear, but now that he had to explain things, it was difficult to put them in logical order.

"It's like this. First of all, I noticed that all the murders were committed after two in the morning, most of them after three."

He could see by the look on the Inspector's face that he hadn't exactly scored a hit, and he hurried on:

"I've been looking up the time of other murders over the past three years. They were nearly always between ten in the evening and two in the morning."

Neither did that observation seem to make much impression. Why not take the bull by the horns and say straight out what was on his mind?

"Just now, looking at my brother, it occurred to me that the man you're looking for might be a man like him. As a matter of fact, I, too, for a moment wondered whether it wasn't him. Wait a moment—"

That was better. The look of polite boredom had gone from Saillard's face.

"If I'd had more experience in this sort of work I'd be able to explain myself better. But you'll see in a moment. A man who's killed eight people one after the other is, if not a madman, at any rate a man who's been thrown off his balance. He might have had a sudden shock. Take my brother, for instance. When he lost his job it upset him so much that he preferred to live in a tissue of lies rather than let his son—"

No. Put into words, it all sounded very clumsy.

"When a man suddenly loses everything he has in life—"

"He doesn't necessarily go mad."

"I'm not saying he's actually mad. But imagine a person so full of resentment that he considers himself justified in revenging himself on his fellow-men. I don't need to point out to you, Inspector, that other murderers always kill in much the same way. This one has used a hammer, a knife, a spanner, and one woman he strangled. And he's never been seen, never left a clue. Wherever he lives in Paris, he must have walked miles and miles at night when there was no transport available, sometimes, when the alarm had been given, with the police on the lookout, questioning everybody they found in the streets. How is it he avoided them?"

He was certain he was on the right track. If only Saillard would hear him out.

The Inspector sat on one of the camp beds. The cloakroom was small, and as Lecœur paced up and down in front of him he could do no more than three paces each way.

"This morning, for instance, assuming he was with the boy, he went halfway across Paris, keeping out of sight of every police station and every traffic point where there'd be a man on duty."

"You mean he knows the Fifteenth and Sixteenth Arrondissements by heart?"

"And not those only. At least two there, the Twelfth and the Twentieth, as he showed on previous occasions. He didn't choose his victims haphazardly. He knew they lived alone and could be done in without any great risk."

What a nuisance! There was his brother, saying: "Here are the sandwiches, Andre."

"Thanks. Go ahead, will you? Don't wait for me. I'll be with you in a moment."

He bundled Olivier back into his corner and returned to the cloakroom. He didn't want him to hear.

"If he's used a different weapon each time, it's because he knows it will puzzle us. He knows that murderers generally have their own way and stick to it."

The Inspector had risen to his feet and was staring at Andre with a faraway look, as though he was following a train of thought of his own.

"You mean that he's—"

"That he's one of us—or has been. I can't get the idea out of my head."

He lowered his voice.

"Someone who's been up against it in the same sort of way as my brother. A discharged fireman might take to arson. It's happened two or three times. A policeman—"

"But why should he steal?"

"Wasn't my brother in need of money? This other chap may be like him in more ways than one. Supposing he, too, was a night worker and goes on pretending he's still in a job. That would explain why the crimes are committed so late. He has to be out all night. The first part of it is easy enough—the cafes and bars are open. Afterward, he's all alone with himself."

As though to himself, Saillard muttered: "There wouldn't be anybody in the personnel department on a day like this."

"Perhaps you could ring up the director at his home. He might remember . . ."

"Hallo! Can I speak to Monsieur Guillaume, please? He's not in? Where could I reach him? At his daughter's in Ateuil? Have you got the number?"

"Hallo! Monsieur Guillaume? Saillard speaking. I hope I'm not disturbing you too much. Oh, you'd finished, had you? Good. It's about the killer. Yes, there's been another one. No. Nothing definite. Only we have an idea that needs checking, and it's urgent. Don't be too surprised at my question.

"Has any member of the Paris police been sacked recently—say two or three months ago? I beg your pardon? Not a single one this year? I see."

Lecœur felt a sudden constriction around his heart, as though overwhelmed by a catastrophe, and threw a pathetic, despairing look at the wall-map. He had already given up and was surprised to hear his chief go on:

"As a matter of fact, it doesn't need to be as recent as all that. It would be someone who had worked in various parts of Paris, including the Fifteenth and Sixteenth. Probably also the Twelfth and Twentieth. Seems to have done a good deal of night work. Also to have been embittered by his dismissal. What?"

The way Saillard pronounced that last word gave Lecœur renewed hope.

"Sergeant Loubet? Yes, I remember the name, though I never actually came across him. Three years ago! You wouldn't know where he lived, I suppose? Somewhere near Les Halles?"

Three years ago. No, it wouldn't do, and Lecœur's heart sank again. You could hardly expect a man to bottle up his resentments for three years and then suddenly start hitting back.

"Have you any idea what became of him? No, of course not. And it's not a good day for finding out."

He hung up and looked thoughtfully at Lecœur. When he spoke, it was as though he was addressing an equal.

"Did you hear? Sergeant Loubet. He was constantly getting into trouble and was shifted three or four times before being finally dismissed. Drink. That was his trouble. He took his dismissal very hard. Guillaume can't say for certain what has become of him, but he thinks he joined a private detective agency. If you'd like to have a try—"

Lecœur set to work. He had little hope of succeeding, but it was better to do something than sit watching for the little lamps in the street-plan. He began with the agencies of the most doubtful reputation, refusing to believe that a person such as Loubet would readily find a job with a reputable firm. Most of the offices were shut, and he had to ring up their proprietors at home.

"Don't know him. You'd better try Tisserand in the Boulevard Saint-Martin. He's the one who takes all the riffraff."

But Tisserand, a firm that specialized in shadowings, was no good, either.

"Don't speak to me of that good-for-nothing. It's a good two months or more since I chucked him out, in spite of his threatening to blackmail me. If he ever shows up at my office again, I'll throw him down the stairs."

"What sort of job did he have?"

"Night work. Watching blocks of flats."

"Did he drink much?"

"He wasn't often sober. I don't know how he man-

aged it, but he always knew where to get free drinks.
Blackmail again, I suppose."

"Can you give me his address?"

"Twenty-seven bis, Rue du Pas-de-la-Mule."

"Does he have a telephone?"

"Maybe. I don't know. I've never had the slightest
desire to ring him up. Is that all? Can I go back to
my game of bridge?"

The Inspector had already snatched up the telephone directory and was looking for Loubet's number.
He rang up himself. There was now a tacit understanding between him and Lecœur. They shared the
same hope, the same trembling eagerness, while Olivier, realizing that something important was going on,
came and stood near them.

Without being invited, Andre did something he
wouldn't have dreamed of doing that morning. He
picked up the second earphone to listen in. The bell
rang in the flat in the Rue du Pas-de-la-Mule. It rang
for a long time, as though the place was deserted, and
his anxiety was becoming acute when at last it stopped
and a voice answered.

Thank Heaven! It was a woman's voice, an elderly
one. "Is that you at last? Where are you?"

"Hallo! This isn't your husband here, Madame."

"Has he met with an accident?"

From the hopefulness of her tone, it sounded as
though she had long been expecting one and wouldn't
be sorry when it happened.

"It is Madame Loubet I'm speaking to, isn't it?"

"Who else would it be?"

"Your husband's not at home?"

"First of all, who are you?"

"Inspector Saillard."

"What do you want him for?"

The Inspector put his hand over the mouthpiece to
say to Lecœur: "Get through to Janvier. Tell him to
dash round there as quick as he can."

"Didn't your husband come home this morning?"

"You ought to know! I thought the police knew
everything!"

"Does it often happen?"

"That's his business, isn't it?"

No doubt she hated her drunkard of a husband, but now that he was threatened she was ready to stand up for him.

"I suppose you know he no longer belongs to the police force."

"Perhaps he found a cleaner job."

"When did he stop working for the Agence Argus?"

"What's that? What are you getting at?"

"I assure you, Madame, your husband was dismissed from the Agence Argus over two months ago."

"You're lying."

"Which means that for these last two months he's been going off to work every evening."

"Where else would he be going? To the Folies Bergère?"

"Have you any idea why he hasn't come back today? He hasn't telephoned, has he?"

She must have been afraid of saying the wrong thing, for she rang off without another word.

When the Inspector put his receiver down, he turned round to see Lecœur standing behind him, looking away. In a shaky voice, the latter said:

"Janvier's on his way now."

He was treated as an equal. He knew it wouldn't last, that tomorrow, sitting at his switchboard, he would be once more but a small cog in the huge wheel.

The others simply didn't count—not even his brother, whose timid eyes darted from one to the other uncomprehendingly, wondering why, if his boy's life was in danger, they talked so much instead of doing something.

Twice he had to pluck at Andre's sleeve to get a word in edgewise.

"Let me go and look for him myself," he begged.

What could he do? The hunt had widened now. A description of ex-Sergeant Loubet had been passed to all police stations and patrols.

It was no longer only a boy of ten who was being looked for, but also a man of fifty-eight, probably the worse for drink, dressed in a black overcoat with a velvet collar and an old grey-felt hat, a man who knew his Paris like the palm of his hand, and who was acquainted with the police.

Janvier had returned, looking fresher than the men there in spite of his night's vigil.

"She tried to slam the door in my face, but I'd taken the precaution of sticking my foot in. She doesn't know anything. She says he's been handing over his pay every month."

"That's why he had to steal. He didn't need big sums. In fact, he wouldn't have known what to do with them. What's she like?"

"Small and dark, with piercing eyes. Her hair's dyed a sort of blue. She must have eczema or something of the sort—she wears mittens."

"Did you get a photo of him?"

"There was one on the dining-room sideboard. She wouldn't give it to me, so I just took it."

A heavy-built, florid man, with bulging eyes, who in his youth had probably been the village beau and had conserved an air of stupid arrogance. The photograph was some years old. No doubt he looked quite different now.

"She didn't give you any idea where he was likely to be, did she?"

"As far as I could make out, except at night, when he was supposed to be at work, she kept him pretty well tied to her apron strings. I talked to the concierge, who told me he was scared stiff of his wife. Often she's seen him stagger home in the morning, then suddenly pull himself together when he went upstairs. He goes out shopping with his wife. In fact, he never goes out alone in the daytime. If she goes out when he's in bed, she locks him in."

"What do you think, Lecœur?"

"I'm wondering whether my nephew and he aren't together."

"What do you mean?"

"They weren't together at the beginning, or Loubet would have stopped the boy giving the alarm. There must have been some distance between them. One was following the other."

"Which way round?"

"When the kid climbed up the drainpipe, he thought his father was guilty. Otherwise, why should he have sent him off to the Gare d'Austerlitz, where no doubt he intended to join him after getting rid of the sandwich tin?"

"It looks like it."

"No, Andre. Francois could never have thought—"

"Leave this alone. You don't understand. At that time the crime had certainly been committed. Francois wouldn't have dreamed of burgling someone's flat for a tin box if it hadn't been that he'd seen the body."

"From his window," put in Janvier, "he could see most of the legs."

"What we don't know is whether the murderer was still there."

"I can't believe he was," said Saillard. "If he had been, he'd have kept out of sight, let the boy get into the room, and then done the same to him as he'd done to the old woman."

"Look here, Olivier. When you got home this morning, was the light on?"

"Yes."

"In the boy's room?"

"Yes. It was the first thing I noticed. It gave me a shock. I thought perhaps he was ill."

"So the murderer very likely saw it and feared his crime had had a witness. He certainly wouldn't have expected anyone to climb up the drainpipe. He must have rushed straight out of the house."

"And waited outside to see what would happen."

Guesswork! Yes. But that was all they could do. The important thing was to guess right. For that you had to put yourself in the other chap's place and think as he had thought. The rest was a matter of patrols, of the hundreds of policemen scattered all over Paris, and, lastly, of luck.

"Rather than go down the way he'd come, the boy must have left the house by the entrance in the Rue Michat."

"Just a moment, Inspector. By that time he probably knew that his father wasn't the murderer."

"Why?"

"Janvier said just now that Madame Fayet lost a lot of blood. If it had been his father, the blood would have had time to dry up more or less. It was some nine hours since Francois had seen him in the room. It was on leaving the house that he found out who had done it, whether it was Loubet or not. The latter wouldn't know whether the boy had seen him up in the room. Francois would have been scared and taken to his heels."

This time it was the boy's father who interrupted.

"No. Not if he knew there was a big reward offered. Not if he knew I'd lost my job. Not if he'd seen me go to the old woman to borrow some money."

The Inspector and Andre Lecœur exchanged glances. They had to admit Olivier was right, and it made them afraid.

No, it had to be pictured otherwise. A dark, deserted street in an outlying quarter of Paris two hours before dawn.

On the other hand, the ex-policeman, obsessed by his sense of grievance, who had just committed his ninth murder to revenge himself on the society that had spurned him, and perhaps still more to prove to himself he was still a man by defying the whole police force—indeed, the whole world.

Was he drunk again? On a night like that, when the bars were open long after their usual closing time, he had no doubt had more than ever. And in that dark, silent street, what did he see with his bulging drink-inflamed eyes? A young boy, the first person who had found him out, and who would now—

"I'd like to know whether he's got a gun on him," sighed the Inspector.

Janvier answered at once:

"I asked his wife. It seems he always carries one about. An automatic pistol, but it's not loaded."

"How can she know that?"

"Once or twice, when he was more than usually drunk, he rounded on her, threatening her with the gun. After that, she got hold of his ammunition and locked it up, telling him an unloaded pistol was quite enough to frighten people without his having to fire it."

Had those two really stalked each other through the streets of Paris? A strange sort of duel in which the man had the strength and the boy the speed?

The boy may well have been scared, but the man stood for something precious enough to push fear into the background: a fortune and the end of his father's worries and humiliations.

Having got so far, there wasn't a lot more to be said by the little group of people waiting in the Préfecture de Police. They sat gazing at the street-plan with a picture in their minds of a boy following a man, the boy no doubt keeping his distance. Everyone else was sleeping. There was no one in the streets who could be a help to the one or a menace to the other. Had Loubet produced his gun in an attempt to frighten the boy away?

When people woke up and began coming out into the streets, what would the boy do then? Would he rush up to the first person he met and start screaming "Murder"?

"Yes. It was Loubet who walked in front," said Saillard slowly.

"And it was I," put in Andre Lecœur, "who told the boy all about the pillar telephone system."

The little crosses came to life. What had at first been mysterious was now almost simple. But it was tragic.

The child was risking his skin to save his father. Tears were slowly trickling down the latter's face. He made no attempt to hide them.

He was in a strange place, surrounded by outlandish

objects, and by people who talked to him as though he wasn't there, as though he was someone else. And his brother was among these people, a brother he could hardly recognize and whom he regarded with instinctive respect.

Even when they did speak, it wasn't necessary to say much. They understood each other. A word sufficed.

"Loubet couldn't go home, of course."

Andre Lecœur smiled suddenly as a thought struck him.

"It didn't occur to him that Francois hadn't a centime in his pocket. He could have escaped by diving into the Métro."

No. That wouldn't hold water. The boy had seen him and would give his description.

Place du Trocadéro, the Etoile. The time was passing. It was practically broad daylight. People were up and about. Why hadn't Francois called for help? Anyhow, with people in the streets it was no longer possible for Loubet to kill him.

The Inspector was deep in thought.

"For one reason or another," he murmured, "I think they're going about together now."

At the same moment, a lamp lit up on the wall. As though he knew it would be for him, Lecœur answered in place of Bedeau.

"Yes. I thought as much."

"It's about the two oranges. They found an Arab boy asleep in the third-class waiting room at the Gare du Nord. He still had the oranges in his pockets. He'd run away from home because his father had beaten him."

"Do you think Bib's dead?"

"If he was dead, Loubet would have gone home, as he would no longer have anything to fear."

So the struggle was still going on somewhere in this now sunny Paris in which families were sauntering along the boulevards taking the air.

It would be the fear of losing him in the crowd that had brought Francois close to his quarry. Why didn't he call for help? No doubt because Loubet had threatened him with his gun. "One word from you, my lad, and I'll empty this into your guts."

So each was pursuing his own goal: for the one to shake off the boy somehow, for the other to watch for the moment when the murderer was off his guard and give the alarm before he had time to shoot.

It was a matter of life and death.

"Loubet isn't likely to be in the center of the town, where policemen are too plentiful for his liking, to say nothing of the fact that many of them know him by sight."

Their most likely direction from the Etoile was towards Montmartre—not to the amusement quarter, but to the remoter and quieter parts.

It was half past two. Had they had anything to eat? Had Loubet, with his mind set on escape, been able to resist the temptation to drink?

"Monsieur le Commissaire—"

Andre Lecœur couldn't speak with the assurance he would have liked. He couldn't get rid of the feeling that he was an upstart, if not a usurper.

"I know there are thousands of little bars in Paris. But if we chose the more likely districts and put plenty of men on the job—"

Not only were all the men there roped in, but Saillard got through to the Police Judiciaire, where there were six men on duty, and set every one of them to work on six different telephone lines.

"Hallo! Is that the Bar des Amis? In the course of the day have you seen a middle-aged man accompanied by a boy of ten? The man's wearing a black overcoat and a—"

Again Lecœur made little crosses, not in his notebook this time, but in the telephone directory. There were ten pages of bars, some of them with the weirdest names.

A plan of Paris was spread out on a table all ready and it was in a little alley of ill-repute behind the Place

Clichy that the Inspector was able to make the first mark in red chalk.

"Yes, there was a man of that description here about twelve o'clock. He drank three glasses of Calvados and ordered a glass of white wine for the boy. The boy didn't want to drink at first, but he did in the end and he wolfed a couple of eggs."

By the way Olivier Lecœur's face lit up, you might have thought he heard his boy's voice.

"You don't know which way they went?"

"Towards the Boulevard des Batignolles, I think. The man looked as though he'd already had one or two before he came in."

"Hallo! Zanzi-Bar? Have you at any time seen a—"

It became a refrain. As soon as one man had finished, the same words, or practically the same, were repeated by his neighbor.

Rue Damrémont. Montmartre again, only farther out this time. One-thirty. Loubet had broken a glass, his movements by this time being somewhat clumsy. The boy got up and made off in the direction of the lavatory, but when the man followed, he thought better of it and went back to his seat.

"Yes. The boy did look a bit frightened. As for the man, he was laughing and smirking as though he was enjoying a huge joke."

"Do you hear that, Olivier? Bib was still there at one-forty."

Andre Lecœur dared not say what was in his mind. The struggle was nearing its climax. Now that Loubet had really started drinking it was just a question of time. The only thing was: would the boy wait long enough?

It was all very well for Madame Loubet to say the gun wasn't loaded. The butt of an automatic was quite hard enough to crack a boy's skull.

His eyes wandered to his brother, and he had a vision of what Olivier might well have come to if his asthma hadn't prevented him drinking.

"Hallo! Yes. Where? Boulevard Ney?"

They had reached the outskirts of Paris. The ex-

Sergeant seemed still to have his wits about him. Little
by little, in easy stages, he was leading the boy to one
of those outlying districts where there were still empty
building sites and desolate spaces.

Three police cars were promptly switched to that
neighborhood, as well as every available *agent cycliste*
within reach. Even Janvier dashed off, taking the
Inspector's little car, and it was all they could do to
prevent Olivier from running after him.

"I tell you, you'd much better stay here. He may
easily go off on a false trail, and then you won't know
anything."

Nobody had time for making coffee. The men of
the second day shift had not thoroughly warmed to
the case. Everyone was strung up.

"Hallo! Yes. Orient Bar. What is it?"

It was André Lecœur who took the call. With the
receiver to his ear, he rose to his feet, making queer
signs that brought the whole room to a hush.

"What? Don't speak so close to the mouthpiece."

In the silence, the others could hear a high-pitched
voice.

"It's for the police! Tell the police I've got him!
The killer! Hallo? What? Is that Uncle André?"

The voice was lowered a tone to say shakily: "I tell
you, I'll shoot, Uncle André."

Lecœur hardly knew to whom he handed the
receiver. He dashed out of the room and up the stairs,
almost breaking down the door of the room.

"Quick, all cars to the Orient Bar, Porte Clignancourt."

And without waiting to hear the message go out, he
dashed back as fast as he'd come. At the door he
stopped dead, struck by the calm that had suddenly
descended on the room.

It was Saillard who held the receiver into which, in
the thickest of Parisian dialects, a voice was saying:

"It's all right. Don't worry. I gave the chap a crack
on the head with a bottle. Laid him out properly. God
knows what he wanted to do to the kid. What's that?
You want to speak to him? Here, little one, come

here. And give me your popgun. I don't like those toys. Why, it isn't loaded."

Another voice. "Is that Uncle Andre?"

The Inspector looked round, and it was not to Andre but to Olivier that he handed the receiver.

"Uncle Andre. I got him."

"Bib! It's me."

"What are you doing there, Dad?"

"Nothing. Waiting to hear from you. It's been—"

"You can't think how bucked I am. Wait a moment, here's the police. They're just arriving."

Confused sounds. Voices, the shuffling of feet, the clink of glasses. Olivier Lecœur listened, standing there awkwardly, gazing at the wall-map which he did not see, his thoughts far away at the northern extremity of Paris, in a windswept boulevard.

"They're taking me with them."

Another voice. "Is that you, Chief? Janvier here."

One might have thought it was Olivier Lecœur who had been knocked on the head with a bottle by the way he held the receiver out, staring blankly in front of him.

"He's out, right out, Chief. They're lugging him away now. When the boy heard the telephone ringing, he decided it was his chance. He grabbed Loubet's gun from his pocket and made a dash for the phone. The proprietor here's a pretty tough nut. If it hadn't been for—"

A little lamp lit up in the plan of Paris.

"Hallo! Your car's gone out?"

"Someone's smashed the glass of the pillar telephone in the Place Clignancourt. Says there's a row going on in a bar. I'll ring up again when we know what's going on."

It wouldn't be necessary.

Nor was it necessary for Andre Lecœur to put a cross in his notebook under Miscellaneous.

—translated by Geoffrey Sainsbury

MISS CRINDLE AND FATHER CHRISTMAS

Malcolm Gray

Christmas comes reluctantly to Much Cluning. Huddling in its valley, the village looks even drearier than usual under grey December skies. There is no tree outside the village hall, and the single string of fairy lights along the High Street hardly creates an air of festivity. The housewives complain about the extra work Christmas brings and the men about the expense. They only do it for the kids, they say. All the same, it is doubtful if they really mean it, or if they would want to see the season abolished even if they could, and a fair number go to church or chapel on Christmas morning.

A few days before Christmas last year, Harriet Richards stood in the yard at her brother's farm giving him a piece of her mind. At twenty-two, Harriet was as generous and warm-hearted as she was pretty. "Do you have to be such a Scrooge?" she demanded angrily.

"Go away," Jason told her coldly. He was nine years older than his sister and he had no use for the season of goodwill. The only good thing about it to his mind was the profit he made on his flock of chickens and turkeys. He was damned if he was going to give any of them away to layabouts who weren't prepared to get off their backsides and work. He said as much to Harriet.

"Layabouts!" she exclaimed furiously. "Do you call old Mrs. Randall a layabout?"

"It's her husband's job to provide for her, not mine."

"When he's nearly eighty and crippled with arthritis?"

"Ach!" Jason said, disgusted.

"And she's not the only one," Harriet went on. "There's Josie Gardner with her three kids. And Bert Renwick and Phoebe," she added, forestalling her brother's attempt to interrupt her. "It's not their fault they can't afford anything but the bare necessities."

"They get their pensions," Jason retorted. "And benefits. They wouldn't get those if people like me didn't pay too damned much in taxes."

"Oh," Harriet said, exasperated, "I don't know how Sheila puts up with you!" And, turning, she started toward the house.

"If you think I breed those birds to feed all the lame ducks in the village, you'd better think again!" Jason called after her.

There were times when she could strangle him, Harriet thought furiously. It wasn't as if he couldn't afford three or four turkeys. By local standards, he was well off. But he seemed to feel that people expected him to give them. It put him on the defensive, and he resented it.

Her sister-in-law was in the kitchen. "Have you and Jason been arguing again?" she asked, amused.

"You could say so." Harriet, still boiling with indignation, explained.

"He works hard," Sheila reminded her. "And he's inclined to think other people don't. There's so much to do at this time of year, he gets worn out."

"He could afford to pay another man if he wasn't so mean," Harriet said bitterly. "Anyway, it's not just this time, it's always."

Soon afterward, she left. Sheila watched her go, thinking.

Later that evening Harriet had a very public quarrel with Colin Loates, her boy friend. Nobody who heard it was quite sure what it was about, but Harriet went home in tears.

*   *   *

Miss Crindle met her in the street the next day. Miss Crindle was a large woman with greying hair and a cheerful manner. Until her retirement three years ago, she had taught at Much Cluning Primary School for more than thirty years, and both Harriet and Colin had been among her brightest pupils. So had Jason, who hadn't been as clever as his sister but by hard work had gained a scholarship to Leobury School and gone on to university. Harriet could have gone, too, but she preferred to stay home and work with the horses her father bred for show jumping.

Colin had been the brightest of the three, a cheeky little boy with charm and a talent for mischief. Miss Crindle had never quite forgiven him for leaving school at sixteen to go into his father's grocery shop.

"And how is Colin?" Miss Crindle inquired that morning.

Harriet looked surprised. "Haven't you heard, Miss Crindle? I thought everybody had. We had a row last night and it's all over."

Miss Crindle noticed that Harriet's left eye was twitching and that she looked embarrassed. All the same, she didn't seem too distressed. She had always been a sensible girl, Miss Crindle thought, and things were different nowadays. In her time, if a girl and her boy friend split up she would be upset for days. "I'm sorry," she said.

Harriet shrugged. "I'll get over it," she said ruefully.

Miss Crindle was sure she would. A girl like Harriet, vivacious and attractive, would find no shortage of young men.

That afternoon, Colin, driving back from Leobury, slewed off the road into a ditch two miles from the village. He explained that he had swerved to avoid a pheasant and skidded, but the popular theory was that his mind hadn't been on his driving, he was thinking about Harriet and their row. Whatever the cause, his car was well and truly stuck and he had to walk to the nearest house and phone the garage to come and tow him out.

*   *   *

They were still doing it when Billy Powis, having run all the way home, blurted out breathlessly to his mother that he had just seen Santa Claus. Mary Powis was busy making mince pies. She laughed but didn't pay too much attention. She was used to her son's tales.

"Oh, dear?" she said.

"But I did, Mum," the seven-year-old insisted.

"Had he got his sledge and reindeer?"

Billy hesitated. He was a truthful little boy and he couldn't really remember, he had been too excited. "He'd got something," he mumbled. More certainly he added, "And he had a sack over his shoulder."

"Where was he?"

"I told you, at the edge of Brackett's Wood. He went into the trees."

"You shouldn't make up stories, Billy," Mary told him mildly. "It's telling fibs, and that's naughty."

"I did see him," Billy persisted. He was learning early that it is bad enough to be suspected when one is guilty, but much worse when one is innocent. "He was all in red, with white stuff on his coat, and he had a big red hood and boots. Like he does when he comes to our school party."

Oh, dear, Mary thought. She decided that the best course would be to ignore her son's tale. "Go and wash your hands," she said.

At the same time, Sheila Richards was trying without success to ring her sister-in-law. Harriet's mother told her Harry was out. She didn't know where, but she didn't suppose she would be long. Sheila thanked her and said she would try again later.

Billy Powis wasn't the only inhabitant of Much Cluning to see Father Christmas. Two other people saw him, and they were grownups. The first was George Townley, the owner of the general store-cum-post office. While Billy was running home to tell his mother what he had seen, George was returning from visiting his sister at Little Cluning. As he drove down the hill into the village, he saw a figure in red with a hood and carrying a sack disappear into the trees beside the road. He was unwise enough to mention it to one of his customers, and soon the story was all over the village. George Townley had started seeing things, and he believed in Santa Claus.

It had been getting colder during the day, and about five o'clock it started to snow. By the time most of Much Cluning went to bed, there was a three-inch covering over everything and it was still snowing. It stopped during the night, but the temperature dropped further.

The second adult to see Father Christmas was Miss Crindle. At one o'clock in the morning of December the twenty-third, she had to get out of bed to go to the bathroom. On her way back, she looked out of the window. It was a fine clear night with a moon. There was never much noise in the valley, but now every sound was muffled by the thick layer of snow.

Just across the road, a figure dressed in scarlet and white, its head covered by a hood, was turning the corner round the back of the Renwicks' cottage. It was bowed under the weight of the sack slung over its right shoulder. Miss Crindle blinked. There were no children's parties at that hour, and any devoted father who was inclined to go to the lengths of dressing up to deliver his offsprings' presents would hardly do so two days before Christmas.

Miss Crindle told herself that if it wasn't a fond father, it must be a burglar. She considered calling the police. But she disliked the idea of being thought an overimaginative old fool and, anyway, everybody knew the Renwicks were almost destitute. No burglar would try his luck there. She climbed back into bed, and the next day she kept what she had seen to herself.

She said nothing even when Phoebe Renwick, who was well over seventy and worn out from caring for her invalid husband, told her her news. When she came down that morning and opened the back door, there on the doorstep there had been a parcel wrapped in gift paper. In it there was a small turkey already plucked and drawn and a tiny Christmas pudding.

"I couldn't believe it," Phoebe said. She was close to tears. "We haven't been able to have a turkey for over twenty years. Not since soon after Bert was first ill and had to give up work. We can't keep it, of course, it wouldn't be right, but it was a lovely thought."

"Of course you can keep it," Miss Crindle told her with spirit.

"No. We were brought up not to accept what we hadn't paid for, or to ask for charity, and we never have, neither of us."

"You call a present charity? Anyway," Miss Crindle added reasonably, "who would you give it back to?"

"I hadn't thought of that," Phoebe admitted.

"You keep it and be glad there are people in the village who think of others," Miss Crindle told her. "You can say a prayer for them in chapel on Christmas morning."

The old lady's eyes moistened. "I will tonight, too," she said.

Busy with her thoughts, Miss Crindle went back indoors and resumed the cleaning she had been doing when she heard Mrs. Renwick calling her. Who was the kind soul who had left the parcel on the old couple's step? She had no doubt that it was the person in Santa Claus costume she had seen during the night, but who was he? Or she?

Not that it mattered: if somebody wanted to do the old couple a good turn surreptitiously, good luck to them. Only why the fancy dress? Such ostentation seemed out of keeping with leaving the parcel secretly in the middle of the night. It was like a disguise, and it made her a little uneasy.

The Renwicks weren't the only beneficiaries of Much Cluning's own Santa Claus: the Randalls, Josie Gardner, and an elderly lady named Willings with a crippled son had found similar parcels at their back doors that morning. By evening the story was all over the village.

Miss Crindle heard it, and she wondered still more.

Neither of the Richards had heard about the parcels. Bracketts Farm was a mile out of Much Cluning
and they'd been busy there all day. Thus there was
no reason for Sheila to suspect anything when Jason
came into the kitchen during the afternoon and asked
her, "Has Mrs. Grundy been for her bird?"

Sheila had been right, he was tired. The woman
who helped deal with the turkeys was ill with flu and
he had been driving himself hard for days. He was
also suspicious.

"No," Sheila answered without looking up from
what she was doing at the sink. "She said she'd come
tomorrow."

Jason swore.

"Why, what's the matter? It doesn't make any
difference."

"It's gone."

Sheila looked up then. "What do you mean?"

"What I say," Jason told her angrily. "It's clear
enough, isn't it? It's been pinched."

His wife stared at him. "Are you sure?" she asked.
But she could see from Jason's face he was. "Have
any of the others gone?"

"I don't know. I was only looking for hers."

"Can't she have another one?" Sheila tried to be
practical, but she knew it wouldn't assuage Jason's
anger.

"Of course she bloody well can't," he retorted.
"The others are all sold, you know that. And you
know how fussy she is."

Sheila did know. Mrs. Grundy lived at Much Cluning Hall and, although she was pleasant enough, she
disliked being thwarted or inconvenienced. Her manner implied that she expected her life to run as
smoothly as the Rolls-Royce her husband drove. Oh,
God, Sheila thought, it looked like being a miserable
Christmas. Jason would be in a foul mood for days.
A terrible thought occurred to her. "Hadn't you better
count them?" she asked.

"I'm going to."

Jason strode across the yard to the big shed where the dead birds, plucked and drawn, were laid out in rows along the shelves. Sheila followed and watched while he counted them. There should be ninety, she knew. Christmas turkeys might be profitable, but they were only a sideline to the main business of the farm, the crops and sheep.

"There are four gone!" Jason shouted. "Four! That's the best part of fifty pounds!" He turned furiously. "I'm going to ring the police!"

"Jason, do you think—?" Sheila asked weakly.

But he was in no mood to pay attention, and she followed him uneasily into the house.

It was nearly an hour before P.C. Tom Roberts arrived. He had been at the site of a road accident four miles away and the theft of four turkeys hadn't seemed like the crime of the century, even in Much Cluning. Clearly Jason Richards didn't agree with him.

"They must have got in during the night," he said. Waiting had done nothing to soothe his anger. "You can see their tracks."

He led the way through the churned-up slush in the yard, past the farm buildings to a small meadow bounded on the far side by a low hedge. It was still freezing hard, and the snow, several inches deep, was crisp and unbroken save for a clearly designed set of footprints leading from the yard to the hedge near the point where it met the road. Jason had said "they," Roberts thought, but there was only one set. Smallish prints, too.

"Looks like he came this way," he agreed. "Was the shed locked at night?"

"No." Jason sounded as if he were daring the policeman to criticize him. "The padlock's fastened with a peg. We've never had anything stolen before."

Roberts walked back across the yard.

"Where are you going?" Jason demanded.

"Don't want to disturb the tracks then, do we, sir?"

Roberts said. He walked along the road and across to the point where, it seemed, the thief had forced his way through the hedge. There was still just enough light for him to make out the tuft of material caught on a twig. He picked it out carefully and frowned. It was bright-red and thin. Hardly the sort of clothing a man would wear to go stealing turkeys on a freezing-cold night. Not what most men would wear at any time, come to that. He tucked the fragment away between two pages of his notebook and returned to where the farmer was watching.

The turkeys must have been stolen on one of the last two nights, Jason told him. He had counted them two days ago.

Tom Roberts lived in the village. He knew about George Townley's seeing a figure dressed like Santa Claus disappearing into Brackett's Wood and about the mysterious parcels which had appeared on certain doorsteps last night. There had been four of them, each one containing a turkey. And four turkeys had been taken from Jason's shed. Roberts was well aware of the dangers of putting two and two together and making sixteen, but it looked to him very much as if some joker had been playing twin roles, Robin Hood and Santa Claus.

Of all the people in the village, he could think of only one who possessed the sort of mind to think up a ploy like that and the cheek to carry it out: Colin Loates. Colin had never been suspected of dishonesty, but he was—what was the word?—unpredictable. Sometimes his sense of humor ran away with him. After all, everybody knew Jason Richards could well afford the loss of four birds, and the recipients of the parcels were genuinely deserving cases. If it had been up to him personally, Roberts would have felt inclined to say, "Good luck to him," and write the case off as unsolved. But it wasn't, and theft was theft, however good the motive. So he promised Jason he would make inquiries and went to see Colin.

*   *   *

He found him at his father's shop, making up orders for the next day.

When Colin heard why he was there, he laughed. "Serve Jason right," he said.

"You've no idea who might have done it?" Roberts asked him.

"Me? No. I don't know why you should come to me about it. You're the one who's supposed to know about all the crime that goes on here."

"Where were you the last two nights?" Roberts asked him.

"What time?"

"Anytime."

"Home in bed."

They eyed each other. Colin seemed to think the whole business was a great joke, and that annoyed Roberts a little. He looked down at the other man's feet. They must be size nines, at least. The boots which made the tracks in the snow on Jason Richards' meadow had been no bigger than sevens. All the same, "Have you got any wellingtons?" he asked.

"Course I have," Colin answered.

"Where are they?"

"In the boot of my car. Why?"

"Do you mind if I have a look at them?"

"Not if you want to."

They went out to the yard at the back of the shop where Colin's old Escort was parked. He opened the boot and brought out a pair of worn grey wellingtons. Roberts studied them. They were size ten.

"All right, thanks," he said.

Colin just grinned. "Do you think I took Jason's turkeys?" he asked.

Roberts didn't answer.

Miss Crindle heard about the theft the next morning when she was doing her last-minute Christmas shopping. It seemed to justify her fears, and she decided that she must talk to Tom Roberts.

"You think the turkeys the Renwicks and the others

got were the ones somebody stole from Jason Richards' shed, don't you?" she asked him.

"I can't say, Miss Crindle," the policeman replied cautiously.

"Of course you can, everybody else is." Miss Crindle swept his objection aside. "And you suspect you know who it was, don't you?"

Roberts eyed his visitor. Muffled up in what looked like two or three layers of jumpers and cardigans under her coat, she looked bigger than ever. It would have been easy to put her down as a silly busybody, but Roberts knew better. Miss Crindle was an intelligent woman. And if she took a keen interest in what went on in Much Cluning, she was no mischief-maker. "We're pursuing our inquiries," he said.

"So I should hope," she told him briskly. "Although I must confess, my sympathies are rather with the thief." She paused, then continued with obvious embarrassment, "I thought I should tell you, I saw Father Christmas last night."

Roberts gaped at her. For a moment he wondered if she had suddenly gone queer. "I'm sorry?" he stammered.

"Somebody dressed as Santa Claus left the parcels. I happened to look out of my window about one o'clock and I saw them going round behind the Renwicks' house. I didn't say anything about it, there didn't seem any point, and I've no wish to be thought mad, but if the birds were stolen—"

"You've no idea who it was?" Roberts asked, recovering a little.

"None," Miss Crindle answered firmly. "I can't even say if it was a man or a woman. I suppose you know George Townley saw them, too, two or three days ago?"

Roberts nodded. "It looks as if whoever took the turkeys was wearing red," he said grimly. "He left this caught on the hedge where he pushed through." He took out his notebook and showed Miss Crindle the fragment of cloth.

She studied it with interest. "It looks like a piece

from a Santa Claus costume," she observed. She gave the policeman a shrewd look. "I suppose you think it was Colin Loates?"

This time Tom Roberts wasn't startled, he knew half the village would be supposing the same thing. "It wasn't him," he said.

"Oh?" Miss Crindle couldn't quite conceal her curiosity.

Roberts was undecided how much he should reveal. He knew the old girl had helped the police when Ralph Johns was murdered and the Chief Inspector had a high regard for her. And he could do with some help now. "The thief left footprints from the hedge across to the shed," he explained. "They were sixes or sevens, and Colin takes tens. I've seen his boots. Besides, when George Townley saw his Santa Claus, they were towing Colin's car out of a ditch along the Leobury road."

Miss Crindle hadn't known that, but she was rather glad. "Have you any idea who it may have been?" she inquired.

"No," Roberts admitted.

Miss Crindle was afraid *she* had, and after Roberts had gone she walked across the road. The Renwicks had few visitors—even the milkman called only every other day—and the footprints in the snow along the side of the cottage were still as clear as when they were made. She studied them thoughtfully, then she went to see Harriet Richards.

She didn't beat about the bush. "What do you know about Father Christmas and Jason's stolen turkeys?" she demanded.

"Me?" The girl looked surprised. "Nothing, Miss Crindle."

"Harriet," Miss Crindle told her sternly, "your eye-lid's twitching. That's the second time it's done it in the last four days."

For some unaccountable reason Harriet blushed.

"Theft is a crime," Miss Crindle continued. "It can have very serious consequences. Sometimes for the

wrong person. You may disapprove of Jason but, even
if you aren't having anything to do with Colin now,
you wouldn't want him to get into trouble, would
you?"

"No," Harriet said.

Miss Crindle nodded. "Good. What size wellingtons
do you take?"

"Sevens."

"And where were you at one o'clock the night
before last?"

Harriet smiled, and for the first time that morning
there was a hint of her old mischief. "At Leobury,"
she answered. "I went to see Pat Dellar. It started to
freeze hard, there was a lot of slush on the road, and
I stayed the night."

Miss Crindle gazed at the girl for quite a long time.
Then, "Think about it, my dear," she said.

On her way home, she met Mary Powis and Billy.

"I've seen Father Christmas," the little boy announced triumphantly.

"Billy!" his mother reproved him. "You thought
you saw him on Monday, and you know he doesn't
come out until Christmas Eve. And only after dark
then." She smiled apologetically at Miss Crindle.

But Miss Crindle was interested. "Where did you
see him, Billy?" she asked.

"By Brackett's Wood," Billy replied.

"What time was it?"

"I don't know. But it got dark soon."

"You aren't the only person who saw him," Miss
Crindle said. "I saw him, too, and so did Mr. Townley."
It was too much, she thought.

When she got home, she phoned Pat Dellar, who
was one of her old pupils. Pat confirmed that Harriet
had spent last night there.

Miss Crindle asked after her parents, they talked
for a minute or two longer, and when Miss Crindle
put down the phone she sat for some time, thinking.
It was clear that Colin hadn't stolen the turkeys. There

was only one set of footprints and he couldn't have worn size six or seven boots. Moreover, he hadn't been the Father Christmas Billy Powis and George Townley had seen. Nor could Harriet have played Santa Claus—she had been miles away when the parcels had been delivered the night before last. So who had?

After twenty minutes, Miss Crindle came to a decision. She made two telephone calls, then put on another cardigan and her coat and went to see Sheila Richards.

"It was all a mistake," Jason said, looking uncomfortable.

P.C. Roberts eyed him stolidly. He was quite sure it hadn't been a mistake, but if Jason was going to maintain it had, there wasn't much he could do.

"The turkeys had been put aside," Jason went on. It would have been obvious to the most obtuse listener that his heart wasn't in it. "They hadn't been stolen at all."

"I see, sir," Roberts said. He was tempted to add something about wasting police time being an offense, but decided against it. "So you don't want us to take any further action?"

"No." Jason almost writhed. Further action was what he wanted above almost everything else, but Sheila had made it all too clear that if he didn't drop the whole business she would leave him. She wasn't given to making idle threats, and Jason had believed her. For all his faults, he loved his wife.

It was Miss Crindle who was responsible. He didn't know what she had told Sheila, but whatever it was it had had a marked effect.

In fact, Miss Crindle had said quite simply that she knew who had taken the turkeys and that she hoped Jason's wife would be able to persuade him to drop the whole matter. She looked down at Sheila's feet. Sheila was nearly six feet tall, and her feet were much larger than her sister-in-law's. "It was Colin, wasn't it?" Sheila said.

Miss Crindle smiled enigmatically.

"But—" Sheila looked distraught "—Jason was sure it was Harry. He said she'd talked about the Renwicks and the Randalls and Josie Gardner a few days ago. She said he ought to give them turkeys."

"It was," Miss Crindle said.

"But it can't have been," Sheila protested. "Harry was staying with Pat the night the parcels were left."

"That wasn't her," Miss Crindle agreed.

"Then who?"

"Colin. It was Harriet's idea. She was very angry with Jason and she thought she'd teach him a lesson and help some people to have a better Christmas at the same time. She suggested it to Colin and he jumped at the idea."

"But they'd fallen out," Sheila objected. "She told me they had a terrible row. I still don't see."

"They took it in turns to cover each other," Miss Crindle told her. "First, while Colin was being towed out of that ditch, Harriet was making sure she was seen in her Santa Claus get up at the other end of the village. They wanted people to talk about Santa Claus being about."

"It's the sort of daft idea that would appeal to them," Sheila agreed miserably. "They've never grown up, either of them."

"We can do with a touch of youthful spirits sometimes," Miss Crindle said. "They didn't look on what they were doing as stealing."

"I tried to phone her that afternoon. Mum said she was out."

Miss Crindle nodded. "She knew Jason didn't lock the shed. She went there that night, took the four smallest turkeys, and carried them across the meadow to Colin, who was waiting in his car. She's a strong girl and it wasn't very far. Colin hid them until the next night, then, while Harriet was safe at the Dellars', he delivered them. *He* couldn't have stolen them, because the footprints in the snow were too small, and Harriet couldn't have delivered them because she was miles away. There was only one set of prints in the meadow and only one round the Renwicks'. Nobody was looking for two people working alternately."

Sheila stared at her. "Except you," she said. "Whatever made you think of it?"

"Well—" Miss Crindle hesitated, then she smiled. "First, their quarrel was a little too public. Harriet and Colin may be high-spirited, but they wouldn't want to have a real argument with half the village looking on. It was almost as if it were being staged for other people's benefit. And when I saw Harriet just afterward, she didn't seem upset at all. Then her eyelid started twitching. It did it again when she told me she didn't know anything about the turkeys. I *knew* she was involved then."

"Oh," Sheila said, understanding.

"It's always done that when she's telling fibs, ever since she was a little girl at school," Miss Crindle said. "When you're a teacher as long as I was, you don't forget things like that. Then, the footprints at the Renwicks' aren't the same size as the others—they must be tens, at least. I tackled Harriet just now, and she told me the truth."

"Oh," Sheila said again. Uneasily she added, "I wonder what Jason's going to say."

"I'm sure you can manage him," Miss Crindle told her.

Mrs. Grundy laughed. "Then I'll have to get another one," she said cheerfully. "Really, Mr. Richards, it doesn't matter at all. To be frank, a ten-pound turkey would have been far too big for just my husband and me. I'm sure Mrs. Gardner and her children will enjoy it much more. But I must insist you let me pay you for it."

Jason met her eye, then looked away. "No," he said gruffly. "That's all right, Mrs. Grundy, I've written those four birds off. They're a present from us. After all, it's Christmas."

Mrs. Grundy nearly fainted.

DEADLY DEALINGS

☐ **BINO by A.W. Gray.** When his seediest client turns up dead, Bino suspects a whitewash of the dirtiest kind. What he finds links his client's demise to a political assassination, and the bodies start piling up. Politics has always been the dirtiest game in town—and it's about to become the deadliest. (401298—$3.95)

☐ **FAVOR—A Stanley Hastings Mystery by Parnell Hall.** The third Stanley Hastings mystery brings the ambulance chaser-turned-private-detective to the seedy backroom poker games and glittery casinos of Atlantic City as a favor—a favor that will get Stanley indicted for grand larceny and named the prime suspect in two murders. (401611—$3.95)

☐ **STRANGLER—A Stanley Hastings Mystery by Parnell Hall.** The first time Stanley calls on a client and finds the guy strangled, he thinks its just one of those things. The second time, poor Stanley knows the deck has been stacked against him.... (402170—$4.50)

☐ **CLIENT—A Stanley Hastings Mystery by Parnell Hall.** Hastings, America's most bumbling gumshoe, snags his first paying client. But then the woman he's hired to tail turns up dead—and the murder weapon turns up in Stanley's car. "Fast-paced ... exceptionally good."—*Mystery News* (402499—$4.50)

☐ **HELL-BENT FOR MURDER—A Joe Binney Mystery by Jack Livingston.** With the help of a sultry small town lady, the deaf detective stirs up a sinister stew of religion, politics and muder. "Fierce and funny ..." —*San Francisco Chronicle* (169158—$3.95)

Prices slightly higher in Canada

Buy them at your local

bookstore or use coupon

on next page for ordering.